The
Next
to Last
Mistake

The Next to Last Mistake

a novel

amalie jahn

Light Messages

To Johnisha, Susie, and Holly.
I'm forever grateful for our friendship.

Infamous

Monday, February 18

I rip a poster off the wall without looking at what's on it and throw it into the pile on the floor. I continue down the science hall past the next bank of lockers and reach for another. This time, however, I accidentally catch a glimpse of my own face printed on the sheet and it stops me dead. There's something so shocking about the photo I simply cannot force myself to look away.

There was a time I might have been embarrassed by the line of sweat I see beading at my brow or how disheveled I look with my bra strap slipping off my shoulder from beneath my shirt, but that's not what draws my attention now. What surprises me instead is the look of sheer joy on my face. The girl in the photo is happy. Enjoying life. Living in the moment. The girl in the picture has momentarily forgotten all the worry and heartache associated with moving to this new place. She's plain old Tess from Iowa having a good time.

Knowing what's written beneath the photo, I don't want to let my eyes drop, but I can't help it. I can't ignore the bold script scrawled across the bottom of the page declaring TESS GOODWIN IS A SLUT. My heart races and bile rises in my throat, but I swallow it down because I can not—I will not—risk showing how this stupid prank has upset me.

After several deep breaths, the anger and sadness wane, and I'm able to toss the sheet onto the floor with the others. Before moving on, however, I notice a piece of tape still clinging to the wall where the poster hung. I need to peel it off because I can't leave any trace of viciousness behind. I pick at the adhesive, slipping my fingernail under the sticky edge, but instead of pulling off cleanly, it only rips in half. Frustrated by everything that's come to pass, I squeeze my eyelids closed to prevent the tears from spilling over, but the persistent voice in the back of my head won't shut up.

You don't belong here, Tess, it says. *And you were stupid to think you would ever fit in.*

chapter 1
Iowa

Thursday, November 8

My best friend Zander is buried in his phone, playing *Clash of Kingdoms* in the passenger's seat beside me on our way to school. Normally I'd be annoyed by his disinterest, since there's nothing I hate more than feeling like his chauffeur. But this morning, his preoccupation with securing a new realm is a relief, leaving him oblivious to both my distracted driving and my somber mood.

As we sputter into the East Chester High School student parking lot in my ancient Volkswagen Jetta, Lacey Pemberton darts out from behind a parked car to where her boyfriend is leaning against the bed of his pickup. I slam on my breaks to avoid hitting her, and Zander finally looks up from his game.

"If any part of you wanted to take her out, that woulda been your chance," he says, clicking off his phone as I pull into an empty parking spot at the far end of the lot. "No one woulda blamed you. She clearly wasn't watching for oncoming traffic."

Although it's sweet of him to express his continued solidarity where Lacey is concerned, retribution for her long-standing aggression toward us is the last thing on my mind.

Yesterday, I might have joined him in one of our exhaustive analyses of her tyrannical hold over the student body. But today? Today the foundation of my life is crumbling beneath me. Her cruelty is no longer relevant.

"I mean, seriously, wasn't it *her* student council who petitioned to have our fancy new crosswalk installed last year? And now she's not even using it? So much for all those 'Safety First' buttons she made everyone wear."

I climb out of the car and slip both arms into my backpack straps. It took extreme willpower not to break down to him on the way to school about the bombshell Dad dropped on me after breakfast this morning. Zander and I share absolutely everything and to keep this secret from him, if only for an hour, feels something like betrayal. But as I stretch my canvas coat closed across my chest and trudge through the parking lot toward the side entrance of the school, I lack the strength to make my announcement more than once. He'll have to hear my news along with everyone else.

"See how easy it is to glance both ways before you cross?" He makes a big show of turning his head to the left and the right before stepping onto the street. "It takes two seconds and you don't have to worry about accidentally getting run over."

Cornflakes churn in my stomach, sloshing around undigested, as I stew about my morning, which started normally enough before taking an unexpected turn. Everything was fine until after breakfast when, instead of heading out to the barn for our typical morning chores, my sister Ashley and I were waylaid by Dad at the kitchen table where he blindsided us with his big news. Now, I can barely keep my knees from buckling as I brace myself against the cab of a classmate's beater pickup, recalling his plan. I'd hoped the initial shock would be worn off by the time we got to school, but the realization keeps hitting me in waves, and I'm forced to slow my pace across the parking lot to steady my breathing.

Zander waits for me by the entrance after noticing I've fallen behind, and I can tell by the suspicious look on his face he's finally realized something's up. "You're not gonna say anything about almost running over Lacey? Really? Come on, Tess, this is the part where you say, 'Accidents are painful. Safety is gainful.'" He laughs aloud. "Remember those signs Lacey hung all over last year?"

He holds the door open, and I manage a weak smile. "I remember," I say stepping into the building.

His eyes narrow as if he's about to ask what's wrong, but before he can inquire, our friend Pete careens through the door behind us, throwing himself onto Zander's back. "Chess club in the house!" he hollers. "You two headed to the library?"

It's a rhetorical question because he knows we are. Along with a handful of other chess club members, the three of us have been meeting in the partitioned corner of the library we call the War Room every morning before first bell since freshman year. Back then, we established the club to help pad our college applications with a non-agricultural-related endeavor. Zander always teases that if there's a spot on Harvard's application for proficiency in artificial cow insemination, he'll be a shoo-in, but we both doubt there is.

Getting into college is the least of my worries this morning, though.

By the time we get to the War Room, our friends Claire and Bruster are already embroiled in a game they've been playing since late-September, and Mike is scribbling furiously onto a sheet of notebook paper. He looks up as Zander collapses into the seat beside him, but instead of joining them as I normally do, I linger just inside the door.

"I swear to God if I have to look at one more tangent or cosine, I might end it all right here in the library. Because at this point I don't care how tall the stupid tree is. I'd actually love if it fell on my head and put me out of my misery."

"Don't you have some fancy calculator for that trigonometry crap?" Zander asks. He pulls his morning pop from his backpack, and I relish the familiar fizzing sound as he cracks it open. "Breakfast of champions," he says to me.

"Yeah," Bruster chimes in without taking his eyes off the chess board, "say that a little louder with all the dairy farmers in the room."

"If milk were caffeinated, I'd make the switch. Until then, I'll start my day with a pop."

Zander's pop of choice is Cedar Falls Cola, which makes me crazy because he will drive miles out of his way to find some instead of drinking a readily-available Coke like everyone else. He likes flapjacks but not waffles. His left foot is two sizes bigger than his right. And he cries at the movie *Rudy* every time he sees it. It's taken me a lifetime to learn everything there is to know about Zander. The thought of ever having to cultivate new friendships seriously makes me want to puke.

I venture a nervous glance at the wall clock over their heads from my post along the periphery of the room. Only fourteen minutes remain until homeroom bell, and several members of the group have yet to make an appearance. I'm considering holding off on my announcement until lunch when Liam, Tina, and Will arrive.

"What's up?" Will says, chucking his backpack onto the floor. He and Zander shake hands in this ridiculous way they assume makes them appear hip but only accentuates how incredibly middle-American they are. I've encouraged them not to do it in public on several occasions to no avail.

"My dad said something about you guys getting a new cultivator," Zander says to him.

Will pulls their game board from the shelf and sets it gently on the table between them, careful not to disturb any pieces. "Yeah. Sorta. It's a used New Holland we're co-opting with the Millers and the Burns. It's way better than the Massey we've been using, though, so hopefully things'll go more smoothly this spring than they did last year."

The guys settle into their game, talking about their dads and the machinery and the beautiful routineness that embodies what it means to grow up on a farm. The milking, feeding, and mucking, ever-present regardless of the season, pressing us forward through the steady monotony of our chore-filled days. The cycle of life. The reaping. The sowing. Births. Deaths. The unexpected cold snap or drought or locust invasion. All these things I can handle. All these things are as much of who I am as who we all are.

But who will I be without my farm, my herd, and everybody I already know?

Just the thought of it causes me to unwittingly blurt out, "I'm moving. To North Carolina. Right after Christmas."

Everyone stops what they're doing as if I've pushed pause on the soundtrack of our morning. Slowly, their faces distort into looks of concern. Brows furrow. Lips purse.

"You're doing what now?" Bruster asks.

I explain again, this time with slightly more detail, trying desperately to talk around the lump that's taken up residence in my throat. "My dad re-enlisted in the Army. It's like some..." I pause, searching for a neutral explanation which doesn't express the actual shock and horror I'm experiencing. "I think he might be having some midlife crisis or something. Because the farm can't support our family financially anymore. And I don't know, some civic duty thing because of the war in Syria."

I force myself to go on, pressing the heels of my hands into my temples and averting my gaze since I can no longer be trusted to look at any of them directly without bursting into tears. Zander, of course, is the worst. He's gaping at me like I've slaughtered his prize pig.

"He already has his orders, and he's been assigned to Fort Bragg in Fayetteville," I say to the floor. "We're selling the farm. We're leaving right after Christmas."

No one speaks. There's only my heartbeat pulsing inside my head and my jagged breathing.

In one swift motion, Zander stands. I don't know what he's doing, but he's coming at me fast. Before I can react, he's got me in an embrace which can only be described as a cross between a headlock and a vice grip, and he's squeezing me. Hard. I'm about to pass out from lack of oxygen when he releases his hold to punch me in the shoulder.

He looks crushed. Worse than the day I told the class he peed his pants in second grade. "That's for not telling me sooner," he says.

It was cruel not to have divulged my secret to him in private on the way to school. In hindsight, it's what I should've done. But I'd been selfish and cowardly, not wanting to rehash the details of my departure half-a-dozen times. "Sorry," I manage, letting myself fall into his arms for the second time. "The whole thing is so…"

I want to say 'stupid' but stop myself. Because is it stupid? Is it stupid my dad wants to provide what he hopes will be a better life for me and Ashley? And is choosing to serve his country in the process such a bad thing?

"Unfortunate," is the word I land on.

The others are watching us now, afraid to speak. Afraid of disturbing what should have been our private moment. Maybe that's the real reason I didn't tell him alone in the car, the second he slid into the passenger's seat. Maybe it's because I was too afraid we'd get stuck, unable to keep going on with our day unless there was an audience encouraging us along.

I wonder how we look to them now, with my head tucked into Zander's chest and his arms clutched tightly around my shoulders. Does it look like we're holding onto each other as though our lives depend on it? Because that's exactly how it feels to me.

"We should have a party," Claire offers, finally breaking the silence. "A farewell send-off over Christmas break."

I smile at her, grateful for the gesture, but it's going to take way more than a party to ease me gracefully out of Iowa.

chapter 2
Sunshine

Thursday, November 8

Life on a farm is perpetual motion. There are no vacations. You can't let something go *just a little while longer* because shirking your responsibilities can ultimately threaten the well-being of the herd. This is why, instead of moping in my room the way Ashley does after school, I pull on my boots and thermals and head out to the barn.

As with any farm, late fall and winter are the slowest seasons, but caring for a herd of fifty cattle still requires considerable daily labor, regardless of the date on the calendar. As a little girl, I was relegated to simple tasks like mucking stalls and filling troughs, but these days I'm responsible for more complicated tasks like calibrating the milking equipment, rotating the cows in and out of the barn, and caring for the herd's general health.

The familiar smell of grain and manure greet me at the barn's entrance, along with the steady whir of the milking machine. Most of the herd have already been through the milking parlor for the second time today and are now back in the pasture, but the last ten remain standing, idly chewing their cud while the machines extract their milk. I walk over to the closest cow, an eight-year-old Holstein with a splotch across her back that Ashley swears resembles the state of Florida.

"Hey, Sunshine," I say, reaching out to rub behind her ears. It's hard not to well up, knowing our days together are numbered, despite our long history.

*

When I was nine-years-old, my dad was the one who dealt with illness and injury, bovine or otherwise. Knowing this, I didn't question the concern in his voice the morning he hollered through the screen door for the rest of us to get dressed and meet him in the barn as quickly as we could. Groggy and still rubbing sleep from my eyes, I ran into the barn, following his voice to the partitioned stalls where cows are kept if they can't stay with the rest of the herd for some reason. Mom and I were surprised to discover, that on this particular occasion, one of the heifers had been separated because she was having difficulty delivering her calf on her own. And although I'd witnessed dozens of calves being born over the years, this was to be the first time I would assist in the delivery.

The pregnant cow, one of the herd's youngest, was stomping her hooves and braying mournfully, clearly in distress.

"The calf is breech," Dad explained as he stood by the heifer's side, patting her neck as if she were the family dog. "I didn't realize until this morning she'd gone into labor overnight, and now I'm afraid she's been trying to give birth for too long." His eyes were frantic, and I felt the weight of his accountability. "I tried correcting the calf's position, but my hands are too big. I can't get a good grip on the blasted thing."

He turned to me then, pleading. "I need you to try and turn the calf so the front feet come out first, or there's a chance we'll lose them both."

It wasn't a question. He wasn't asking if I could or if I would. He was telling me to slide my tiny nine-year-old hands into the cow and turn the baby around.

I didn't hesitate.

After several minutes trying to distinguish hind hooves from front hooves, I finally felt the smoothness of the calf's snout and was able to begin correcting the presentation from breech to head-first. Slowly, laboriously, the calf twisted within its mother's womb, and once I was convinced I'd done it properly, my dad instructed me to pull.

Moments later, I held the calf in my arms as Dad tried in vain to resuscitate it, covering its mucus-laden snout with his entire mouth while the heifer looked on. Sadly, the calf would not survive.

"Remember this, Tess," my mom said, handing me a tissue to dry my eyes as we shuffled back to the house in the pale light of morning. "Let the pain be a reminder—you can't get attached to these animals. They're a commodity. Nothing more. Don't waste your tears on the herd."

But as I lay in bed that night, I couldn't stop thinking of the mother cow. Of how woefully she'd watched as we'd carried her baby away. Her soulful eyes haunted me as I stared at the ceiling—I couldn't let her spend the night alone. And so, after slipping on my coat and boots over my pajamas, I snuck out of the house, cringing as the screen door scraped against the jamb.

I found her back in the barn, lying on her side amongst a fresh pile of straw, no longer damp with birthing fluids. She lifted her head to greet me, and I recognized for the first time how her spot *did* sort of resemble Florida. I could see it now, if

I turned my head to the side, even if it was a stretch.

I'd never been to Florida, but I'd heard it was a sunny place.
"I'm going to call you Sunshine," I said as I spread a blanket
on the ground behind her and propped myself against her
back. "I'm sorry about your baby. But I promise to always be
your friend."

*

Standing with her now, I remember my pledge and feel
the overwhelming urge to look away. Down the line are Greta,
Flower, Minnie, Daisy, Maggie, Bella, Penelope, Annie, and
Muffin. I smile to myself because despite my mother's counsel,
every cow on our farm has a name.

Names that will be lost forever the moment we move away.

"Have a good day at school?" Dad asks from the doorway.
Like always, he's come to help me disconnect the udders from
the machinery now that the milking is complete, acting as if
this morning never happened.

But the dull ache in the pit of my stomach confirms it most
certainly did.

I shrug and continue scratching Sunshine's neck, unable
to look at him directly. The tension pulls between us, tight as
barbed wire, and I can't believe he's going all business as usual
on me. Should I follow his lead or confess how devastated I am
about every facet of his plan, forcing me from the only life I've
ever known? Would it do any good to tell him how brutal it
was holding myself together all day, tears threatening to spill
over every time I noticed my own pained expression mirrored
in Zander's face across the room?

He strolls past me over to the main line and clamps it shut.
I lean down beside Sunshine to release her from the teat cups.

"I know it's hard for you to wrap your head around why
I've made the decision to sell the farm, but the truth is, it's

been a long time coming."

This is news to me. The possibility he would consider a life outside the farm seems impossible. My dad loves being a farmer even more than I do. At least, I thought he did.

"You never told us things had gotten so bad financially," I say, grateful he's broached the subject so I didn't have to. "Why didn't you say something before?"

He flushes a particularly finicky line and shakes his head. "Your mom and I didn't want..." He hesitates then, fumbling with the tube's connection before continuing. "I guess we didn't want to worry you girls unnecessarily. The truth is, we were hoping the finances would work themselves out. But like I told you this morning, milk consumption is down across the country. Big farms are getting bigger and making it harder for smaller farms like us to remain solvent."

He lifts his head, and under the brim of his hat there's apprehension in the lines of his face I hadn't noticed this morning. Were they there all along or did my ignorance prevent me from seeing them before now? It's clear he doesn't want to leave the farm any more than the rest of us. He's disappointed in himself. Embarrassed even.

"Your mom was the one who encouraged me to re-enlist. Believe it or not, we loved military life, in some ways as much as we love this one. The Army can provide for us in ways the farm no longer can, and with the problems in the Middle East..." He switches off the pump, and it falls silent. "Let's just say our country needs my particular set of skills now more than ever. In fact, if it weren't for my unique decoding abilities, the Army might not have agreed to take me back. But they did, so I'm trying really hard to think of it as a good thing. And I know it's gonna be hard for you to leave Zander and the herd behind, but I hope maybe someday you'll see this move as the opportunity it truly is."

This simple acknowledgment of my sacrifice lifts some of the resentment, and a bit of the anger I've been harboring against him slips away to reveal a twinge of pride. Our move will allow him to defend the Syrian people while providing for our family at the same time. No one could be more selfless than my dad. This understanding, however, doesn't ease the tightness in my chest as I move down the line, taking care to give each cow an extra rub or scratch or pat. Our days together are still numbered, regardless of the reasons why.

"Your sister's got herself all worked up, though, hasn't she?" he says, forcing levity into the conversation. "Your mom warned me she was gonna be piss and vinegar, and boy she wasn't lying. You'll work on her for me, huh?"

Like the invitation to right Sunshine's calf inside her womb, this isn't a request I can deny. It's an assumption of action. And, of course, I'll do my best.

"I'll talk to her," I tell him, releasing the last cow, Muffin, from the equipment. "But no promises. It'll be hard to convince her it's all gonna be okay when I'm having a hard time convincing myself."

He turns to me, and our eyes meet. They're glassy in a way I've never seen before. "I'm so sorry," he says, "for uprooting all of you like this." He unties Muffin from the rail and swats her rear, encouraging her out of the parlor into the field. "Even you, Muffin old girl."

chapter 3
Bur Oak

Saturday, November 10

As one of the smaller parcels in our area with just under 120 acres, the entire western perimeter of our farm runs along Zander's property line, which is nearly triple the size of ours. Because of its larger scale, his farm includes a sign and a moniker—*Robert's Farmstead Dairy*—while ours remains a nameless entity. The point at which the properties meet is marked by a lone, sprawling bur oak, sixty feet tall and visible from both of our houses. Mere proximity isn't what brings Zander across the barren cornfield to where I'm perched among the lowest limbs this morning, though.

"It's freezing out here," he calls from below, craning up at me with his hand at his brow, shielding his eyes from the morning sun.

"I figure I better enjoy the cold while I can. Before I ship off to the balmy South."

Instead of venturing a reply, he begins climbing the tree, scrambling to the same branch we've been sitting on together since we were tall enough to hoist one another up.

"You know," he says as he settles in beside me, resting

his head on my shoulder, "it gets cold in North Carolina, too. You're not moving to Miami."

I sigh. "It feels like I'm moving to the moon."

He pulls me closer, wrapping me into the folds of his coat, and I can't stop myself from molding into the hollow of his chest. It would be better if I didn't need him so much, but he's a habit I'm not inclined to break.

"It'll be better than the moon," he says. "For one, I hear there's oxygen in North Carolina. And also, other people. Plus, think about how close you'll be to the ocean."

I haven't considered my improved proximity to the beach. I've never even seen the ocean before.

"If you take me to the shore, I'll totally come visit you," he adds. "Maybe this summer, after planting and before harvest."

I envision the two of us walking along the beach together, dipping our toes in the frothy surf. As pleasant as the image is, everything about it seems wrong. We don't belong there. We belong here. On the farm. Milking cows. In Iowa.

"Do you even have a proper bathing suit?" I ask him.

"I have cut-offs," he says with a shrug.

I smile. The idea of him swimming in the ocean is ridiculous, even if he could pass as a surfer with his shaggy, sandy hair.

He pulls out his phone to check the distance from Fayetteville to the closest beach, and seeing it reminds me of one of my numerous concerns for the future. "You do realize that once I move, you're gonna need to use the call function of your cell if you wanna hear my voice," I say. "A long-distance friendship can't survive on emojis alone, and I'm worried actual phone conversations might kill you."

He dated Gabby Landford through most of our sophomore year, and she was chatty. Refused to text and called him every night at eight o'clock to talk for at least an hour about 'nothing.'

Zander's words, not mine. By contrast, he and I never talk on the phone and barely even text—only enough to coordinate driving arrangements or confirm homework assignments.

All our communication is done in person.

That is, until after Christmas, when there isn't going to be any more *in person.*

"If you're referring to my horrible phone calls with Gabby, you know I hated talking to her because I never had anything important to say."

"Oh, and you're gonna have important stuff to say to me?" I hope my sarcastic tone masks the desperation in my voice. If our long-distance conversations feel compulsory, he might opt out the way he did with Gabby. Being cut out of his life is not an option. My heart will not allow it.

His reply comes without hesitation, calming my nerves. "Are you kidding? Of course, we'll have things to talk about. I'll have to fill you in on everything going on back here. Like if the chess club finally gets the funding to go to regionals. And about Lacey and her cronies and how your farm's getting on."

I try to imagine what talking on the phone with him will be like, but my brain gets stuck on the semantics of *your farm* because it clearly isn't going to be my farm anymore. Or ever again.

And if I don't live on the farm next door and I don't have the same homework and I'm no longer a member of the same chess club, how long will it be before Zander and I don't have anything to talk about anymore?

I don't respond, but he continues, almost as if he can read my mind. "We have sixteen years of history together, Tess. Nothing can take those memories away from us. You're always gonna be a part of my life, even if you're no longer a part of my days."

I turn to face him, struggling to keep my balance on the

branch. He isn't smiling, but his eyes are warm, and I reach out with my finger to trace the scar cutting across his temple through his left eyebrow—the only remaining physical evidence of his fall from the silo when he was eleven. For a farm boy, he certainly has a way of knowing the right things to say.

One of the many reasons he's always been my lone confidant.

"I have no idea how to make new friends," I confess to him now. "What if no one in Fayetteville likes me?"

He shakes his head like he's considering blowing me off before meeting my gaze. I want him to tell me I'm crazy and have nothing to worry about. I want him to say people will love me, and I'll make a ton of new friends on the first day. But he doesn't. Because we don't lie to one another. We never have. I didn't lie to him when he asked if he was any good at playing the guitar in seventh grade (he wasn't), and he didn't lie to me when I asked if he liked my pixie haircut the summer we turned fourteen (he didn't).

And so now, instead of coddling me the way a pseudo-friend would, he tells me the truth.

"It might suck, Tess. It might suck big time. Those kids, they aren't gonna be like us. I mean, probably not. Because Mid-West kids and East Coast kids are pretty different, right? But here's the thing—you're smart and fun and super pretty, and I'm betting you'll find at least one other person there who gets you."

I let my chin drop to my chest, embarrassed not only by the way his compliments raise heat to my cheeks but because of how worried I am about moving on without him. Leaving the farm and the herd wouldn't be nearly as scary if he could come with me. But without him around to act as my relationship liaison, my inability to make small talk and fear of rejection are going to seriously inhibit my capacity for making new friends.

"I'm not a typical girl, Zander. And I can almost guarantee there isn't gonna be another dairy farmer/chess wiz waiting to be my new best friend in Fayetteville." The whine in my voice is grating even to my own ears, so I can only imagine what Zander must think of the self-indulgent pity party I'm having for myself. It doesn't stop me from continuing, though, burying my head into his chest. "What if they all hate me?"

He doesn't immediately respond, and my trepidation hangs in the air between us—an inadequate articulation of how nervous I am about being a potential outcast—a country bumpkin in a sea of cultured urbanites. It's one more thing to add to the growing list of reasons I can't sleep at night.

He nudges me with his shoulder. "No one is gonna hate you. There's literally nothing about you to hate. Except maybe the fact that you're a total spaz."

He's working the deflection, trying to get me to laugh.

"The only reason I fit in here is because of you, and our school is full of nothing but farm kids. How am I ever gonna find someone there?"

He shakes his head but falls short of rolling his eyes. "You'll talk to people. Get to know them. And let them get to know you. Be yourself and give it some time. If they still don't get you after you've given them a chance, I'll be here to listen. But you can't go in with a defeatist attitude. You gotta be positive. You gotta believe you're gonna find new friends."

I sigh. I want to tell him I don't want to find anybody else. Instead, I say, "You're not gonna be easy to replace."

He chuckles, lifting his foot in the air. "I know. I wear a size fourteen. These are mighty big shoes to fill."

I can't help but smile. "You're a dork."

"The dorkiest," he replies.

We sit together in silence for what seems like a long time

but is probably only ten minutes, until my fingers get so cold I can barely feel them. When I tell him I need to go home—to help with the herd, finish my history report on why the United States entered WWI, and start packing—he climbs down first and grabs me by the waist to lower me to the ground beside him.

There's an awkwardness between us that's never been there before, as if neither of us wants to say goodbye, even if we're only heading across the field to our respective houses. I kick at a clump of dirt with my shoe, hands buried deep in my coat pockets. He gives my arm a sympathetic squeeze before heading toward his house, but stops a moment later, calling over his shoulder.

"I'm going with Bruster and Pete to Mason City to see the new Spielberg movie tonight. You wanna come?"

I remember the tentative plans the guys set before my dad released his bombshell. In a few short weeks, Zander and I won't be going anywhere together ever again. I stifle the thought.

"The alien one?"

He nods.

"Sure. I'm in."

"Pick you up at six," he says.

He ambles across the field, tall and lanky, more man than boy, and it reminds me of how he once was, a carefree kid with skinned knees and a farmer's tan, running back and forth between our houses. I add this older version of him now to my mental scrapbook of memories, an image to call upon when my recollections of him begin getting fuzzy around the edges, as they certainly will in the months to come.

chapter 4
New Year's Eve

Monday, December 31

Pete hands me a pair of ridiculous looking glasses which are designed so you look through the date into the promise of the coming year.

"Claire gave out noisemakers, too, but they only came in a pack of six so there aren't any left," he explains to me as I follow him from the foyer down the stairs into Claire's basement.

"It's okay," I tell him. "These glasses are more than enough excitement for me."

It seems I'm the last to arrive as everyone else is already scattered around the room in groups of twos and threes. Zander's in the corner, embroiled in what appears to be a particularly serious game of foosball against Mike and doesn't even look up as I enter the room. Since our conversation at the oak tree in November, things have gotten seriously awkward between us, which is why I wasn't surprised when he didn't offer me a ride to tonight's party or ask for me to pick him up on the way.

Over the course of the past several weeks, I've felt a not-so-subtle shift in our friendship. After Thanksgiving, he started catching a ride to school with Bruster instead of tagging along with me. Around the same time, he stopped walking me to each of my classes and began making excuses for why he couldn't come over on Wednesday nights to play chess. The worst, though, was during the final week before Christmas break when he abandoned his post beside me in the cafeteria. As much as all the others hurt, this final snub felt most like a kick in the teeth. Because barring illness, we'd eaten school lunch together every day for the past eleven years.

I know in my heart as I look at him now that he's only bracing himself for what's to come. Preparing for the days I won't be able to drive him around or walk with him to class or sit beside him as we eat our chicken tenders and pineapple tidbits. It's merely self-preservation. A means of protecting his heart. And maybe I should be grateful he's been pulling away for the both of us. But acknowledging this and accepting it are two entirely different things.

Resisting the urge to go to him now, I head in the opposite direction to the card table covered in three half-eaten bags of chips, a bowl of crusty queso, and a double-duty sheet cake with 'We'll Miss You Tess' and 'Happy New Year' written across the top. At least I earned top billing with whoever decorated the cake. I help myself to a chip as I count the people dispersed around the room. Along with the eight other members of the chess club, there are a few stragglers who obviously weren't invited to any other New Year's parties around town.

"Surprise!" Claire yells, jumping off the second-hand sectional to give me a hug. I smile because she must realize the party is anything but a surprise since she's been discussing it ad nauseam with anyone who'll listen for the past three weeks.

Bruster hands me a Solo cup, and I thank him. "What's in it?" I ask.

"Does it matter?" he says over the music, and I shrug in

agreement before taking a sip. It's warm and fruity and burns the back of my throat. The evening might be less painful if I chug it down, but I want to remember every moment of the last night I'm ever going to spend with these people, so I decide to nurse it instead.

I'm still standing awkwardly in a corner alone with my cup when Zander finally notices me, nodding in my direction from across the room. Looking at him hurts deep down, and I'm struck by an insatiable longing. There's a hopelessness in the way he stares at me now as if he wishes I would get on with my leaving instead of dragging out the inevitable with my continued presence.

I force myself to turn away, unable to muster more than a wave before accepting an invitation to sit on the sofa between Tina and Claire. Ryan Seacrest is on TV announcing the *New Year's Rockin' Eve* performances. The people in New York look cold.

"I love Katy Perry," Tina says, commenting on the night's scheduled musicians. "I would love to dye my hair that color."

"You should do it," Claire tells her, grabbing for another handful of Doritos.

Tina rolls her eyes. "Like my mother wouldn't kill me. Can you even imagine?"

If I had to choose two girls from East Chester who might legitimately dye their hair teal, Tina and Claire would be the last two I would pick. Of course, there aren't many who would consider doing something so edgy. Edgy is one thing the kids from our town are not.

Claire turns to me then, as if she's just remembered I'm leaving in the morning. "So how long's the drive to Fayetteville?"

I've been dreading this conversation. The one where we all finally talk about my forced relocation across the country.

Until now, everyone's been avoiding the topic, like not talking about it might keep it from happening. But the time has come. My last night in Iowa. I guess they figure it's now or never.

Never would have been preferable.

I sigh. "My dad says it's like eighteen hours or something, but we're taking two days to get there."

"Your mom's staying behind, though, right?"

"Yeah. To finish with the movers. Dad insisted Ashley and I leave with him tomorrow so we can register for school by the end of this week and start classes next Monday. He's freaking out about us 'getting behind on our studies,' so we'll be sleeping on the floor 'til Mom and the movers show up sometime next week."

Our new residence is a sore subject, and although I've been trying not to worry about living in a neighborhood, it's making me claustrophobic already. I realize, as I chance a glance over my shoulder in Zander's direction, I'm going to have new neighbors and none of them will be him. My mouth goes dry, and I bite at the inside of my cheek to keep the tears from spilling over. Someone new will be moving into my house, too. Probably a replacement best friend for Zander.

"Are you excited about your new school?" Tina asks, pulling me from my thoughts back into our conversation. It takes a second for my brain to switch gears, and as I shift my gaze away from the foosball match, I'm certain 'excited' is the last word I would use to describe how I feel.

"It's gonna be different," I say diplomatically. Although I'm in no mood to discuss my deep-seated feelings of inadequacy associated with not fitting in at my new school, for some reason, I go on. "I'm nervous about making friends. I don't know quite what to expect."

"Totally understandable," Claire chimes in, always happy to hijack a conversation. "Because *we've* all known each other forever, right? I mean, since kindergarten at least. Except for when Jessica moved here in second grade. Or was it third? Either way, I can't imagine having to start over again. Especially with a bunch of military kids who don't know anything about life on a farm. What are the chances you'll have anything in common with them?"

Although I attempt to keep the shock off my face, I must still appear horrified because before I can engage my brain to formulate a suitable response, Claire continues. "But I'm sure you'll find someone to hang out with. And you always have Ashley, right? Sisters are the best."

If Claire's intent for this party was to help me feel better about my transition out of Iowa, it's definitely not having the desired effect. Maybe it was overly optimistic of me to hope my classmates might gush about what an amazing opportunity I've been given or perhaps express jealousy over the path of my new life, even if they had to lie to my face. So far, they're only making things worse.

Tina must sense my unease, cutting her eyes away from the television to change the subject. "Did you guys find a buyer for the farm and the livestock?"

"The auction's in February," I tell her, realizing as I say it there isn't a single pleasant topic for us to discuss. The long drive. The new school. The sale of my farm. It all hurts. And now, despite their commiserate faces, I'm done with the party. I'm done chit-chatting about how my world is imploding all around me.

All I want to do is go home.

"Well, I'm sure my dad will go. He can't resist a good livestock auction." She takes out her phone and scrolls through her contacts. "I wanna make sure I've got your number because we should totally keep in touch. Call and text and whatever. And you follow me on Snapchat and Instagram, right? Promise you'll post lots of pictures of the Army stuff in Fayetteville once you get there."

Claire's forced lightheartedness only makes me want to bolt even more. "Absolutely," I say, the level of enthusiasm in my voice far surpassing my actual excitement. "I'll definitely keep in touch."

The girls turn back to Ryan Seacrest and his *Rockin' New Year's Eve*. We've officially reached the point in our friendship where there's nothing left to say. To discuss homework or relationship drama or even the basketball team's unexpected winning season would be a waste of breath. These things no longer connect us. We sit together in strained silence, watching the crowd of spectators in New York City who have assembled to welcome in the promise of a new year. I can't help but resent their revelry.

"I'm gonna go check out what the guys are up to," I tell them at a commercial break, even though I'd have to be deaf not to hear them freaking out over the foosball match on the other side of the room.

With my mostly-full cup in hand, I make my way to where Zander and Mike are still duking it out. As hard as I try, I simply can't stay away.

"Game point," Mike says.

"You wish," Zander replies. "Somehow points keep ending up on your side. I know you're cheating."

"I never cheat. It's not my fault you suck."

Their banter continues, back and forth between them as if I'm not even there. The tiny ball ricochets around the table, flying from one end to the other until Zander finally shoots it into Mike's goal.

"And that, my friend, is how you do it," Zander says, spinning his red players in a display of triumph. He glances at me, a mischievous grin on his face. "You wanna play?"

His simple offer splinters the tension between us, causing a hairline fracture in the carefully crafted blockades we've both constructed to save us from ourselves. Part of me wants to decline nonchalantly as if I can't be bothered with so many other options at my disposal. But instead, I cave immediately. How can I resist? Especially since it's not only our final opportunity to be together but my last chance to beat the master at his own game.

"First one to ten," I say.

Having already warmed up, he scores against me quickly. Twice. But before long, my hands remember the rhythm of the strikers: forward, mid, defense, goal. Between shots, I notice beads of sweat gathering at his hairline. He really wants to win.

I wish the moment could last forever. I wish I could keep living *this* life. The one where Zander and I battle over foosball and chess and who gets the last chocolate donut at the bake shop.

But time keeps moving forward and before long I'm surprised to discover I'm up by three points. Mike and Pete dog Zander from the sideline.

"After all these years you're gonna let her beat you now?"

"Don't be nice to her," Mike warns. "She'll never let you live this down."

My body tenses. In an effort to rile up Zander, Mike's distracted me instead. I lift my head to glare at him. I want to yell in his face. I want to tell him it doesn't matter if I win or never let him 'live it down.' Because who cares about bragging rights when you live 1,200 miles away?

With my concentration broken, Zander scores again, the ball hurtling so quickly into my goal, I don't even realize what's happened.

"Your turn," he says, smirking.

I fish the ball out of the return and toss it onto the table.

Immediately, he scores another goal.

And another.

And another.

"Game point," he says.

I want to win. I do. Because in all the years we've been hanging out in Claire's basement, I've never beaten him, and it would feel amazing to finally take him down. But in that moment, my palms sweaty against the handles, I know we may never play another game of foosball in Claire's basement together again.

And I can't do it.

The ball drops one final time, and I ease off the rods. In less than ten seconds, Zander emerges victorious, dancing around the room like a lunatic, high-fiving the others.

"Tough break, Tess," he says, giving me a sympathetic pat on the back. "Maybe next time."

I force a smile. His words are meaningless—something nice to say since there will probably never be a next time. "Good game," I manage.

I slink off to the food table and test the salsa. Not surprisingly, it's mild, like everything else in Iowa. The people. The pace. The entire way of life. I wonder if I'll ever adjust to a spicier existence.

I dip another tortilla chip into the queso, remembering the weather forecast on the radio on the way to the party. With predictions of overnight temperatures in the single digits, Dad's probably already moving the herd into the barn and might need help raking extra straw for dry bedding to keep them warm. I'm weighing my allegiance to my friends with my commitment to my dad when it hits me: I'm wasting my time in Claire's basement, because the truth is, Zander's been right all along. If I'm gonna go, I should get on with it. Stop dragging out the unavoidable and leave already.

I excuse myself, announcing I have to use the bathroom upstairs, and with one final glance over my shoulder, grab my coat and keys from where I dropped them earlier at the foot of the stairs and head up. I don't wave. I don't give hugs. I don't even say goodbye. I bolt out the front door into the arctic air, which catches in my lungs and nearly stops me in my tracks.

*

I find Dad where I expect, pitchfork in hand, piling additional layers of insulation for the cows to sleep against. He's bundled in his heaviest coat, and his face is barely visible beneath his thermal mask.

"Need some help?" I ask, sliding the barn door shut behind me.

"Thought you were at your farewell party? Gotta be getting close to midnight, doesn't it?" he asks, without looking up from his work.

I shrug. "I left a little after eleven o'clock. There wasn't much left to say, and I figured you could probably use an extra set of hands here."

He stops shoveling, and I can tell there's some underlying sentiment he wants to express but doesn't. Instead, he says, "It's supposed to be cold like this for a few more days, and I can't expect your mother to keep up with the herd while she's dealing with the movers. I hired Dean Reynolds to take care of things until after the auction and Zander's dad offered to help as well, but I wanna make sure the girls are ready to deal with this cold on their own as best they can. I'm gonna fill all the troughs with double the feed both inside and out in the fields. I also wanna keep this bedding nice and thick. They hate being cooped up inside, but it's too cold for 'em out there."

I grab another pitchfork from the storage closet and begin lobbing straw into the stalls. As the herd looks on, we work in silence, relishing the strain of our muscles and the satisfaction of protecting the creatures who can't protect themselves. It occurs to me, as we toil side by side, being a soldier might be more like being a farmer than I initially supposed, and my dad is going to make a great one.

With two of us working, it doesn't take long to fill the stall floors. "If you load the troughs in here, I'll take care of the ones in the field," he says once we finish.

"Sounds good," I agree.

He slides the door shut behind him while I head off in the direction of the feeders. Usually, the herd eats outside. In the summer, the cows feed on the grass in the pasture, but in the winter, we haul hay bales or grain into the large metal troughs scattered throughout the property. Most of them are outside, but there are some inside, too, for occasions such as this.

As I dump bags of grain into the troughs, I find myself lingering, pausing beside each cow to say goodbye. It seems strange I'm more inclined to have a proper farewell with them than my friends, but perhaps it's because the cows, ignorant of our diverging futures, haven't begun looking at me with sadness in their eyes. I scratch Greta behind the ears. Lay my cheek against Daisy's snout. And by the time Dad reappears from the pasture, I'm weeping into Sunshine's neck.

"They're gonna be fine," he consoles me, placing both hands on my shoulders. When I don't respond, he pulls me away from her, and I crumple into his chest, crying with unrestrained desperation. He strokes my hair, quietly shushing me like I'm a child with a busted-up knee, and although his reassurances are inadequate, they're comforting just the same. Once my breathing returns to normal, I find the courage to lift my face, hoping to draw strength from his composure. Instead, his tear-stained cheeks betray him.

"We're gonna be fine. All of us," he tells me, and I get the feeling saying the words aloud is as much for his benefit as my own. "Once we get past this hard part of leaving, I'm sure it's gonna get easier."

"It's gonna be great," I offer in an effort to ease his guilt.

He wraps his arm around my shoulder and leads me toward the barn door. "You always have been my optimistic girl, haven't you," he says.

I shrug but absorb the warmth of his praise.

Before leaving the barn for the last time, he turns back to face the herd, calling to them in a voice racked with guilt. "Good night, Ladies," he says. "And Happy New Year."

It's almost one o'clock in the morning by the time I crawl into bed. Even after a hot shower, my cheeks and toes are still cool to the touch, and I welcome the warmth of my flannel sheets. I wonder briefly before closing my eyes if we'll even need them in North Carolina but decide I don't care. I'm keeping them either way.

I'm almost asleep, barely conscious of drifting off, when I'm startled by a noise outside my window. Before I have a chance to turn on the light and investigate, the sash slides open and someone steps into my room.

I hope beyond all hope I'm not dreaming.

"Zander?" I ask, not wondering if it's him but why he's here.

He's all the way in the room now, standing at the foot of my bed. "Did I wake you?" he whispers.

"No," I tell him. He blows into his hands, and I lift my blankets, inviting him under the covers to warm up.

"It's colder than a polar bear's butt out there," he says, snuggling against me in my tiny twin bed like we're still six-year-olds, camping outside in each other's backyards. I wrap my arms around him and he settles against my shoulder. "You left your own party."

"It wasn't really *my* party," I say. "More New Year's than anything else."

"The cake was good. Red velvet. You would've liked it."

There's so much I want to say. Apologies I want to give. Promises I want to make. But the words are jumbled around in my head, and I'm afraid if I speak everything will come out all wrong.

"I didn't have anyone to kiss at the ball drop," he says eventually, and I wonder if whatever was in his Solo cup has gone to his head.

"Tina and Claire were there," I say.

He chuckles grimly and his voice turns serious. "We've been together every New Year's since we were babies, you know that?" His words settle over me, and I strain under the weight of them. Heavier still is the burden of what he doesn't say: *And this might have been our last.*

"I'm sorry," I say, feeling the need to explain, "but it was so cold and I knew my dad was gonna need help with the herd and..."

He rolls over to face me, placing a finger over my lips. "It's okay, Tess. I get it. It's been hard being around each other for the past few weeks. I didn't realize the anticipation of you leaving was gonna suck so bad. I didn't know how horrible I was at long goodbyes." Now he's the one who's apologizing. "I guess I didn't know what else to do. I figured this day might be easier for both of us..."

"If you left me before I had the chance to leave you?"

"Something like that," he says with a sigh. "It wasn't intentional. I guess I've been sorta messed up in my own head, thinking about not having you around. You're the best part of my days."

I blink back tears I don't realize are already spilling down my cheeks. His admission is true for me as well—something we've always taken for granted.

"It's only eighteen months, then we'll both graduate and head to college together like we always planned. You and me. It's not that long, right?"

"It's not that long," he agrees. "But it'll never be the same, not having you right next door."

His body is relaxed against mine, and I'm reminded of all the nights we spent together growing up, head to foot and back to back, me teasing him for his stinky feet and him making fun of my retainer. "Maybe someone better will move in here," I laugh between sniffles. "Some Victoria's Secret supermodel, schlepping around manure in waders and a thong."

He chuckles, too, and I imagine him smiling in the darkness. "As tempting as she sounds, I still wouldn't willingly trade you for her."

There's something unspoken in his words, a tiny invitation across a boundary we've never crossed. But I can't cross it now. I won't. There's no reason to take something painful and make it complicated as well.

"I should go to sleep," I tell him. "We're leaving after the morning milking, and I gotta be alert enough to drive."

He stirs under the covers and his warmth leaves my side. As he stands over me, silhouetted in the moonlight cascading through my window, I hear him sigh. Then, he leans down to place a kiss on my forehead like a father tucking in his child.

"Bye," I say.

"Bye."

"Love ya."

"Love ya back."

And then he's gone, back through the window out into the night. I assume, in the wake of our farewell, it's going to take me hours to fall asleep, but the next thing I know my alarm is going off, and it's time to slide the chessboard of my past life on to the shelf and begin another match.

chapter 5
Fayetteville or Bust

Tuesday, January 1 – Wednesday, January 2

Zander isn't waiting for me on the porch or the end of the driveway as we head out. I don't expect him to be, but part of me hopes I'll have one more chance to wave goodbye. Apparently, he's satisfied with our farewell from the night before, and I decide, as we pass his house, he's probably smart to have stayed away. We both suck at goodbyes.

Dad takes the lead as we travel the familiar roads out of town, but since his Ram 1500 has way more pick up than my Jetta, Ashley and I quickly lose sight of him once we hit the interstate.

"You gotta keep up," Ashley instructs from the passenger's seat as she flips stations on the radio. "You don't even know where we're going."

"I have Google maps on my phone," I tell her, nodding to where I've propped it on the dash. "And besides, Dad won't leave us stranded."

"Wish he woulda left us," she mumbles under her breath.

This is about how the entire trip to Fayetteville goes, with me concentrating on keeping up with Dad through lane shifts, construction, backups, and detours, while Ashley makes disparaging remarks every fifteen minutes, like clockwork.

"There's not a single good radio station in Indiana."

"Why don't you have a USB port in this car?"

"I'm hungry."

"I have to go to the bathroom."

"Ohio's ugly."

"There's a sign for Fayetteville! No, wait. Whose idea was it to put another Fayetteville in West Virginia?"

"Pull over! This road's too curvy. I'm gonna puke!"

"Is this North Carolina? Where are the palm trees? I thought we were moving to the South. This is totally messed up."

By the time we arrive at the gated entrance to Fort Bragg on Wednesday afternoon, I'm pretty sure that if I have to spend another minute on the road with Ashley, someone is going to die.

"Thank God!" she says as we spill out of the car, both of us stretching our arms above our heads to work out the kinks associated with eighteen hours of road travel. It's warmer than home but not as summery as we were expecting. All the same, I'm happy to strip off my heavy coat and Ashley seems to be as well.

"Wait here," Dad calls to us from across the main entrance parking lot. Given the steady stream of civilians and soldiers flooding in and out of the building, I expect him to be gone for quite a while. Instead, he returns in less than five minutes with a pass for the dashboard of my car. "This will let your POV on base for now until you get an ID card next week. We'll get TLE for a few nights and have been assigned a room with Army lodging until our permanent quarters are ready. We should get keys to our housing Friday or Monday sometime after my in-processing is complete." He looks around then, taking it all in as if he's come home to an old friend. "Things are a lot different from the last time I was here."

The perplexed look on Ashley's face confirms she and I share the same bewilderment over Dad's account of our situation. Peppered with an unintelligible smattering of military jargon, it's almost as if he's speaking a foreign language. "How about explaining all that again, only this time in English," I say.

Dad chuckles to himself, considering a broader explanation. "Your car is a POV. A personal operating vehicle. TLE is temporary housing, like a hotel. And in-processing means checking into my assigned unit," he clarifies. "In fact, if I can still find my..."

He's stopped short by the sound of a bomb going off. Ashley and I jump into the air, nearly knocking each other down.

Dad laughs. "Artillery fire," he says. "You girls are gonna have to get used to it. They set off all the big stuff around here. Howitzers and mortars. Air defense. Lots of little artillery, too. SAW. 50 Caliber. AT4s."

"English, Dad," I scold.

"Weapons. Guns. Firearms."

"It sounds like a war zone," Ashley says. "I miss the peace and quiet of the farm already."

I glare at her, but Dad seems unfazed. "Before you know it, it'll be background noise, and you won't even notice it anymore." As another round of shots rings out, Ashley and I jump a second time. "Come on, you two. Let's leave your car here for now, and I'll show you around a little bit before it gets dark."

I'm not thrilled about the prospect of being back on the road, especially cramped into the front seat of Dad's truck next to Ashley. Binge-watching the final season of *Unbreakable*

Kimmy Schmidt on Netflix in the hotel sounds like a better idea, but Dad's enthusiasm is infectious and before long I'm almost as excited as he is.

"What's over there?" I ask, pointing to a large building with an overflowing parking lot.

"That's AAFES and the PX," he says quickly, before remembering my anacronym-free mandate. "Uh, it's the grocery store and a place sorta like a Walmart but only for military people."

"Oh, great," Ashley deadpans, "all my shopping needs in one convenient place."

I ignore her, noticing another building ahead. "Are we staying there? The Landmark Inn?"

"No. We're staying over at Moon Hall. There's more temporary housing further on post." We drive a couple of miles, and he points out a library and a golf course. "There are two 18-hole courses here on post. This one is Ryder and the other one is Stryker."

I can't believe how big they are compared to our little 9-hole course in Iowa.

We come to a traffic circle, and after a couple more turns he points out an ice rink, a gymnasium, and Womack Hospital.

"It's huge," I say.

"They treat a lot of people there," he replies, taking a right-hand turn onto Normandy. "And Ashley, here's where you'll go to school for the rest of the year, Albritton Middle School."

From the truck's center seat, Ashley cranes around me to look at her new school. Her eyes widen, and although she doesn't mention it's twice the size of my high school back home, I can tell she's gobsmacked. Or maybe terrified. Either way, the moment passes quickly because before we're even completely past, she's already scowling again, arms folded across her chest.

"My school's not on base, right Dad?" I ask as we continue on Normandy. "It's a public school."

"Right. Since there's no DOD high school here on base for military kids, all the high schoolers go to M.A. Hopkins, a public school off post. If we get housing in Casablanca like I'm hoping, it won't be too far of a drive for you to get there." He leans around Ashley to look at me. "We'll go there tomorrow or Friday at the latest so you can have a look around."

If Ashley's middle school is any indication of the size of the schools around here, I don't know how I'm going to navigate the building or the student body.

I'm still worrying about school when Dad announces, "This is the 82nd Airborne area of post, where I'll be stationed while we're here."

The street is long and straight and would remind me of home if it weren't for all the brigade headquarters and barracks lining both sides.

"Here's where I'll be working," he says as we pull in front of a rectangular, two-story cinderblock building. "313th MI Battalion."

There are soldiers everywhere, some marching in formation, some strolling along the sidewalk dressed in combat fatigues similar to the camouflage Zander wears hunting with his dad. Except for the hats, that is.

"What's with the red berets?" Ashley asks before I have a chance to comment.

"They're actually maroon," Dad replies, "and they're only worn by airborne divisions like the 82nd. The 75th Ranger Regiment wear tan ones and Special Forces wear green."

Still processing my dad's seemingly endless supply of non-farming-related knowledge, we turn a corner and begin to double back on a parallel street. The first thing I spot is a billboard which reads:

82ⁿᵈ Airborne Division Public Safety Message Center

39 DAYS NO DIVISION FATALITY

I read it a second time, certain it can't seriously be tracking soldier deaths. Dad sees us reading the board and chuckles nervously under his breath.

"I'd almost forgotten about that," he says. "It's, uh, supposed to give everyone an incentive to be safe because if the division goes 82 days without a fatality, everyone gets a day off." He smiles as though this is perfectly normal, incentivizing the practice of staying alive.

Before we've fully passed, I glance at the sign again and it hits me—my dad is putting his life in danger by simply being here. Because soldiers die. Apparently so often they need a billboard to keep track.

My stomach lurches, and I'm furious with myself for having been so short-sighted. How could I have spent the last six weeks so focused on myself when my dad was getting ready to lay his life on the line for his country, the way one of his fellow soldiers did thirty-nine days ago?

Oh my God. He could die. People die here.

Dad clears his throat as we continue driving past the division headquarters and apparently feels the need to keep explaining, since both Ashley and I have fallen completely silent. "You gotta consider, with how many men and women from the division are serving both here on base and abroad, that's still a pretty good success rate. I mean, you can die anywhere, right? Crossing the street. Choking on a hot dog. Jim Tucker died in that combine accident not too long ago, remember?"

He's trying to put us at ease. To help us feel safe in the face of truly mortal danger, but blaming fate doesn't seem quite fair in this instance. It's not that simple for me.

"Oh, look! A bowling alley!" Ashley cries, having already

moved on from the subject of our father's possible demise. Apparently, it *is* that simple for her. "Can anyone go there or only soldiers?"

"Everyone can go there, spouses and dependents too," Dad says, clearly grateful for the change in conversation. "You and your friends can ride your bikes up here on Friday nights. They used to make the best cheesesteaks around."

The first time Dad took me bowling at Sidetracks back in Iowa, he helped me carry the shiny purple ball from the rack to the lane because I could barely carry it, even with two hands. He taught me to keep my wrist straight so the ball wouldn't sail off into the gutter. He cheered the loudest the night I scored my first spare.

"It's got something like twenty-four lanes," he continues, his voice thick with pride. "Way bigger than the one back home."

The moment he says it, I can tell he wishes he could take it back, because what was meant as a comment to highlight how much bigger and better these new lanes are, comes out instead as a jab at the life we left behind back in Iowa.

We fall into silent contemplation as we continue our tour. Every building we pass illustrates how different our lives are about to become. There are no farms. No crops. No silos. No tractors.

Just lots of soldiers and loud guns.

We cross what appears to be an interstate, and Dad turns into a residential section. "This is Casablanca," he tells us. "My first choice for our housing. We'll have to take whatever they assign us, but there's some availability in here."

A sidewalk runs parallel to the street and along tiny patches of green as far as I can see. The houses are practically on top of one another. Then I notice some actually are.

"Are those supposed to be one house or two?" Ashley asks.

"Two houses. They're connected to save land. It's called a duplex."

"Are we gonna have to live in one of those?"

Dad speeds up, past the houses, as if he's finally seeing the neighborhood through our eyes, how intrusive it all seems, and he's embarrassed. "Maybe. I already told you, I don't know for sure."

I stare out the window as we continue through the neighborhood. Each house looks exactly like the last: one brick rancher after another with fading shingles and a smattering of shrubbery beside the stoop. The grass, what little there is of it, is neatly trimmed inside the squares of yard, and each house has a concrete path leading to the front door. I try to imagine myself living in one of these houses, but it's nearly impossible.

Finally, I say to Dad, "It seems like a nice place."

"It is," he says, reaching around Ashley to pat me on the shoulder. "And I think you're both going to be surprised how much you'll like it here if you give it a chance."

chapter 6
M.A. Hopkins

Friday, January 4

Dad spends all of Thursday and most of Friday in-processing while Ashley and I hang out in our hotel room watching bad daytime television and eating a bunch of junk food he let us buy at the commissary. It's fun for a while but by Friday afternoon, we're at each other's throats. Ashley's scowl has returned because she can't figure out why her friends haven't texted her back all morning. When I remind her they're in school, she repays my kindness by throwing a pillow at my head.

"You always have an answer for everything," she says. "You're such a know-it-all."

Over the years, I've become immune to Ashley's insults. Her words no longer sting the way they did when we were younger. As she rolls her eyes and grabs another Twizzlers from the bag, what upsets me more than her teasing is her initial reservation. Because while I do have an answer for why her friends aren't texting her now, I have no idea why Zander didn't return my texts last night.

Bad reception? Too much farm work? Extra homework?

Forgotten friend syndrome?

I'm checking my phone for the hundredth time for a response when Dad breezes in, carrying an armful of fatigues and two pairs of combat boots. "Well, I'm finished," he says tossing it all onto his bed. "Passed my physical. Signed into my unit. Even got all the patches sewn on my BDUs."

I glare at him and he acknowledges his verbal transgression. "Battle dress uniforms. BDUs," he says again, handing me a pair of camouflage pants.

"Who cares about the clothes. What'd you do to your hair?" Ashley asks for the both of us. His curl-laden, shaggy mop of hair my mother's constantly hounding him to cut is gone. Completely gone.

"It's called a high and tight. You like it?"

Ashley makes a face. "It makes your forehead look really big. And your ears," she adds.

"The better to hear you with, my dear," he teases, hurling himself across the room to tickle her.

"Stop!" she screams, squealing with delight. "Your forehead is blinding me!"

"Never," he cries, tickling her even harder.

Once the two of them settle down, and I'm able to look past his lack of hair, I ask, "So did we get our house?"

"Yes," he says, pushing himself onto his elbow so he can reach into his pocket for the key. "And it's not a duplex. It's a single-family home, so you should both be happy about that."

"In the neighborhood you showed us?" Ashley asks.

"Yeah. Casablanca."

There's visible relief on her face. She's warming to the idea of being here, because the truth is, there are worse places to live than in one of the homes in Casablanca, even if it's still not anywhere as good as the farm.

"Can we go to the schools and see the house this

afternoon?" I ask.

"Yes, to both," he says, hopping off the bed. "I was thinking we'd hit the house first, then the high school, and finish off at the middle school."

*

Less than fifteen minutes later, we pull into the driveway of our new house. It's a modest, brick, one-story with a quaint stoop and black shutters. There's a carport big enough for one car and a large maple in the front yard.

"This is it," Dad says, stepping out of the car. "Come out and meet your new house, girls."

Inside the front door is the family room. A pass-thru gives us a glimpse into the kitchen which seems modern enough, with dark stained cabinets and stainless-steel appliances.

"Mom will be happy there's a dishwasher," Ashley says, stepping into the room.

Although it's technically an eat-in kitchen, there's not nearly enough room for our old farmhouse table. Dad's eyeing the space, clearly thinking the same thing.

"We can always put our table in storage and get something smaller to fit here," he says. "We don't need that big 'ole thing anyway, just enough seats for the four of us is all."

He's trying to act like it's no big deal, but it is. The table is as much a part of our family as the cat or the cows. It's seen every Thanksgiving turkey and Easter ham. Every craft project, school project, and baking disaster. It's been carved into, spilled on, finished and refinished. It's where Mom fed me my first spoonful of rice cereal and Dad taught me to play chess during a massive ice storm when I was six.

"We won't get rid of it then?" Ashley asks, inspecting the refrigerator's ice dispenser.

"Nah," Dad tells her. "Folks on base don't have sheds,

but there are plenty of self-storage places around. Whatever doesn't fit in this house, we'll put into storage. Won't be here forever and we might get lucky and have room for it at our next post."

Ashley eyes him suspiciously. "Next post? Aren't we just staying here?"

Dad takes a deep breath, puffs out his cheeks, and proceeds to blow the air out slowly through his lips. He's obviously trying to be patient about our ignorance with regard to the inner workings of the military.

"That's not how it works in the Army. You can't stay in one place forever, remember? I told you in the beginning, it's really common for military kids to move around a lot. I'll be stationed here for a while, and in a few years, they'll move us somewhere else. I wouldn't worry too much about it, though. By the time we make a third move, you'll be off on your own somewhere."

"Back in Iowa," she says, glaring at him from across the kitchen.

"Fair enough." He throws his hands over his head in mock surrender. "Wherever you want to go." Officially tabling the conversation, he takes a step toward the hallway and waves over his shoulder for us to join him. "Come on. Let's take a look at the bedrooms."

There are three altogether: one for me, one for Ashley, and a master suite for Mom and Dad. Ashley quickly claims the larger of the two bedrooms, which is fine with me since I prefer the one with the extra window.

"Come look at the bathroom!" she calls from down the hall. "There're two sinks!"

Sure enough, along with a toilet and tub/shower combo, there are in fact two sinks. "Good," I tell her. "Now I won't have to wait an hour while you primp like a Kardashian every morning."

"And I won't have to look at all the nasty toothpaste you leave caked beside the drain," she counters, before sticking her tongue out at me.

"Real mature," I say.

"Real mature," she mimics in a sing-song voice.

"Hey, girls," Dad calls from somewhere on the far side of the house. "Come check out the backyard."

There's a deck about half the size of the one we had at the farm, but it's big enough for a table, four chairs, and a grill. The best part, though, is the tree line because if I block the neighboring houses from my peripheral vision, I can almost imagine we're living in the woods.

"Won't it be pretty in the spring once the leaves come back?" Dad asks optimistically.

Ashley and I both agree it will, and as we huddle together in the yard, I'm struck by the absurdity of my situation. About how ridiculous it is that I'm standing in North Carolina staring at an outcropping of trees I'm supposed to pretend is a forest.

I want to run next door to tell Zander about it so we can both have a good laugh. But of course, I can't. Because now he lives 1,200 miles away.

"Can we go to the school?" I ask.

*

According to the nameplate on the outside of the building, M.A. Hopkins High School is named after Moses Aaron Hopkins, a former slave and educator who served as the U.S. Ambassador to Liberia from 1885 to 1886. I try to picture where Liberia is located in Africa and draw a blank.

"So, this is it," Dad says as we enter through the front door of the building. It's almost two o'clock and even though classes are still in session, quite a few students are milling around the hallways.

A dull ache sets in just below my ribcage. "I don't belong here," I say, although I hadn't intended on speaking the words aloud.

"Sure, you do," Dad reassures me as he places his arm protectively around my shoulder and leads me into the front office, while Ashley, mouth gaping, trails along behind.

"Can I help you?" the secretary at the front desk asks in a warm, southern drawl. Dad enquires about completing my enrollment paperwork while I stare at my shoes and try not to feel out of place.

The nametag on the secretary's lanyard states the petite, middle-aged black woman with a head of fiery red curls is Mrs. Rhoda Fields. I'm envious of the causal back-and-forth of her conversation with Dad—the way he seems completely unashamed by his obvious Mid-westernness. His confidence is probably a byproduct of the time he spent outside Iowa during his prior years of service. But I've spent my entire life isolated in such a homogeneous part of the country, it's difficult for me to imagine myself fitting in anywhere else. Listening to Dad laughing with her about how glad he is to be back 'in the land of sweet tea' gives me hope, though, that perhaps all I need is time. Time to get to know the people and find my place among them.

Now, Mrs. Fields turns her attention to me. "Tess Goodwin, you said? Let's see what I've got." She flips through a large stack of folders in the file cabinet beside her desk. "Well, now look here. Seems like we've got a folder all printed out for you already. Makes it easier when we know kids are comin' in advance, and we sure thank you for that," she says, smiling broadly at my dad.

"My pleasure," he says, in his most affable tone. "We want to get her settled in as quickly and painlessly as possible."

"Well, now that I can understand. Got two kids of my own here. One in the ninth and one in the twelfth. I'm sure Tess here will be fine." She pulls several papers from the folder with my name and hands them to Dad. "All I need is for you to sign and initial these here, and Tess will need to do the same," she says, handing me a pen. "Last thing I need from you is a copy of her vaccination schedule."

Dad and I sign the forms, and he hands her a copy of what appears to be my shot record, which surprises me because I didn't even know I had one.

As I'm handing Mrs. Fields back her pen, another African American woman and man emerge from the back of the office. "Oh, Dr. Emmett and Dr. Conner, say hello to our newest student. This is Tess Goodwin from Iowa."

Dr. Emmett, who's nametag states she's the principal, rushes over to take my hand, shaking it firmly between both of her own. She's tall and thin and strikingly beautiful, in a fitted pantsuit and matching pumps. The warmth of her smile immediately puts me at ease.

"We're so glad you're with us." She glances at Dad, giving him an understanding look. "We get all the kids from Bragg here, so we know how hard transitions can be. You let me know if there's ever anything I can do to help you feel more at home."

Dr. Conner, the assistant principal, shakes Dad's hand and turns to Mrs. Fields. "Did you get her set up with a buddy?"

"We were just getting to that," she says, plunging into the depths of yet another file cabinet. "And as a matter of fact, I already have someone in mind."

After a round of goodbyes, the principals excuse themselves into the hallway, and Mrs. Fields comes up with a manila envelope. "Okay," she says, more to herself than to us. "We keep a list of students who volunteer to help show new enrollees the ropes, and I just had someone sign up last month who I think will be a perfect match for you, Tess. You can come here to the front office first thing Monday morning, and I'll make sure she's waiting for you. Lemme just see if I can find her here on the sheet." She slides her finger down the page until it stops at the name she's looking for. "Ah, yes. Here she is. Leonetta Jackson."

chapter 7
First Day

Monday, January 7

Instead of stepping into the school's front office, I hesitate beyond the threshold, folding and refolding my schedule between my hands like a master origamist, questioning every decision I've made since the moment Dad announced we were moving to Fayetteville. I glance through the doorway, pondering the unlikely series of events that brought me to the lobby of M.A. Hopkins High School in the first place, wondering if speaking up about my true feelings back in November would have made a difference. Would I be spending the day with Zander instead of a stranger if I had been firmer in my resolve about not wanting to leave Iowa?

The only other student in the office doesn't look up from her book as the door closes behind me with a gentle click. She's sitting in a chair against the back wall, her nose buried in a copy of *Girl With a Pearl Earring*. Her face is concealed behind a chin-length bob woven with streaks of purple and blue. A wrist-full of gold bangles jingle as she turns the page.

If Zander was here he'd walk right up and ask if she's my mentor, but of course, I don't want to disturb her because interrupting is impolite. Without him, I lack the courage to introduce myself, so I'm still standing there like an idiot when Mrs. Fields finally looks up from her desk.

"Leonetta?" she says. "Your buddy, Tess, is here. Now put down your book and show this nice girl around."

I'd worked myself into a frenzy over the weekend worrying about two things: why Zander still hadn't texted me back and whether Leonetta was going to like me. A tiny part of me thought perhaps she'd be another Midwestern transplant since Mrs. Fields had promised the two of us would be 'a perfect match.' Looking at Leonetta now, with her perfectly shaped eyebrows and rich, ruby lipstick, I brace myself for her disappointment. There's no way she's gonna want to spend the day with some freckly farmgirl who doesn't even have her ears pierced, and I halfway expect her to ask Mrs. Fields to reassign me to someone else.

"Nice to meet you," she says instead, smiling brightly as she slips her book into her bag before hoisting herself from the chair. "D'you just get into town?"

I follow her like a puppy into the hallway now teeming with students, hurrying in every direction. "Yeah. Last week," I say, the relief of her tentative acceptance spreading through me, casting away a few of my initial concerns.

She asks me where I'm from and about the reason for our move before holding out a perfectly manicured hand. "I need your schedule so I can help you find your way to class. I'll be staying with you all day, making sure you get from place to place."

I'm simultaneously relieved and dismayed as I hand her the paper. Relieved she'll be navigating for the next seven hours but dismayed I'll be on my own by this time tomorrow.

"So, uh, it turns out I'm in three of your four classes," she says, her voice laced with something like relief. "Plus, we both have second lunch."

The mention of concurrent lunch assignments sparks a tiny flame of hope inside me. Perhaps her acknowledgment will result in an invitation to eat together later in the day. Back at East Chester, I never worried about having someone to sit with: Zander was always by my side. But then again, with so few students, there was never a need for more than one shift, guaranteeing we'd always be together. I'm still pondering how many students necessitate multiple lunches when Leonetta stops abruptly in front of what appears to be a computer lab. "They already assign you an email address?" she asks.

"Yeah. When I enrolled last week. They set me up with a Chromebook, too."

She takes a step back as a kid carrying a printer exits the lab. "D'you test it out to make sure it works?"

I shake my head. "Didn't know I needed to."

"It's alright," she says with a sigh. "We can try it later. Half the time they don't load properly. You know how glitchy school computers can be."

I purse my lips and swallow down the urge to panic. "Actually, we just had textbooks at my old school. I don't know anything about using a Chromebook."

She nods sympathetically and continues moving down the hall with purpose, shuffling along in her flats. "Don't worry about it," she says. "If it's not working, I'll just give you access to my stuff 'til we can get it sorted."

"Really?" I can't believe she would do that for me. We don't even know each other.

"Yeah, of course. It's no big deal. Being late to Krenshaw's class is definitely a big deal, though, so we better hurry up."

Neck craned and eyes wide, I must look like a tourist walking beside her, trying to get a sense of the school's overwhelming expanse. I'm still wrapping my head around the enormity of the building, which seems to go on endlessly in every direction, when she stops beside a classroom door. "This is you. First period. The only class we don't have together. Don't worry, though, I'll be back before the bell rings to take you to your next class." She turns to go but abruptly changes her mind, pivoting on her heel. "And just FYI, this is American History with Ms. Krenshaw. She's a triflin' heifer. Don't sit in the front row or the back row. Pick somewhere in the middle. Promise me."

I promise, thankful for this unsolicited advice, but as I enter the room, I'm suddenly nervous, imagining how one should handle a 'triflin' heifer.' I'm familiar with the protocol for regular heifers but the trifling kind? Not so much.

The room is divided into five rows of seven, and one of the only available seats is on the far side of the room by the windows, but it's toward the middle, so I grab it. The rest of the class carries on, raucous and disorderly, and I busy myself with my new school supplies to avoid drawing attention to myself. I'm doodling mindlessly on the first crisp sheet of paper in the spiral notebook Dad bought me at the PX when someone slips into the seat beside me.

"Hey," a girl says, startling me from my sketch.

I lift my chin to respond only to find her rustling through her shoulder bag.

"Hi," I say back, my voice thin and tentative.

"This your first day?" She pulls a laptop from the bag and dives back in without making eye contact.

"Yeah."

"You from Bragg?"

"Yeah. Well, I'm actually from Iowa. But we just got here. To Fort Bragg."

She finally looks up from her gigantic purse, lip gloss in hand, eyes wide with disbelief. "Iowa? Isn't that out west somewhere? Like one of those tornado states?"

"You're thinking of Kansas or Oklahoma," I tell her. "But we sometimes get tornados. And there are a lot of farms."

She's back in her bag again, searching for something else. "D'you live on a farm?"

"Yeah. A dairy farm."

"That's cool," she says, returning from her bag a third time, this time with a pack of Orbitz gum. She holds out a stick. "Wanna piece?"

I thank her and take the gum.

Ms. Krenshaw arrives a moment later, and by the stern look of her, Leonetta's warnings were not without merit. "You people have three seconds to get your tails in your seats or I'm passing out ASDs."

I glance at the girl beside me, and she rolls her eyes in a show of solidarity. Ms. Krenshaw's barking around the room, clearly taking some sort of informal attendance. She stops once she gets to me.

"Tess Goodwin?" she asks.

"Yes, Ma'am."

"Grab a map supplement from the shelf back there. And hurry up."

I weave my way through desks, backpacks, and indifferent stares to the back of the room, where, after several moments of searching, I select a book from the stack.

Since they're discussing World War I, a subject my old class covered in the fall, I find myself zoning out, reflecting on how nice Leonetta and the Orbitz girl are and what I would be doing back home if I hadn't been dragged out of Iowa. It's earlier there because of the time change, so instead of being in school already, I'd still be out in the barn for the morning milking. I'd trade Sunshine for Ms. Krenshaw in a hot minute.

Halfway through class, Orbitz girl leans over, whispering

across the aisle. "You should definitely be taking notes. Krenshaw's tests are legendary."

I give her a small smile. "I already did World War I back in Iowa. The stuff she's covering is review."

With a shake of her head she returns to her laptop. "Must be nice."

When the bell rings, signaling the end of first period, I have a page full of doodles but not a single note from the lecture. Everyone else is on their feet before it's even done sounding, and when I glance to my right to ask for Orbitz girl's name, I'm disappointed to discover she's already gone.

Out in the hallway, Leonetta's right where I left her. "How bad was Krenshaw?" she asks as I fall into step beside her.

"She's definitely not winning any Miss Congeniality awards."

Leonetta nods. "I told you. Triflin' heifer."

We push through the crowd of endless backpacks, past banks of lockers, and dozens of classrooms. The silence between us stretches uncomfortably so I scramble for a topic to keep the conversation going. "I did meet the girl who sat beside me. She seemed nice."

"What's her name?" Her tone is accusatory as if I've done something wrong.

"I dunno. She didn't tell me."

"Then what's she look like?"

Her hair was short, cropped close to her head in the back and longer in the front. She had rings on her fingers and wore a beautiful linen shirt—completely appropriate for Fayetteville but so different from the jeans and cotton t-shirts I'm used to wearing around the farm. Also, she was black, but it feels inappropriate to add this as part of her description, so I decide not to say anything at all.

"I don't remember anything specific. Why?"

She sighs heavily. "You gotta be careful who you talk to around here. Some a these girls 'ill spit on ya as soon as look atcha."

I smile. It's funny how wherever you go, there are always *those* people. "I know about mean girls," I tell her as we come to a stairwell. "We have them in Iowa, too."

She shakes her head. "Oh no, you don't either. You don't have girls like this. They'll eat an innocent little thing like you alive. Triflin' heifers, the lot of 'em."

Hearing this makes me cringe, but then again, it's nice to know she sees herself in opposition to those who would be interested in consuming me. I open my mouth to admit how out of place I feel but decide against it. The last thing I want is to be labeled as some sort of outcast on my first day.

"The girl seemed pretty nice. She gave me gum." I say finally. "Hopefully we'll see her again today, and I can point her out."

Leonetta grunts as we start up the stairs, and I don't know if she's grunting at me or from overexertion, but I pretend not to notice and follow behind, discreetly checking the stairwell sign. Number seven isn't somewhere we've been before. I sidle up beside her at the top of the stairs.

"Hey. By the way. I might need your help getting around again tomorrow because I have no idea how we got to first period." I look around and notice we're in yet another unfamiliar hallway. "In fact," I continue, "I have no idea where we are now."

"Were you homeschooled or somethin' before this?"

I can't help but smile at the notion. "No," I tell her. "But my high school was small. Like way smaller than this. They should really give new students a map or something to help navigate this place. Otherwise, I may end up locked in some decommissioned mop closet never to be heard from again."

She laughs aloud, presumably at my joke and not at the image of my decaying body in a closet. Her loud, guttural guffaw takes me by surprise but also works to ease my fears. Is it possible I'm making my first friend?

"Don't worry about finding your way," she says. "I'll walk you around for as long as you need. It's all part of my job." The tone of her voice suggests she's relieved by the premise of an extended assignment, and it strikes me that the benefits of our pairing might not be one-sided. Perhaps Mrs. Fields saw me as a good match for Leonetta as well.

"You involved in any clubs?" she asks as we continue to second period.

"I was in the chess club back home. Or, back in Iowa," I say, correcting myself. I wonder how long it will take before I stop thinking of Iowa as home.

"My dad tried to teach me to play as a kid, but I never got the hang of it."

"My dad taught me," I say, perhaps a little too enthusiastically. "I can totally teach you."

"That'd be cool," she says with a smile.

"Is there a chess club here?"

She shrugs. "Not that I know of, but there could be. If not, you could always join the gospel choir with me. Do you sing?"

"Only in the shower," I tell her.

We arrive at Mr. Hogan's second-period chemistry class and file in with the rest of our classmates. Just inside the door, I spot the Orbitz girl from American History, and I nudge Leonetta to get her attention.

"There's the girl from the other class," I say, motioning toward her with my eyes as nonchalantly as I can. "The one who sat beside me."

Leonetta smiles. "Oh, that's Alice. She's good people. Lucky break," she says. "Come on. Let's get you a seat."

Because it's chemistry, the class is paired at lab tables, but unfortunately for me, everyone's already matched. Leonetta leads me to the front of the room and introduces me to Mr. Hogan, a bald, doughy man wearing a pair of quirky horned-rimmed glasses and a bow tie. He shakes my hand and issues me a tray of lab equipment.

"It's nice to meet you, Tess. We've got a group of three," he says, pointing to a table in the back corner of the room, "so one of them will need to break off to partner with you."

Leonetta squeezes my arm, and by the looks on the faces of the three girls I'm about to divide, this is not going to end well.

"Tess can partner with me and Desean," she offers, her voice desperate.

"No. No, that's silly. Working in pairs makes things easier." He raises his voice to call across the room. "Monika, come join Tess up front here at this empty table," he instructs.

There's an audible groan from Monika as she snatches her bag off the floor and waves begrudgingly to her former partners. She struts to the front of the room, glaring daggers at me, and I can tell she's definitely one of the girls Leonetta warned me about.

We sit side-by-side for the entire class period without looking at one another. Her anger is palpable, radiating from every pore in her body, but she doesn't say a word. She doesn't glance in my direction. And she definitely does not offer me a piece of gum.

*

By the end of class, I'm sweating profusely, perspiration pooling under my armpits as if I've been mucking stalls for five hours in the middle of July. The stress of sitting next to Monika made it difficult to concentrate on Mr. Hogan's explanation of covalent bonds, and I'm beyond relieved to see Leonetta waiting for me outside the door after the bell.

"Oh, girl," she says. "I was hoping he wouldn't do that, but he did, and you got stuck by the worst of them. Monika is the most triflin' of the heifers."

"I noticed," I say.

"It wasn't such a big deal today on a-count-a we weren't doing any lab work, but once you have to work together on an assignment, you're gonna have to watch out. That girl'll sabotage you. Seen her do it before."

I don't know whether I should be grateful or disheartened by her overtly honest opinion of my situation. I decide, as we lumber along through the throng of students on their way to third period, it's probably better to know the truth so I can prepare myself for the worst.

Leonetta's trying to tell me something more about Monika, but the hallway seems busier than it was at the previous class change, and before long we're overtaken by the mob, separating us from one another.

Luckily, I find her waiting for me at the next stairwell where she explains about the overcrowding. "First lunch is at the beginning of this period. We go in the middle of class with second lunch, and third shift goes at the end. That's why it's so crazy. Folks can't wait to get their lunch on." She stops suddenly halfway down the steps as if she's forgotten something important. "Did you pack or are you gonna buy?"

I pat my back pocket where I stashed the five-dollar bill Dad left me on the kitchen counter. "I'm buying."

She nods approvingly. "Okay. That's good. Make sure you stay with me through the line, though. That way Cecilia'll give you the good stuff."

"Is there bad stuff?" I ask, although I'm not sure I want to know.

"Let's just say there's the stuff the school system buys for us to eat, and then there's the stuff Cecilia fixes. You will never eat another slice of cold, greasy school pizza again."

Although I don't necessarily mind the rectangular anomaly that is school pizza, my stomach is already grumbling for lunch, and I'm eager for class to get underway.

"Anything I need to know about this class?" I ask, following her into the room.

She shakes her head. "Nah. Not really. This is English with Mrs. Alexander. Her husband is stationed at Bragg. He's a colonel, I think. Anyway, she's real nice, but this is her last year, so don't get too attached." We take two seats next to each other in the front row. "You like to read?" she asks, and I remember she was reading *Girl with a Pearl Earring* while she waited for me in the office.

"I do," I tell her, "but back home, on the farm, there wasn't a lot of time for it. I mean, I read for my assignments and all, but there's always a lot of work to do on a farm." I don't add that any free time I did get was usually spent playing chess with Zander.

"Oh," she says. The disappointment in her voice makes me wish I had some literary point of reference to relate.

"What are you reading in here?" I ask.

"*A Raisin in the Sun.*"

My heart leaps since it's something I've read. "Lorraine Hansberry, right? About the Younger family and the insurance check and trying to decide what to do with the money?"

"Yeah. That's the one," she says. "Have you read it?"

I nod. "And I loved it. What about you?"

Before she can answer, Mrs. Alexander appears at the front of the room, wearing a cheery sundress and a welcoming smile on her face.

"Ah! You must be Tess," she exclaims, seeing me in the

front of the room. "Welcome to Hopkins. I'm glad you've met Leonetta." She gives her a wink. "How's your day been so far?"

It's easy to understand why Leonetta likes her, and I admit, to both her and myself, my day's been fine.

"Well, let me get you set up with our anthology," she calls over her shoulder as she scoots down an aisle to the back of the room, her head of corkscrew curls bouncing with every step. "The rest of you turn to page 191, and we'll pick up where we left off Friday, discussing the symbolism of Mama's plant."

The first half of class flies by, with Leonetta contributing to most, if not all, of the discussion. I watch her light up as she shares her opinion about how the plant is the only thing the family has left, but the mother still nurtures it despite a lack of sunlight in the hopes of sustaining its life. It seems as though, somehow, the nurturing aspect of the symbolism is something she relates to, but before I have time to consider it further, the bell rings, and it's time for lunch.

Instead of bolting out the door with the rest of the class, Leonetta hangs back as everyone else funnels into the hallway. Once they're gone, she approaches Mrs. Alexander's desk.

"What can I do for you, The Divine Miss L?" Mrs. Alexander asks.

Leonetta crimsons in response to the teacher's pet name, the affection between them undeniable.

"Mrs. A, I was wondering, do we have a chess club here at school?"

My breath catches in my throat and I hold it, realizing immediately the significance of this moment.

"Hmm." Mrs. Alexander glances out the window, trying to recall. "I don't think so," she says finally. "But I'm happy to find out. Why do you ask?"

Leonetta motions in my direction. "Tess was in a chess club at her school back in Iowa, and I thought maybe she could join one here, too."

Our teacher nods. "That's a lovely idea. And Tess, if you want, you're welcome to join my literature circle as well. We meet after school on Tuesdays. Leonetta here is actually one of our founding members."

Leonetta looks at me, the pride visible in the broadness of her smile. "You should definitely come."

I don't know her well enough to speculate about the nature of her invitation—whether she's just an inclusive sort of person or if she genuinely wants me around. Either way, I'm grateful, so of course, I accept her offer.

By the time we make it to lunch, the cafeteria is jam-packed, the serving line extending most of the room's length.

"Holy crap," I say, "how are we ever gonna make it through this line with enough time to actually eat?"

Leonetta ushers me quickly to the end of the line and hands me a tray. "It moves fast," she tells me. "Plus, Cecelia will take care of us."

As we shuffle toward the counter, I glance around the cafeteria and am struck by the pronounced segregation. There are large groups of black students huddled together, and interspersed between them, smaller pockets of white, Latino, and Asian students as well, each isolated from the next. It's like back at East Chester with the jocks and the brains and the stoners. Only here at Hopkins, it seems as though race is the great divider, some sort of voluntary isolationism. Watching the close-knit groups makes me all the more grateful to have Leonetta by my side.

True to her word, three minutes later, we're already to the serving portion of the line. She leans down to whisper in my ear. "See the woman with the hot pink hair net on the end there? That's Cecilia. Don't take any food from anybody else 'til we get to her. Follow my lead."

I shake my head as each of the other cafeteria workers offers me the standard fare: corn dog nuggets, tater tots, Salisbury steak. Finally, we reach the end of the line, my tray still empty.

"Two plates today, Cecilia," Leonetta tells the woman. "One for me and one for Tess. She just got here from Iowa."

Cecilia grins at me, as if I've just been let in on the world's best secret. "Oh lawd, girls, are you in for a treat today," she says over her shoulder as she shuffles off into the kitchen. A minute later she returns with two steaming plates of food. "Pork chop, collards, and homemade macaroni salad," she says, handing them to us. "Woulda had some biscuits, too, Netta, but our flour delivery got delayed this week. Anyway, y'all enjoy. And it's nice to meet ya, Tess. I'm sure I'll be seeing a lot of you around."

I thank her and follow Leonetta to the seating area, which I'm discouraged to discover has limited availability. I figure, though, she probably has a place she always sits, like Zander and I did back at East Chester.

I glance around for a familiar face, realizing how strange it is that she hasn't introduced me to any of her friends. Is it possible she doesn't have any?

Does she typically eat alone?

I'm still pondering her seemingly isolated existence as we make our way to what appears to be the last two open seats, nestled squarely between the wrestling team and mathletes. Taking my seat, I laugh quietly to myself, disbelieving of the irony in traveling 1,200 miles only to find the exact same kids I left behind—the jocks and the geeks—and am both annoyed and comforted by the universality of cliques.

The pork chop appears to have been marinated in an

unfamiliar spice, so I pick it up with my fingers to examine it more closely before tearing off a tentative bite with my teeth. "Oh my God, this is amazing," I say. "What's on it?"

Beside me, Leonetta uses her utensils to cut off a corner of the chop. She shrugs. "Dunno. Cecilia won't share her recipes with anybody. Says they're her great-great-great grandmomma's recipes from when she was a slave down in Louisiana, and she's probably gonna take 'em to the grave with her."

"Well, that would be a tragedy because this is delicious," I say through a mouthful of my second bite.

"You oughta try the collards," she says. "And don't worry, 'cuz she's already put in the perfect amount of Tabasco. You won't need more."

I stop chewing, holding my chop in mid-air. "What's Tabasco?"

Now she's the one who stops eating. "You kiddin'."

I shake my head. "No. I've never heard of it before."

She laughs aloud, and I'm afraid she's going to spit her food across the table. "Girl, you sure got a lot to learn about livin' in the South." She clears her throat in mock seriousness. "Number One: Thou shalt douse Tabasco, also known as hot sauce, on pretty much everything, including, but not limited to, eggs, chicken, collards, and jambalaya."

"Should I be writing this down?" I ask.

She nudges me in the arm with her shoulder. "Just try the collards," she says.

The collards are bitter and spicy, and I've almost convinced myself I don't like them when I take another small bite to appease Leonetta who's watching me with rapt anticipation. By the third bite, the richness of the flavors begins to grow on me and before long, I've cleaned my plate.

"So, Tabasco," she says, grinning through a mouthful of

her own collards.

"It's the heat, right?"

"Yes, the heat."

We chat together for a few minutes about my friends back in Iowa before I decide to ask about her typical seating arrangements. "Am I keeping you from sitting at your regular spot?"

She shakes her head but doesn't look up from her food.

"Oh," I say. "Then who do you usually eat with?"

She bows her head, wiping her face with her paper napkin to keep from welling up. I mentally slap myself for saying anything. "I'm sorry," I say before she's able to respond.

"No. It's fine. It's just that recently, I've been sittin' by myself, readin' my book. But I used to sit with my best friend, Tanya. We met at the end of eighth grade and spent two and a half years together here. But her family PCS'd right after Thanksgiving."

"PCS'd?"

"It stands for a 'permanent change of station.' They were military and she moved away, just like you."

Immediately, I think of Zander. About how I permanently changed my station, leaving him behind. But unlike Leonetta, he isn't completely alone. He has the guys.

My heart aches for her, and I struggle for the words to make it better. "Well, you've got a new lunch partner now if you'll have me," I tell her. When she finally looks up, I don't know whose smile is bigger, mine or hers.

*

After lunch, Leonetta drags me into the hall, insisting I be the one to lead her back to English. We're both surprised when I'm able to get there without making a single wrong turn.

"You'll know this building like the back of your hand by the end of the week," she tells me as we take our seats together at the front of the room.

By the end of class, we've finished our dissection of *A Raisin in the Sun*, and after Mrs. Alexander assigns our reading homework for the night, she stops us as we're filing into the hall.

"I asked some of the other teachers in the faculty room about a chess club, and we don't have one," she tells me. "But I bet Mr. Wilson might be willing to sponsor you if you're interested in establishing one."

"Mr. Wilson's our geometry teacher," Leonetta tells me. "We're heading there now. He's really nice and really smart. He stays after school most days to tutor kids who need extra help, so I bet he'd let you hang out and play chess in the back of his room if you want."

Just as Zander and I were relegated to the corner of the library back at East Chester, I'll be facing the same partitioned existence here. Apparently, regardless of the locale, chess doesn't take priority on anyone's hierarchy of afterschool activities.

I thank Mrs. Alexander, and Leonetta leads me to geometry, where I notice Orbitz-girl Alice sitting beside another girl I recognize from English. Their heads are knitted together across the aisle and they're engrossed in conversation over a small spiral-bound notebook.

"Who's the girl talking to Alice?" I whisper to Leonetta as we weave our way down the row in their direction.

"Summer Phillips," she says. "Why?"

"Is she nice?"

She shrugs. "Don't really know her that well. Why?" she asks again.

We snag two seats behind them and without thinking I say, "She and Alice are the only interracial friends I've seen today, that's all." It doesn't occur to me until I hear it coming out of my mouth how my comment might be misconstrued, but before I have a chance to explain myself, Mr. Wilson strolls in. Craning my neck to properly view his face, he reminds me of the basketball players Dad and I watch during March Madness—unimaginably tall and thin, with hands the size of dinner plates.

"What's going on, Geometry?" he calls to the class, illuminating the smart board at the front of the room to reveal what I assume are the answers to the weekend's homework assignment. "Check your proofs quickly and holler at me if you have any questions. One similar to number six threw a bunch of you last week, so hit me up if you're still having trouble with triangle bisection."

Alice and Summer have stashed away their notebook and are now checking their assignments with the rest of the class. Alice raises her hand, and as Mr. Wilson lumbers over to her desk he notices me.

"Overheard we were gettin' a new addition today," he says with a smile, teeth gleaming. He leans down, practically bending himself in half to shake my hand. "You're Tess, right?"

"Yes, sir."

"Good to have you," he says. "If you have time after school today, I'd love to chat with you about your situation."

I have no idea what he's talking about. "Sir?"

He smiles again, explaining further. "You know, to get an idea of what you've been taught so far this year at your old school, to check for gaps between what we're studying now and what you already know. Geometry-wise," he adds.

"After school today?"

He nods. "Or tomorrow. Or anytime this week. Before school even, if that would work better for you."

Ashley's expecting me to be home after school today

and will probably worry if I don't show up. And I'm already looking forward to Mrs. Alexander's literature circle tomorrow afternoon.

"I was actually taking Algebra II back in Iowa, but none of the Algebra classes fit into my schedule here so I guess they just put me in geometry and figured I'd catch up."

His eyes widen. "Catch up? What are these guidance counselors even thinking? Dear Lord, we definitely need to talk, Tess. The sooner the better."

"Do you think we can meet after school on Wednesday?"

He nods. "I'll clear my schedule."

As we've been talking, Alice has completely turned around in her seat and is now watching us intently. For a second, I think she's upset that I've kept Mr. Wilson from answering her question, but her curious expression confirms she isn't annoyed by the delay. Once we're through, she speaks with him briefly, and as he ambles back toward the front of the room, she swivels around to face me again.

"You've never taken geometry before?"

I shake my head. "Nope."

"But you already know what we're covering in history?"

"Right," I say, wondering what she's getting at.

"How would you feel about tutoring one another?"

Her question takes me by surprise. "Really?"

She sighs heavily, shaking her head. "I'm practically failing history because Ms. Krenshaw's such a craptastic teacher, and it's killing my GPA. I'm a wiz at geometry, though, so I was thinking maybe we can help each other out. I work after school at Krispy Kreme but maybe we could get together at night or on the weekends or something?"

The desperation in her voice is unmistakable, and I'm definitely going to need the help in math.

"Sure. Let's do it," I say.

"You're the best," she replies enthusiastically, ripping a sheet of paper from her notebook. "This is my cell." She hands me the paper which includes her name, the ten digits of her phone number and a heart, all hastily penned in her flowing script. "Call or text me tonight, after seven," she says.

I open my mouth to respond, but Mr. Wilson's at the board now, explaining the proof for an isosceles triangle on the coordinate plane. I have no idea what he's talking about, but I begin taking notes with the others just the same. Halfway through the explanation, I must be exceptionally focused because when Leonetta snatches Alice's sheet off my desk, I nearly jump out of my seat. I don't have time to ask what she's doing because a moment later she returns the paper, sliding it beneath my notes. Now her name and number appear beside Alice's in large block letters.

I turn to acknowledge the gesture and find her eyeing me expectantly as if she's overstepped some unspoken boundary and is now second-guessing herself. I tear a corner off the bottom of the sheet, scribble my own digits, and slip the note back onto her desk. She returns my smile, visibly relieved.

After the exchange, class plods along through a blurry fog of confusion, and I'm relieved when the bell at the end of class also signals the end of the school day. Students flood into the hallways, more rambunctious now than they were at the start.

"You survived," Leonetta says as we shove our way toward the student parking lot.

"It was good," I admit, surprised by how good it actually was.

"I'm glad," she says. "And hey, if you want I'll text you tonight, and we can go through your Chromebook together to make sure you've got everything you need."

We already discovered my Quizlet login doesn't work, so there are bound to be other issues. "That'd be awesome," I tell her. "Thanks. And you can text me anytime. I literally have nothing going on."

"Okay." She hesitates then, chewing the inside of her cheek. "You want me to meet you in the office again tomorrow morning?"

There's a hopeful edge to her voice, but I really want to see if I can make it on my own. "How about if we meet at Ms. Krenshaw's. I'll try to get there by myself, but if I don't make it by the warning bell, come look for me in the office."

She agrees, and as we go our separate ways, she to her car and me to mine, and I'm struck by how easy spending the day together was. How effortless. How despite our obvious differences, we somehow managed to discover common threads between us, creating a tentative connection. In light of this observation, as I pull out of the parking lot, I'm forced to acknowledge that maybe fitting in here won't be as difficult as I thought, and for the first time since November, I'm no longer dreading the days to come.

chapter 8
Go-Kart

Thursday, January 10

The sky fades from blue and red into a vivid shade of violet as Ashley, Dad, and I stand in the driveway waiting for Mom to arrive.

"How far out was she?" Ashley asks, pulling her sweater tightly across her chest.

"She called from Sanford about forty-five minutes ago, so unless she's lost, she should be here any minute."

It's clear from the way she's pacing Ashley's impatient to go back in the house, but Dad already made it clear we're to wait outside for Mom's arrival. She's scuffing the toe of her sneaker against the front stoop as Mom's Jeep Wrangler rounds the corner at the end of the street.

"She's here!" Ashley cries, racing across the lawn in her direction.

Dad waves furiously as she pulls into the driveway, opens the driver's side door, and throws herself into his waiting arms. Watching their embrace is awkward, and I can't help but feel as if their reunion should be in private and not out on the driveway for the whole neighborhood to see. Despite my mortification, however, the two of them seem completely unfazed by their public display of affection.

"I don't know how I'm going to handle being apart for months at a time," Mom murmurs into his chest. "It was hard being away from you. I'm not sure this was such a good idea."

Dad tucks a loose strand of hair behind her ear and whispers something as he gathers her under his arm and leads her toward the house. It's an act I've witnessed between them hundreds of times, but on this occasion, it feels strangely sacred, a reminder to pay special attention to the joy they take in simply sharing the same space. "Girls," he calls over his shoulder from the door, as if he's suddenly remembered we're there, "come show Mom around."

Inside the front door, Mom embraces us both, first Ashley, then me. "After you've given me the grand tour, I want to hear all about the first week at your new schools," she says to us.

The tour, as it turns out, isn't so much grand as it is short, and after Mom gives her Good Housekeeping Seal of Approval to our new digs, we all end up in the kitchen: Dad perched on the kitchen counter, Mom leaning against the fridge, and Ashley and I on the floor with our backs against the wall where the table should be.

"The school is huge," Ashley's telling her. "I have like thirty-one kids in my homeroom and there's barely enough seats for everyone. I already met these three girls, Kenna and Madison and Jillian, and we're all going to the base movie theater tomorrow night. They go every weekend. It's only a dollar, and Dad already said I can go. Madison's mom is driving us."

"What's the movie?" Mom asks, giving Dad a small smile and a wink, which is code for 'I told you so.' She'd known, despite the protests, Ashley would take to her new surroundings like a duck to water.

"We're seeing the new Disney, but before you say I've

already seen it, I haven't seen it here, with these people, so I'm going."

Mom feigns a defensive posture. "If Dad already said, then Dad already said. We all know his word is the law around here." She's joking but there's the tiniest drop of pain in her voice. If he hears it, Dad doesn't let on.

"Tell her about your school, Tess," he pipes up, readjusting his position on the counter. "Tell her about chess club."

Mom's eyes brighten. "Do they have one you can join? A real one?"

I shake my head and begin explaining. "They don't currently have one, but Mr. Wilson, my geometry teacher, said he's willing to sponsor me if I want to start one. We can meet in his room after school, and he already did some research and found out there are a bunch of schools in Raleigh and Durham we might be able to compete against. Like, a real match and everything."

"That's terrific," she says, yawning. "Sorry. It's been a long day." She slides her back down the length of the refrigerator and crosses her legs beneath her on the floor. "Ashley told me about her friends, but what about you? Anyone new and exciting?"

She's worried for me because it's no secret I've never been particularly good at making friends. Every friend I had back in Iowa came to me via Zander. He was always the liaison.

"Actually, yeah," I tell her. "The school paired me with a buddy which sounds totally middle school—no offense, Ashley—but it turns out the girl they put me with is very cool. Her name's Leonetta."

Mom raises an eyebrow. "Interesting name."

"Yeah," I say, feeling the need to come to Leonetta's defense against my own mother's judgment. "It's actually a sweet story. Her dad's name is Leon and since he never had a son to call

Leon Jr., he decided to name his daughter Leonetta instead."

She nods, considering this. "That is sweet, but there has to be more to this new friend of yours than her name, as unique as it may be. Is her family military?"

"No. They're townies," I tell her, remembering the word Leonetta used to describe the city's permanent residents. Mom waits patiently while I consider other relevant information. Does it matter she's physically the exact opposite of me? She's tall and I'm short? She's voluptuous and I'm a beanpole? She's black and I'm white? Does it matter she wouldn't last half an hour with Zander and me on the farm, repairing loose tractor gaskets and digging manure out of the cows' hooves or that I don't know the difference between a chittlin' and a corn fritter? I decide immediately none of those things matter. What matters instead is how kind she's been to me. The compassion she's shown for the difficulty of my situation. How open and giving she's been of herself, despite the fact we're little more than strangers.

The first few days, a nagging voice in the back of my head kept trying to convince me she wasn't being nice because she liked me—she was just taking her position as an 'incoming student liaison' a little too seriously. Now, though, I'm starting to believe she actually enjoys hanging out with me.

Maybe making new friends won't be as hard as I thought.

I'm not ready to admit any of this to my family, though, so instead I say, "She's super smart. Loves to read. She's a part of this literature circle our English teacher, Mrs. Alexander, runs on Tuesday afternoons. She invited me to come with her, and it was actually a lot of fun. She's also a part of the school's gospel choir, and she asked me to join, but..."

"You can't because you're not black," Ashley finishes for me.

I narrow my eyes, offended on more than one level. "I was

going to say I'm not joining because I can't sing. And for your information, anyone can join."

"I think you sing beautifully," Dad interrupts, in an obvious attempt to ward off a sibling dispute. "You sing to the herd all the time."

I want to correct him. I want to remind him I *sang* to the herd, past tense. But I don't, because what would be the point. Instead, I continue to fill Mom in on my week.

"Anyway, Leonetta's coming over this weekend to help me set up all the apps on my Chromebook, and I hope you don't mind, but I invited her to stay for dinner..."

"Can we order pizza?" Ashley asks.

"Sure. Now stop interrupting your sister," she says, turning to me. "Go ahead, Tess."

Ashley and I glower at one another before I continue. "There's also this other girl named Alice. We're in a couple of the same classes, and it turns out we could both use some help. So, I'm gonna be tutoring her in history, and she's gonna be tutoring me in math. We're planning to meet here a couple nights a week if that's okay."

"Fine with me," Mom says, throwing a quick glance at Dad across the room. "It sounds like you've gotten off to a good start with these girls."

"Yeah," Dad adds. "You're really lucking out in the friend department, huh?"

I consider Dad's use of the word 'luck.' It probably *was* nothing more than plain, dumb luck that brought Leonetta and Alice to my doorstep, but at this point, I'll take it.

"Oh, and speaking of friends," Mom says. "I can't believe I forgot, Tess. There's something out in the car for you."

She heaves herself off the linoleum floor and hurries outside, returning a moment later, envelope in hand. "The movers found this under the mat on the front porch. It's got your name on it. I can't imagine who it's from."

She's being facetious, of course. The chicken scratch barely passing for legible handwriting is quite obviously Zander's. I take the envelope, feigning disinterest, but the tiny smirk playing at the corner of Mom's mouth suggests she sees through the façade.

I take a step out of the kitchen. "I'm gonna go..."

Dad lovingly rolls his eyes. "You're excused," he says, motioning with his hands toward the hallway.

I stretch out across the sleeping bag and air mattress, the lone furnishings occupying the center of my room. They've been acting as a makeshift bed in the absence of my own mattress and box spring which, along with the rest of my belongings, are due to arrive in the morning. I carefully slide my finger under the closed portion of the envelope, noting it's sealed and not merely folded under. Whatever he's written inside must be personal, and I consider tossing it aside without opening it. There's got to be a reason he's ignored every text and call I've made to him for the last week, and since I'm barely handling my own unsettled emotions, I'm not sure I'm ready to confront whatever excuses the letter might contain.

But a moment later, the envelope's on the floor and a sheet of notebook paper, creased into three distinct sections, is in my hands. I unfold it and begin to read.

Hey Tess –

I watched the movers at your house last night from our tree and saw them taking out the TV and the sofa and your dad's recliner. It was weird, watching them deconstruct your house, room by room, piece by piece. And every time they'd bring something out, I'd think to myself: remember when I used to sit on that with Tess or watch that with Tess or use that with Tess? I felt like a totally creepy stalker the whole time, and my dad kept hollering at me from the garage to help him fix our broken snow blower (I know, again, right?!) but I couldn't tear myself away. It was like watching a car crash, I guess. You know it's gonna be ugly but you can't not look.

Anyway, I was still watching when they brought the go-kart you and I made in fourth grade outta the tool shed. Remember that thing? I'll never forget how you negotiated with Mr. Yearling for that old lawn mower engine of his. You were like a flea market trader, bargaining him down to two days' worth of weeding and raking for it. Back then I thought doing all the work wasn't gonna be worth it, but it totally was. Now, when I think about that weekend, all I can remember is how much fun we had. The snake we found under the crawl space. The giant pile of leaves we burned in a barrel to roast hot dogs over. And until I was just now thinking about it, I'd forgotten the poison ivy I got all over my arms. Watching them drag the kart out made me remember all those afternoons we spent building it and all the fun we had driving it through the fields that fall.

It was killing me, seeing it again, without you around. And that was before I realized it wasn't going into the moving truck. It was going to the dump. The dump, Tess, can you believe it? I'm hoping you didn't know they were getting rid of it, or maybe you didn't think about it at all, so that's why I hope you don't mind what I did next because last night, after everyone else was asleep, I snuck over to your house and pulled it outta the trash heap. It's in our barn now, behind the feed. And with your blessing, that's where it's gonna stay. Cuz I thought maybe someday you'd want it back. Or at least I was hoping you might.

So anyway, I hope you're not too mad I haven't called or texted since you left. I read this article online about how you should give people time and space to get acclimated if they're adjusting to a new situation. It seemed like sound advice at the time, but after purposely ignoring a bunch of your texts, I'm starting to realize maybe you needed a friend more than you needed space. Now I feel like a jerk, and I'm scared you might be too mad at me to answer when I do call, which is why I've written this letter instead. I want to hear how the move went and how everything's going at your new school. As for here, everything is pretty much the same. Except for the part about everything being completely different.

Text me if you get a chance.

Z

I set the letter on the floor and stare out the window at someone who I assume is one of my new neighbors, a stranger, walking her schnauzer in the glow of the streetlight. My mind is swimming, swirling, trying to make sense of the wash of emotions bubbling to the surface.

The dog stops to poop in our yard.

As I watch the woman cleaning the mess, I am struck by the many implications of Zander's confession. That his recent unresponsiveness was born of compassion instead of pain or selfishness, as I had wrongfully assumed, is certainly a relief, but I'm also moved by the longing he must have felt as he watched my house being emptied. Was it mere nostalgia that inspired him to save the stupid go-kart from the trash? Or was it something more? Something deeper?

I tuck the letter into the bottom of my sleeping bag—the only place I have to hide it—and slide my phone from my back pocket to send him a text. My fingers hover over the screen not knowing exactly what to say or how to say it. Should I pretend everything's great? Tell him I got his letter, and I'm glad he kept the go-kart. Should I tell him about Leonetta and her purple and blue striped hair and affinity for Tabasco? About how Alice and I are going to be tutoring each other, and how there's a possibility I might finally compete in a legitimate chess competition on an actual team? Should I mention Summer Phillips and how much he would like her because as it turns out she's beautiful and charismatic and snarky but not in a mean sort of way?

I don't realize I've bitten my cuticle below the quick until I taste blood. I wrap my finger in my t-shirt to stop the bleeding and toss my phone onto the floor. As much as I want to reach out to Zander, I can't. I'm too afraid. Afraid he'll stop being the person he's always been now that we're apart. And so instead, I suppress the sadness and the longing and the homesickness and return to the kitchen to be with my family.

chapter 9
Converging Coordinate Planes

Wednesday, January 16

I slide the last of my jeans into my bottom dresser drawer and peel the tape from the seams of the cardboard box to break it down. It's about the hundredth box I've emptied over the past week, and it feels good to be done. At least my bedroom finally feels like a bedroom instead of the Fed Ex distribution center it's resembled since the movers arrived.

The clock on my nightstand reads 6:49 pm. Alice will be here any minute, and I still haven't looked at our math homework, much less prepared any history notes to review. I slide my geometry book out of my bag and flip to the assignment—using the distance formula on the coordinate plane.

Super.

Maybe she'll want to do our homework together, I think.

Moments later the doorbell rings, and I usher Alice into the foyer—or, more accurately, foyer-like space. She's stately and elegant, looking more like a full-grown woman in her slacks and blouse than the sixteen-year-old she is. Standing beside her in my frayed jeans and faded Hy-Vee t-shirt makes me feel like the *before* photo in one of those make-over shows. Alice, however, doesn't seem to notice.

"I'm sorry I'm early," she says breathlessly, slipping off her coat. "But my little brother Foster was driving me crazy, and I had to get out of the house. I bolted outta there as soon as my mom got home from work."

"It's okay," I say, taking her jacket and tossing it across the back of the nearby sofa. "I haven't even looked at the history assignment yet so it'll give us a few extra minutes to work on it together."

I lead her into the kitchen where the light from the overhead lamp is bright, and my mom and Ashley are still cleaning up from dinner.

"You must be Alice," Mom says, setting down her dishtowel as we enter the room.

"It's nice to meet you, Mrs. Goodwin," she says, easing onto one of the kitchen chairs around our newly acquired dinette table. "You have a beautiful home."

I have no idea why she says it. The house is far from beautiful and even further from being a home. Boxes still litter the floor space and the walls are devoid of my mom's beloved photographs and hand-made wreaths. Still, the simple gesture, the sincerity with which she says it, endears her to me.

We start with our history assignment, a five-hundred-word essay on the repercussions of Russia's entry into the First World War on August 1, 1914. I end up having to backtrack, explaining to her about Russian interests in Serbia, but after about twenty minutes she's able to construct a good outline of dates and facts to use for the essay.

"How hard would it be for Ms. Krenshaw to actually explain all this stuff to us like you just did?" she asks rhetorically, tucking away her history notes and extracting her math text and a pack of gum from her bag. She offers me a piece as she has on every occasion since the first day we met. "It helps me focus," she says, popping a stick of Wintergreen in her mouth.

I peel mine from the wrapper, relishing the minty coolness against my tongue. "Is there some sort of guarantee on the label, because when it comes to math, God knows I need as much help as I can get."

She laughs, but after attempting the first two problems together, I can tell by the look on her face she's realized I wasn't kidding about my geometric ineptitude or the need for divine intervention. It's clear she may have taken on a project beyond her level of tutorial prowess. She's getting frustrated, and so am I. It's as if I've walked in on a theatrical performance in its final act without any prior knowledge of the characters or plot.

"You're completely lost," she says, closing her book. "Which means we need to get back to basics. I need to teach you how to use a coordinate plane."

"Okay?"

"Okay. So, let's think about this for a minute. You play chess, right?"

I nod.

"Then let's start there. Bring me a chess board—an old one if you've got it—and a few pieces."

Mom gives me a strange look over her shoulder as I make my way to the family room, where, after a brief scan, I spot the container I'm looking for at the bottom of a stack of boxes beneath the window. I shimmy it out without causing an avalanche, and inside, I'm relieved to find my collection of chess boards. I flip through them (there are eleven) and choose the rattiest, a cardboard one with peeling edges and a gaping crack in the spine.

Shoving the remaining boards back into the box, I come across the homemade wooden one with tiny brass hinges and perfect squares of inlaid cherry and birch. The board is my father's and was my grandfather's before him. It's the board Dad taught me to play on, where I slid my first tentative pawn from one square to the next.

Although I was only six, I remember the details of that game as if I'm still a small child, sitting on his lap while he coached me through the logistics of every move. I recall the way he encouraged me to think carefully about the long-term implications of each decision, seeing forward not just to the next move, but the one after that and the one after that, predicting what he might do in response to my own moves. Reminding me even though pawns can only move vertically one or two spaces, they can capture diagonally. It was the first time I remember him using The Face, the one he reserves for when I'm falling into one of his traps. He never told me outright what I was doing wrong but encouraged me instead to discover and remedy the situation on my own. I lost that first game and many more in subsequent years. He never let me win, refusing to lure me into a false sense of security in the hopes of bolstering my confidence. How it frustrated me as a child to never win. To always presume to be so close to victory, only to be placed in check, blindsided by my instructor.

Looking at the board now, as beautiful in my hands today as it was a decade before, I understand my dad's resolve. Why he never gave in to the temptation to let me beat him, as I'm sure he probably wanted to on many occasions, his daughter sitting across the table from him on the verge of tears. Because once the day finally arrived, a year ago in November of my sophomore year, the legitimate victory was the sweetest, most glorious moment of my young life. I ran, without stopping to relish Dad's congratulatory hug, across the field and past the tree to Zander's, where news of my victory was celebrated with unmitigated exuberance and ice cream. If he had let me win at seven, or nine, or twelve, before I was able to reasonably beat him on my own, our hours together would have been tarnished, marred by the inauthentic and underlying belief I would never be truly capable of it on my own. With this knowledge and understanding, I return to the kitchen, armed with a clearer perspective of my undertaking with Alice, only to find her chatting like old friends at the table with my mom.

"There are ten cousins in all," Alice is saying, "and I'm the oldest. It's mostly fun, watching them grow and learn, but it's hard to get anything done when we're all together, you know what I'm sayin'? Especially school work. And the little ones are the neediest. Poor little Patsy can't even tie her own shoes."

Mom smiles sympathetically and glances up, realizing I've stepped into the room. "Tess, did you know Alice's family keeps a plot of farmland down the road on the other side of Spring Lake? You said you grow soybean and sorghum and cotton?"

Alice nods.

"Tell Tess about the farm's history. It's fascinating."

I can't imagine Alice, with her chewing gum and chic hairstyle and fitted slacks working on a farm. I slip onto the empty chair beside her as she begins to explain.

"The land was my great-great-grandfather's, bought with his own wages after the emancipation. He was a butcher, not a farmer, but he kept the land planted every year for his kids to harvest. By hand, of course. Said he didn't want them to forget where they came from. Said he wanted to make sure they had a physical connection to their past. Anyway, when he died, he passed the land and the tradition on to his kids, and my great-grandfather and great uncles did the same with their families. To this day, my dad plants every spring and my brother and I harvest every fall. It's a small plot. Not nearly as big as the one my dad and his brothers and sisters picked, but still, it's enough to get your muscles burning." She holds out her hands, and I can make out scars on her fingertips. "My cousins are secretly plotting to sell their portion of the land once it's our time, but who knows? I might join the Black Cotton movement."

"Black Cotton?" I ask.

"Yeah, there's this amazing fifth-generation cotton farmer here in North Carolina who started this company, Black Cotton, as a way for other black, small-acreage cotton farmers to sustain profitability. But they don't sell the cotton to the clothing industry; they sell it as décor, like in bouquets and stuff." She narrows her eyes at me. "Have you ever seen real cotton before? Like still on the stalk?"

I shake my head.

"Most people haven't," she says, smiling. "It's actually quite beautiful. Maybe you'd like to help us with the harvest in the fall and you can see it for yourself?"

That Alice is willing to share this part of herself with me fills my farmer heart to overflowing. "I'd love that," I tell her.

Smiling satisfactorily to herself, Mom backs out of the room. "I guess it's a good thing Alice asked about our farm back in Iowa," she says, revealing the origin of their conversation. "Kinda cool you both know a thing or two about agriculture."

There's a tug. The pull of an invisible connection strengthening the bond between us. I wonder how many threads it will take to seal our friendship and how many connections we'll discover as the days go by. Surely there are others.

I wonder how many threads run between me and Zander, tying us to one another across the miles. Hundreds? Thousands? And I wonder how long it will take for them to dissolve once our lives are no longer intertwined as they once were.

"You found a chessboard," Alice says, startling me from my thoughts. For a moment, I'd forgotten I was still holding it.

"Yeah, and it's an old one so we can do whatever you want

with it."

She unfolds the board on the table and pulls a black Sharpie from her bag, dividing the board into four equal segments, bisecting it across the middle in both directions. "It's a coordinate plane," she says.

My eyes widen with understanding. "So, this one's the X-axis and this one's the Y-axis," I say pointing at the lines she's drawn.

"Exactly," she confirms, gathering the handful of pawns I've dumped on the table. "And we're going to use these chess pieces to plot the points."

We continue through our assignment in this way, physically plotting the shapes on the plane then plugging the coordinates into the distance formula for each mark. It's slow work but after half-an-hour, it's beginning to make sense.

"The shape isn't changing in size, it's just changing position," I say.

"Yes. The formula gives the translation."

"So, this one is..." I pause, drumming the eraser of my pencil against the table. "(x -6, y 3)?"

I'm overcome by a sense of relief at completing the assignment and even more relieved I came to the correct conclusions on my own. "Yes. You've totally got it," she tells me.

She glances around the room, landing on the microwave clock over the stove. "It's getting late," she says. "I promised Foster I'd be home in time to read with him before bed. We're halfway through the third Harry Potter. My mom had two fits and a hemorrhage when she found out I was reading it to him, but I convinced her the series isn't *of the devil*." She rolls her eyes, chucking her belongings into her bag before heading toward the front door. "Moms, right?"

"Right," I agree, the tug of another thread gathering between us. A thread I hope is one of many more to come.

chapter 10
Stenos and Strippers

Friday, January 18

Cecilia slides our plates of lasagna and string beans across the serving counter to Leonetta and me, and as the aroma wafts upward, I'm thankful, as I am every day, I'm no longer stuck eating standard lunch fare. Leonetta is pleased by how willingly I've taken to Cecilia's cooking and teases it's all part of her master plan to assimilate me into a true southern belle, but I'm just happy I don't have to eat limp, greasy fries anymore. We turn the corner from the line to the seating area and are discouraged to find our usual seats are occupied.

"A bunch of teams must be leaving school early today because of away games. Our shift always ends up being mad overcrowded on those days," Leonetta explains, scanning the aisles for other options.

We're still shuffling aimlessly around the perimeter when I spot Alice and Summer laughing together in the center of the room. There are two seats across from them, and I signal to Leonetta to follow me. Shimmying in their direction among the minefield of backpacks while praying I don't tip anything off my tray onto someone's head, I'm still distracted by the segregation of the lunchroom. Black kids with the black kids. Latino kids with the Latino kids. White kids with the white kids. It's hard for me to wrap my head around the idea of skin color being so tied to making kids who they are. Being such a huge part of their identities, like belonging to an exclusive team or a club. Back in Iowa, white was the default setting for everything, and I never gave my skin color a second thought. But it's hard not to think about it here, and I can't help but wonder if Leonetta has ever *not* had to think about race.

Race doesn't appear to be an issue for Alice and Summer's friendship, though, with their heads nearly touching as they share chips from the same bag of Lays.

"Can we sit with you?" I ask, approaching from the opposite side of the table.

Alice looks up from their notebook and smiles. "Of course," she says.

As Leonetta and I set down our trays, it's clear we've interrupted them. I'm hesitant to say anything, but Leonetta speaks right up. "Whatcha doing?" she asks, taking her first bite of lasagna.

Alice and Summer glance at one another, an unspoken dialogue between them to determine whether to include us in whatever they're discussing. Only a second passes before Alice slides a spiral-bound steno across the table, carefully avoiding our lunches. The wire is across the top of the notebook, and it's opened to a page in the back. Along the top of the sheet, I recognize Alice's handwriting. It says, 'Eleven Reasons to Never Date a Private.' Below, there are seven completed bullet points and four blank spaces.

"Why eleven?" Leonetta asks as if the number's the most pressing topic to discuss.

"Ten seems a little predictable and twenty of any one thing is way too many to think of. So, we always have eleven,"

Summer explains.

Leonetta sets down her fork to flip through the notebook. "You have a lot of these lists."

"We've been working on them for over two years," Alice explains. "There are sixty-three altogether."

I'm impressed by the longevity of their friendship, given the transient nature of the area. Perhaps Summer's a townie, too.

"Nah. Life-long military kid. But this is our third year at Bragg," she tells me. "It won't be long until we head somewhere new. I honestly can't believe we're still here. It's the longest we've been stationed anywhere. My dad's set to pin Colonel this spring, though, then he'll get his new assignment." As she says this, her eyes cut from Alice who's stopped eating and is biting at her lip.

My heart aches for them and the inevitability of their separation. To spare them from thinking about it further, I change the subject. "So, what's the deal with this list? Why shouldn't I date a private?"

I scan the first entries: 1. Work crazy, stupid hours. 2. Never call when they say they will. 3. No sexy facial hair.

"Summer's dating a private," Alice tells us. "But he's a jerk."

"He's not *that* bad," Summer says defensively. "And he's super cute."

"Because looks are the most important thing," Alice teases.

Summer rolls her eyes, takes a bite of pizza, and continues, ignoring her friend. "I met Travis at the Fort Bragg fair last June. I got sick on the Centrifuge, and he showed up outta nowhere to hold back my hair while I stood there puking into a trashcan beside the grandstand. He was so sweet. Got me a drink of water and stayed with me until I felt well enough to walk back to my parents' car."

"That's disgusting," Leonetta says.

Summer shrugs. "We didn't start dating right away, even though he gave me his number, in case I ever needed someone to hold back my hair again. But I didn't call because the last thing I wanted was to get involved with some private."

"Ergo, the list," Alice chimes in.

"Yeah, I mean, I'd grown up hearing horror stories from my dad about these eighteen-year-olds and how they're all Hooah and think they're total badasses and will pick up any girl they can find because they can. So, I didn't call. But then, a week later, I ran into him in the PX with my mom. And he was all like, 'I didn't think you could look any prettier than when you were puking into a trashcan, but I was wrong. You're even prettier when you're well.'"

Now it's Alice's turn to roll her eyes. "Yeah. And can you believe she fell for that line?"

I did because I might have, too. "What's this one about?" I ask, pointing to number six on the list. "Date strippers."

"You gonna tell them?" Alice asks, narrowing her eyes at Summer.

She finishes off her pizza and takes a sip of Diet Coke before beginning. "A few weeks ago, we were at the Mexican place on Bragg Boulevard for dinner and his stupid phone starts buzzing. He's gotta keep it on all the time in case someone from the unit needs him so I'm totally used to it, but this time it was driving me crazy. Buzzing, buzzing, buzzing non-stop through the entire meal. I kept waiting for him to call back whoever it was because, with the way his phone was going off, I was sure it was someone from Division. But he never did. He just sat there like a statue ignoring it." She takes another sip of her pop and continues. "Later that night, in the car on the way home, he got out to pump gas and left his phone on his seat. I was so curious about why he never responded to the incessant buzzing, I snooped. The same number called him fourteen times while we were eating and had been calling over and over for weeks."

"Who was it?" Leonetta interrupts through a bite of beans.

"A stripper, of course," Alice explains.

"No," I say, horrified some guy would betray Summer. I've never even seen a strip club, let alone met a stripper, and the idea of being deceived by someone who I thought loved me was unimaginable.

"Yeah. Turns out he gave her his number back in the fall when he was out at some club with the guys. He tried to feed me all this BS about how he didn't want to go to the club in the first place and how his buddy gave her his number. He swears he's never returned her calls, but his call history doesn't lie."

She takes a nonchalant sip of pop, as if she couldn't care less about the whole ordeal. If Zander was ever disloyal to me I'd be heartbroken. But then again, Zander's not my boyfriend. And I'm not Summer.

"Are you two still together?" I ask.

She sighs heavily, plucking the steno pad off the table, tossing it into her bag. "Yeah. I guess so. I mean, like I said, I'm only gonna be here like, what, four or five more months, tops? So, I figured, what's the sense in having some drama-filled break-up? Might as well enjoy the free meals and trips to the movies while I can, then cut ties once we ship out. No harm, no foul."

Everyone's packing around me, but I've been so engrossed in Summer's story I've forgotten to eat. I scarf down what I can, encouraging the others to go on without me. By the time I finally leave the cafeteria, the hallways have emptied, and my thoughts return to Summer as I make my way back to English. Part of me is envious of her callous attitude. Of her ability to separate her emotions from the reality of her boyfriend's infidelity. Perhaps she's able to remain steadfast because she's not in love with him, and never really was, which would account for her blasé attitude. On the other hand, if she does genuinely love him and is still unmoved by his deception, what does that say about her? I'm inclined to think, however, she's suffering far more greatly than she's letting on and is only putting on a good face for the rest of us.

Does she cry when she's alone?

Would I if I was her?

I start down the stairs to the first floor, barely mindful of my location, my head swimming with thoughts of my dad, who was once a young private himself here in Fayetteville. Was he like the guys Summer's father described: eighteen years old, full of piss and vinegar, only looking for a good time? Was he like Travis?

He and my mom flew here from Iowa so many years ago, with the simple dream of starting a life together on their own terms, away from the prying eyes of small-town, middle-America. What would Mom think of Alice and Summer's list describing 'Eleven Reasons to Never Date a Private?' Would she agree with them or did she see things differently? Of course, there's no way Dad would have left Mom sitting home alone while he went out with the other privates to strip clubs. He'd loved her then. He loves her still.

I have vivid memories of Mom and Dad talking about 'The Army Years'—from the beginning of their marriage until just after I was born. They were high school sweethearts, but Dad had no interest in becoming a farmer, like his father and grandfather before. Looking for an alternative to small-town life, he was seduced by the enlistment officer who met with all the guys in his class during the spring of his senior year, convincing him, in lieu of farming, the Army might be a perfect match.

Without their families' blessings, they were married by

a justice of the peace at the Des Moines city courthouse on the morning of June 11, three days after their high school graduation and only hours before boarding the plane that flew them swiftly from their sheltered lives in Iowa to the great unknown of North Carolina. It was the first time Mom had ever been on a plane, out of the state, or away from her parents.

But they were young. And they were in love. And they were determined to make a life for themselves out in the world.

Over the years, Ashley and I have listened to the story of those early days so many times, the memories seep from our pores as if they are our own. How they arrived in Fayetteville with four borrowed pieces of luggage and an envelope containing $1046.39 of cash, comprised of graduation gifts, Mom's babysitting money, and Dad's savings from years of working odd jobs around the local farms. To this day, I have no idea how they survived. On ramen, stale bread, and faith, Mom's always said.

Lost in my thoughts, I've wandered into an unfamiliar hallway. Panic sets in, not only because I'm late but also because I'm lost and have no idea how to get back to the cafeteria much less English class. Standing paralyzed in the center of the hall, I hear Leonetta bellowing from somewhere back in the direction from which I've just come.

"Netta?" I call back.

Her heavy footfalls clomp down the nearest stairwell. "Tess?" she replies.

"I'm here," I tell her. "Don't move. I'll come to you."

I follow her voice back down the hall, and as I turn to climb the nearest staircase, she's there, grinning at me like the Cheshire cat.

"Eight days," she says, shaking her head. "I thought I'd lose you way before this. Day three. Day four, maybe. And to be honest, I thought you had this place licked. I was feeling pretty good about my mentoring abilities."

"Thank God you're here," I gush, rushing up the stairs to throw my arms around her. I can't believe how relieved—and how stupid—I feel. "How'd you know where to find me? How'd you figure out I was lost?"

She trudges up the steps in front of me. "I didn't know where to find you, but I figured after ten minutes passed and you still weren't in class, something was up. Luckily Mrs. Alexander isn't Ms. Krenshaw, so she didn't hesitate to let me head out. Been looking for you all this time. What the heck happened?"

I shrug. "I guess I took a wrong turn outta the cafeteria. I was thinking about stuff and forgot to pay attention to where I was."

"Thinking about what stuff?" she asks once we're both at the top of the staircase, walking side-by-side.

I want to tell her about my parents, their humble military beginnings, and how they left the Army because of me, but it somehow feels too personal for the hallway or maybe for our fledgling friendship. Instead, I say, "I was thinking about Summer and how her boyfriend lies to her and talks to other girls behind her back. I guess I'm hoping all guys aren't like that. They can't be, right?"

"Wouldn't know," she says matter-of-factly.

I don't know Leonetta well enough to judge whether she's had much experience with guys. It's possible she's never had a boyfriend.

That would make two of us.

"Zander, the guy I told you about from back home... I mean, back in Iowa, isn't a jerk. At least, I don't think he is."

She tightens her face, glancing at me suspiciously as if I've been withholding valuable information all this time.

"He isn't my boyfriend if that's what you're thinking," I tell her quickly. "Remember? He's the guy from next door. I've known him since we were babies. Anyway, he's dated a couple girls and was sweet to all of them."

"He was *never* your boyfriend?" she asks.

I'm staring at my shoes, leather Merrells, which probably still hide traces of the herd between their treads. Zander owns the exact same pair, but the men's version, in his size. We bought them together on a rare trip to the Merle Hay Mall in Des Moines before school started in the fall. With summer job money burning holes in our pockets, we'd set out back-to-school shopping, just the two of us, in his father's pickup. After the two-hour drive, listening to practically every song on Zander's playlist—Miranda Lambert, Blake Shelton, Big & Rich—we'd window-shopped until lunch, realizing our paltry savings weren't going to go very far, and we were going to need to be selective about what we ultimately chose to purchase. Somehow, he'd convinced me the Merrells, on sale for $69.95, were a sound investment. Looking at them now, I'm sure they weren't, because wearing them away from the farm feels excessive, like driving around Fayetteville on snow tires. The truth is, I'm only still wearing them because they remind me of him.

"No," I tell her. "We never dated. It wasn't like that between us."

I hate myself for using the past tense, but I still haven't spoken to him since he snuck into my bedroom New Year's Eve, and in the days since, everything about him is starting to feel distant.

"I'm sure there are good guys in the world who won't lie to us or break our hearts," she says as we approach the door to our English class. "I'm just not sure where to find them."

chapter 11
Apologies

Sunday, January 20

I'm sprawled across my bed reading *The Bluest Eye* in preparation for Tuesday's afterschool lit circle when my phone rings. I dog-ear the book and scootch across the bed so I can grab the phone off my nightstand. I assume it's Leonetta calling to chat or Alice confirming our evening study session, so without looking at the screen, I answer with a lighthearted, "Hey."

"Hey, yourself."

For a second, my heart stops beating inside my chest. It's Zander, and his voice is like a cool glass of water on a hot, summer day. I don't appreciate how much I've missed hearing his voice until it's reverberating inside my head: familiar, supportive, cheerful.

Exactly like home.

"Zander," is all I say, because there seems to be an unfortunate disconnect between my brain and my mouth. Or maybe it's my heart gumming up the works.

"I hope it's okay I'm calling," he says. "I figured your mom probably already gave you my letter but you were too pissed off at me to call, so I decided to do what I should have done at the beginning and reach out."

He says it all in one breath as if he's rehearsed, and I can't help but feel a pang of remorse for the angst in his voice. Why didn't I text him all week?

"Oh," I say, trying not to fumble over my words. "It's a great time actually. And I'm definitely not upset. Been busy I guess, what with the forced cross-country assimilation and all."

It's a flat out lie, but he laughs heartily, and I'm amazed at how hearing it can simultaneously fill my heart and break it.

"So, how bad is it?" he asks, all the awkwardness of our days apart seemingly forgotten. I can imagine him sitting in his kitchen, rocking on the back two legs of the chair with his dirty feet propped on the table, his mother having a fit.

"It's not as bad as I thought it'd be," I say, but then worry it might hurt to know I'm doing alright without him. "There's no one here like you, though," I add.

"Well, alright," he says. "That's not a bad start considering A) you're not going to find anyone like me and B) you thought you were going to be completely miserable. Please tell me you're not sitting alone at lunch, though."

"I'm not a pariah," I say with a laugh, "so no, I'm not sitting alone. In fact, I met a few girls who've been really nice to me. They even seem genuinely interested in what my life was like back on the farm, asking about the move and the cows, and you know, all the other stuff I left behind." Of course, I don't mention what I've told them about *him*. Instead, I go on about Leonetta and Alice and Summer. How willing they've been to find space for me in their lives, no questions asked. And I tell him about lit circle and tutoring and Summer's crummy boyfriend. And also, how I ended up getting lost because the school's so freakin' big.

"I'm glad you're getting things figured out." He sounds

sincerely happy for me—a reminder of why, until now, I never needed to look any further than my backyard for a best friend.

"I am," I tell him. "But I've had a lot of help. Leonetta's been watching out for me, giving me tips about our classes and the kids to avoid like Monika Moore. I keep trying to figure out why she cares so much, but all I can come up with is that maybe she just needs a friend as much as I do."

"Who's Monika Moore?" he asks.

I regret having brought her up because the last thing I want is Zander's pity, but since I'm on a roll, quenched by his attention like someone marooned in the desert, I can't keep from sharing everything. "Ugh. She's this girl who has it out for me already," I continue, remembering our most recent run-in. "I got stuck sitting next to her on the first day of chemistry, and now she hates me. Like seriously hates me."

"Why in the world would she hate you?"

"I brought the class size from twenty-seven to twenty-eight, thus eliminating the need for Monika and her two lackeys to remain a group of three. I'm the reason our teacher split them up, and now instead of getting to hang out in the back of the room with her friends, she's stuck in the front with me."

"That sucks."

"Yeah. It sucks big. And now, it's like she's doing everything in her power to make me as miserable as I've made her. You'll never believe what that triflin' heifer did to me last week..."

"Trifling what? Did you just call her a cow?" he interrupts.

I smile, acknowledging how Leonetta's expression likens someone to an actual cow. Leave it to the dairy farmer.

"Netta calls everyone who's been mean to her a triflin' heifer. I have no idea why. It's something she says, and I guess I've picked it up."

"I like it," he says. "Mind if I use it? We got a few triflin' heifers around East Chester, don't you think?"

"If you're talking about Lacey, then yeah. And it's not trademarked, so I don't see why not." I tell him about how Monika purposely switched my zinc with silver nitrate during our independent lab assignments, so instead of creating bubbles with the hydrochloric acid the way everyone else did, I concocted a ridiculous goopy glob.

"She sounds like a real piece of work."

"She's awful," I agree.

"Why does she keep harassing you like that?"

I'd been asking myself the very same question. "I dunno. Maybe she's bored, and it gives her something to do. Whatever it is, I hope she gets over it soon."

There's a brief pause as I consider changing the subject to the state of our farms. Part of me wants to know what's been going on out of sheer curiosity and the desire to hold on to whatever thread of commonality we might still claim to share, but the other part would prefer to be left blissfully unaware. Because do I want to know if my herd was divided piecemeal to the highest bidders or if some of the older cows were sent to slaughter? Cows like Sunshine and Bella. If he never tells me, I can continue to live with my current memories of how I left the farm—exactly the way it was my entire life. Exactly the way it had always been with Zander.

The farm, to include all the livestock, people, and buildings it encompassed, served as the backdrop of our friendship from the beginning. It was the third amigo to what, from afar, most would have considered merely a duo. The farm made our friendship what it was. Had we grown up in a skyscrapered city or even some sprawling suburb with street lights and sidewalks and carefully manicured lawns, we would have been different.

Our friendship would have been different. But we didn't. We grew up amongst the cornfields and the tractors and the silos.

The silos were always something of a forbidden fruit, looming over the rest of the farm like great sentinels, and although we had access to most other areas of the farm, the silos were a place we were prohibited from venturing. Which is, of course, what made them all the more alluring, especially to Zander.

After Sunshine's birthing tragedy, I became a vigilant midwife, terrified of allowing another calf to die during my watch, which is how Zander and I came to find ourselves in the dairy barn after school one afternoon in the spring of our sixth-grade year, tending to one of the pregnant cows. I'd been unaware, as I checked Daisy's cervix for signs of dilation, that Zander had been eyeing the rickety, metal ladder which led from the base of the silo to the very top.

"You dare me to make it all the way up there?" he'd asked.

"No," I told him, without a moment's hesitation. "We're not allowed to climb the silo."

"Yeah, but the view's gotta be amazing," he said. "I bet I could see all the way to Landon's farm on the other side of town. Heck, I bet I could see all the way to Hutchins."

Hutchins was the next town over, and although I doubted he'd be able to see that far, I still couldn't help but wonder how the world might look from up there.

"It's not safe," I told him flatly, as I felt the calf's hooves poking into Daisy's extended midsection, trying to assess if the baby was in the proper birthing position.

"Yeah, but our dads do it all the time," he said, lifting himself from where he'd been resting on the ground, brushing the dirt off the seat of his jeans, "and nothing ever happens to them. I bet they wanna keep the view to themselves."

"They don't go up there to admire the views, just to check

the…" I began to say, but the words weren't even out of my mouth before Zander was halfway to the silo.

I was torn then, between calling after him to get him to stop, and knowing if I did, it would surely attract my dad's attention. I watched him clamber up the first set of rungs, amd my voice caught in my throat, not knowing whether to remain silent or rat him out. Indecision became my decision, and I kept quiet as he climbed higher and higher, scaling the side of the silo like some rogue Spiderman. My dad's words from months before, about his intention to replace the standard, open ladder with a safer, enclosed one, came back to me, and as he reached just above the halfway point, I cried out.

"Zander! Please come back down."

But he didn't reverse course. He didn't even stop or look back. Instead, he scrambled higher until I could no longer make out the logo on the back of his John Deere t-shirt. Then the unthinkable happened. Four rungs from the top, his foot slipped.

I watched in horrified silence as he fell, plummeting to the ground at an alarming speed. The thud of him hitting the earth crushed my soul, and I didn't realize I was screaming until the shock of my dad racing past jolted me out of my daze. I followed him to where Zander landed, atop a filthy pile of straw recently mucked from the barn. His body was crumpled into an unnatural position, with his hips twisted to the right and his shoulders curled to the left. He was unconscious, and there was a deep laceration on his right arm where he'd grabbed for the ladder on his way down. There was another gash on his face, across his temple, where he'd hit his head. For some reason, that injury, more than any of the others, caused my knees to buckle. His perfect face was irreparably marred.

Dad was bent over him, checking for a pulse, and when he gazed up at me, shielding his eyes with blood-covered hands, there was no mistaking the desperation in his eyes. "Go call 911. Tell them what happened. Tell them he has a heartbeat but his breathing is shallow. Tell them our address. Tell them to hurry."

*

Remembering Zander's brush with death and the days I spent sitting vigil by his bedside at the hospital, weeping over him, begging him not to leave me, my heart aches with the depth and breadth of our friendship. I want to ask if he misses me. If he's lonely. If he thinks about me as often as I think of him.

"How's the chess club?" I ask instead, unable to broach such a personal line of questioning for fear of the unfavorable response such an inquisition might elicit.

"Claire and Bruster finally finished their game," he says.

"Claire won, didn't she?"

"No surprise," he says. "I honestly thought she was going to let him win last week because she has a thing for Will now and was sick of spending her mornings tied to Bruster, but darned if she didn't stick it out to the end and beat that sad sack."

"Will? Seriously?" Although it's no surprise Claire beat Bruster, I can't believe she's interested in Will, the same guy who still picked his nose and ate it well into the eighth grade.

"Love sees no faults."

"He ate his boogers, Zander."

A screen door slams on Zander's end of the line, and his dad bellows for him to come outside to the barn. "I gotta go," he says, scrambling across the kitchen. "I promised I'd change the oil in the tractor this afternoon." He pauses and I can tell he doesn't want to hang up. "And I'm a man of my word, as you well know."

I pick at my cuticle. I'd been fine, all those days, all

those weeks, all those hours since leaving Iowa. Or at least reasonably fine. But now, having to say goodbye again, if only over the phone and if only until next time, feels like peeling a scab before the wound beneath is fully healed.

"I know. A man of your word." I repeat. I want to say goodbye but can't let him go without knowing there's definitely going to be another conversation in our near future. I need something specific to look forward to. "Hey. As long as it wouldn't be too Gabby-ish, what if we call each other around this time every Sunday afternoon to catch up?" I ask. "Since things are so busy for both of us during the week and all."

"Definitely not too Gabby-ish," he says. "And that's actually a really good idea."

Relief washes over me as his dad calls again for him to get off the phone. "I guess we should say goodbye now before you get in trouble. But I'll call you next Sunday, and you can tell me more about Claire and Will and the boogers."

He laughs and my heart leaps. How many years I took his laugh for granted. The ease of it. The way it makes me feel safe and connected. But now...

"Okay," he says. "It's a date. I'll be home, here, waiting by the phone."

"Okay," I say.

There's a beat of silence as both of us wait for the other to end the call. Finally, I say goodbye.

"Bye," he says, and before I can even catch my breath, the line disconnects and he's gone.

chapter 12
Blond Hair, Blue Eyes

Tuesday, February 12

By the time I skid around the corner into Mrs. Alexander's room like some ridiculous cartoon character, the rest of the literature circle is already seated, books on their laps, deep in conversation. They're used to my late arrival, since I always check in with Mr. Wilson about our math assignment at the end of the day, but they greet me warmly with nods and hellos as if I'm an old friend instead of a recent interloper.

Like the cafeteria, which serves as a representative microcosm of student life, most of the extracurriculars at Hopkins are as segregated as the lunch tables, each of the races keeping very much to themselves. Lit circle, however, is different, and I'm certain Mrs. Alexander's commitment to mutual acceptance and understanding is the reason for its diversity, both in its members and its reading selections.

Our reading lists in Iowa were comprised of the classics I assumed were the staples of every American high school: *Jane Eyre, The Scarlet Letter, The Great Gatsby, Catcher in the Rye*, and *Death of a Salesman*. Only now, after spending time with the members of Mrs. Alexander's lit circle, have I become aware of how sheltered my existence has been, realizing the works I've been exposed to are primarily representative of *white* American literature, not the least bit indicative of the breadth and scope of what our country's diversity of authors has to offer.

As I slip silently into the last open seat beside Leonetta, the group is already mired in a deeply philosophical discussion on the final chapters of *The Bluest Eye*, by Toni Morrison, a title I'd never heard of before moving here. With no point of reference from which to contribute, I've spent every session listening, enthralled by the group's analysis of the main character, Pecola Breedlove, a young black girl who believes having blond hair and blue eyes will make her pretty, and beauty will ensure perfection in every aspect of her life.

Lashanda, a senior with a sharp tongue but a soft heart, smacks her novel on her leg as she glares across the circle of chairs at Rashida. "You're telling me you never thought once about straightening your hair or using makeup to contour your nose?"

Rashida shrugs. "I'm a proud, black woman," she says, tossing the long dreadlocks she keeps tied with a frayed length of fabric behind her back. "I don't need to conform to white beauty standards."

"That's one of the points Morrison is trying to make," Mrs. Alexander interjects. "That you see yourself in opposition to traditional white beauty justifies her point, Rashida. She believes it's a travesty there are *any* conventional definitions of beauty in our society. But we continue to be bombarded by them, maybe even more today than when this was written. So, who maintains these standards?"

"White people do," Leonetta chimes in. "Because white people control the media and powerful corporations. They control what we see and how we see it. They tell us what's pretty and what's not. They decide what constitutes *regular* shampoo and what ends up on a special aisle labeled *ethnic*."

I hold my breath. It's the first time I've heard Leonetta use the word 'they' in an 'us against them' sort of way. I hate imagining us on opposing teams. The black team versus the white team. I want us to be on the same team. But I have to admit she's right. Our entire country was established on a foundation of racial hierarchy and the media is just one of many systems perpetuating it to this day.

Looking around the circle, I'm painfully aware that although I'm not the only white person in the group, I am the only one with blond hair and blue eyes. This makes me want to speak up. To defend myself against any presumed alliance with the media. Because after all, aren't they the ones shoving images of unattainable, idealistic beauty down everyone's throats? And it's not my fault I was born with blond hair and blue eyes any more than it's their fault they were born with black hair and brown eyes. But listening to the continuing dialogue between Leonetta and the others, it occurs to me I'm in no position to take offense. This part of the conversation isn't about me.

And maybe some discussions are best left to the people they most concern.

"So, Leonetta, you would argue in parts of tribal Africa, where the western world hasn't infiltrated with its biased, lofty opinion of blond hair and blue eyes, those traits aren't valued there? Do natural curls and fuller figures epitomize their definition of beauty?"

"Yeah. They probably do," she says. "They learn to appreciate the black features they're exposed to. Not hate them, like we're taught."

The group nods in agreement. "I tend to concur with you, Leonetta," Mrs. Alexander says, "but I'd like to ask you all again—if you believe the definition of beauty is influenced primarily by white, western culture in our society, who is ultimately responsible for maintaining that definition? What do you think, Tess?"

I swallow hard to clear my throat, wishing she hadn't called on me. "We all are," I venture, my voice barely above a whisper. "We let the media in as little kids. We let them tell us what's pretty and what's not. And we believe them. We believe their advertisements and their television shows and their movies. And even though I happen to be white, with the blond hair and blue eyes Pecola dreamed of, I'm not unaffected by the media. I believe what they say about needing to be tan to be beautiful, even though my mom's had dozens of cancerous lesions cut off her skin. I believe them when they tell me I need bigger boobs and a smaller waist. None of us are immune to the media's constraining definition of beauty. We're all on the same side in this, and we're all losers in their commercialized game against us. Ms. Morrison is speaking for the black community through Pecola's story, but I think in some ways, she's speaking for all of us. For anyone who's ever felt less than."

Roy, the SGA sophomore class president, turns to me, shaking his head. "No way, Tess. Morrison wrote this book about racial self-loathing, so you don't get to play the 'we're all in this together' card because I can almost guarantee you've never hated yourself for being born white. You can't even compare our situations. When you're white, you don't need to think about race, and you don't need to overcome negative racial stereotypes. People don't assume things about you simply because of the color of your skin. Like, you don't have to worry about whether people think you're a thug even if you're not. I gotta work hard to prove I'm smart and honest and reliable. When was the last time you had to prove anything about yourself to anyone?"

By the tone of his voice, I expect to see hatred or anger in his eyes, like the characters of Maureen and Geraldine from the novel, but instead, there's only despondency; the pain associated with constantly having to prove his worth.

"You're right," I tell him. "You're absolutely right. I don't agonize about any of that stuff or face those sorts of prejudices. The truth is, before moving here, I didn't know much about what it means to be black. There weren't any black kids at my old school and the only exposure I had to black culture was media-driven stereotypical nonsense. Now, though, thanks to you all and our discussions here, I'm beginning to see the truth." I swallow hard, willing myself to go on. "At the same time, because everyone's personal experiences are different, none of us can truly understand what it's like to be another person, no matter how hard we try. And that's okay. Because we don't need to live other people's lives or walk around in their shoes to respect and love them, do we? We just need to try to understand. And I think, with the help of this group, I'm starting to."

I see a few timid smiles around the circle before my gaze returns to Roy. He isn't smiling. He actually looks a little sick.

"You know, Tess, that's the same crap I hear all the time. *We're all the same. Everyone has their own struggles, blah, blah, blah.* But the differences matter. There are still a lot of people in this country who believe all races are treated fairly and given the same opportunities. That sort of ideology gives them a free pass to ignore the systemic injustice that's plagued our country for hundreds of years. But in some of the most mundane, daily ways, my life as a black man is inherently harder than a lot of white people's simply because of the color of my skin. And I'm not asking for any special treatment because of it. But I would like to be judged on my character instead of my race." He sighs heavily and closes his eyes, pinching the bridge of his nose. When he opens them again, I can see his profound exhaustion.

"Life can be hard if you're white. There's no denying that. But it won't be hard *because* you're white."

A lump rises in my throat, and I blink back the tears threatening to spill over. I probably have no right to feel hurt by what Roy's said, but I do because I'm human and no one likes being confronted. He's right, of course, and it occurs to me I still have a lot to learn about what it means to be black. I have a lot to learn about my place in the world. And so maybe in order to understand more fully, I need to keep listening.

The group is silent, still contemplating our exchange before Mrs. Alexander finally speaks up. "Both Roy and Tess might be on to something here. Roy would argue Pecola is bound to her blackness through no fault of her own. It's an issue for her specifically as it relates to whiteness, and there's an implicit bias for her in this which causes her great pain. On the other hand, wouldn't you also agree the general themes of love and acceptance were pervasive throughout the book? That all any of the main characters wanted was to be loved for who they were, regardless of their appearance or past, as Tess suggests?"

"I guess," a guy named Will says tentatively. "But what happened to Pecola, the tragedy of her life, stemmed from her blind subscription to the image and values of white culture. She never questioned it which ultimately led to her undoing."

"It wasn't just Pecola," Leonetta points out. "All the characters were victims of their circumstances, in one way or another. But knowing where they came from, their backstory, it helped me, as a reader, to understand why they did the things they did." She closes her book and her eyes before going on. "We need to make sure we understand other people's backstories before making judgments about their lives. Know where they come from. Where their heads are. Try to appreciate their motivations."

Mrs. Alexander leans forward in her seat, resting her elbows on her knees. She's smiling, self-satisfactorily, and I can tell she's pleased with our discussion. "So, what does this mean for the twelve of you sitting in this room? What lessons can we carry away from Morrison's work?"

Her question strikes me with such directness, it's as if I'm experiencing literature for the first time. I've read hundreds of stories over the years purely for enjoyment without ever acknowledging there might be something more the author wanted from me. Was it possible an author could ask something of her audience outside of mere enjoyment and understanding? Could an author expect a reader to foster change in his or her own life based on the ideas presented in a book?

Sarah Hill, one of the other white students in the group, clears her throat. "We talked last week about how Ms. Morrison used the primer excerpts to point out how different Pecola's black world was from the white world of Dick and Jane. But maybe in addition to recognizing the differences, like Pecola did with the white picket fence and the blue eyes and the red dress, all the things she didn't have, we should also focus on the stuff that makes us alike. The stuff that binds us. Like searching for love and acceptance. We all want those things, right? No matter our color or culture."

"Exactly. Using those universal truths to build the foundation of our relationships makes it easier to understand and accept the differences," Rashida says, smiling at Sarah. "We're not so different once we strip away everything contrived by society, but it's important to understand why the differences exist, what effects they have on our lives, and most importantly how to celebrate them."

"Yeah. And while we're at it, screw the media," says Lashanda. "Who cares what they say. We should appreciate each other for who we are, not who society tells us we oughta be. That goes for you too, Snow White," she adds, pointing at me. "Wear your damn sunscreen."

*

Leonetta is strangely quiet on the way to the other side of the building following lit circle. I get the sense there's something she's not saying. Something she's holding in.

"Do I make you feel that way?" I ask as we head downstairs to the first floor.

"Which way?"

I tuck my thumb into my hand to keep from picking at my cuticle. "Like Roy feels."

She hesitates, not looking at me as she adjusts the bag slung across her shoulder. When she eventually speaks, though, her voice is steady. "Not really."

I nod, letting the truth settle over me like fog in the pasture on a winter morning. 'Not really' isn't no, but she's too nice to call me out because we're friends and she knows how important she is to me. She's protecting my feelings at the expense of her own.

Now, our strengthening bond, growing day-by-day one connective thread at a time, compels me to respond. "I can do better, Netta."

She stops at the end of the hallway and looks up, her eyes soft. "I know," she says. "And you will. But right now, you better get your butt home because you and I both know it's probably gonna take you all night to get your geometry homework done."

We're still laughing about my mathematical incompetence, halfway to our cars on the far side of the student parking lot when Summer pulls up beside us in her cherry red Honda Civic. "I'm meeting Alice at the mall tonight after dinner," she tells us through her open window. "Some kid on the basketball team, Derek Something-Or-Other, invited her to go to the big party at Calvin Watkins' after the championship game Friday night. She says she doesn't have anything to wear so we're gonna go shopping. Wanna come with?"

Before I have a chance to process, Leonetta asks, "To the mall or to the party?"

She shrugs. "Both I guess."

Leonetta looks at me expectantly, obviously wanting to tag along. I, on the other hand, am loathe to accept an invitation to the mall as shopping has never been high on my list of priorities. It's clear, however, if I'm going to survive here in this brave, new world, I need to continue venturing outside of my comfort zone. I've already taken a chance on the food and the after-school activities, so why not consider a trip to the mall?

"So, you girls in?" Summer asks, and as I consider her anticipatory gaze, it dawns on me the others don't need me to be enthusiastic about the actual shopping. They want me to come along because they like me. Because they enjoy being with me. It's not so much about the purchasing of goods as it is about the camaraderie. The being-included in a way I'd never imagined I would be moving here.

"I'm in if Netta's in," I tell her at last. "As long as I can get my math finished in time."

"I'm in," Leonetta says without the slightest hesitation.

"Then meet us in the food court at seven," Summer says. "And don't be late!"

As Summer pulls away, we continue across the lot to where our cars are parked adjacent to the track. Out of nowhere, a pickup with a bed full of students speeds past, nearly running Leonetta down. They miss hitting her by less than a foot.

"Why you tryin' to be ghetto, new girl?" one of the guys calls from the back, and although I don't know him, I do recognize the girl laughing beside him from history class.

Triflin' heifer.

Leonetta's still shaking as they careen around the corner, nearly tipping sideways onto two wheels before disappearing down the road. The moment passes but I remain frozen, watching helplessly while Leonetta attempts to steady herself.

"You okay?" I ask, gathering the armful of books she's scattered across the asphalt.

She nods, but I can tell she's still unnerved.

"Was that John Frasier?" a voice calls from behind us. "Because if it was, I'm gonna beat his ass."

Rashida runs toward us in her long bohemian skirt, her shoulder bag draped casually across her chest and flip-flops slapping noisily against the pavement.

"I don't know who it was," I tell her once she reaches us. "But we're okay. Just a little shaken."

Rashida places a hand on Leonetta's hunched back, soothing my friend who's struggling to compose herself. "We need to report this to the principal. She needs to know what those maniacs did."

Leonetta shakes her head defiantly. "No," she says. "Let it be."

"They can't get away with harassing you two," Rashida continues with the same righteous tone she used against Lashanda back in lit circle describing herself as a 'proud, black woman.' Watching her now comforting Leonetta, I have no doubt she is.

Leonetta straightens, collecting her books from my arms. Her shirt is askew across her shoulders revealing her bra straps, but she doesn't adjust it. Instead, she says, "It's like we talked about today. Society only wins if we let it and snitching on those idiots to Dr. Emmett will only confirm they've upset us." She looks at me then for the first time since the incident, raising her chin in defiance. "We'll be friends with whoever we want, and if they don't like it, it's on them."

Back in my little town in Iowa, Lacey hated me because she was jealous of my friendship with Zander and the nasty episode between us in the eighth grade proved it. Here in Fayetteville, more of the same. There's a good chance I'm never going to live in a place without ignorant jerks. They're everywhere, and they come from every walk of life.

But no one back in Iowa ever tried running me over with a moving vehicle. Not even a tractor.

chapter 13
Sizzle

Tuesday, February 12

It's a relief to see Leonetta's car already parked in the mall lot as I make my second pass down the aisle closest to the entrance. I'd been afraid our traumatic afternoon might cause her to reconsider coming out, but since she's already waiting inside, I give up on finding a dream spot and ease my car into the next available slot.

A quick scan of the food court finds her sitting across from Summer and Alice at a table near Subway, and I snag a free sample of bourbon chicken from a Japanese restaurant employee as I weave my way in their direction, sidestepping dozens of bag-laden and tray-wielding shoppers.

"Oh, yay!" Alice says as I collapse into the seat beside Leonetta. "I was hoping you'd make it."

"Thanks for the invite," I say. "This party's a big deal, huh?"

Thinking back, I don't recall a single party back in Iowa that required special attire. For the most part, dressing up meant arriving in something other than boots and overalls.

Alice and Summer share a conspiratorial glance, nonverbally deciding who's going to fill me in. "Calvin Watkins graduated from Hopkins last year, was a member of the basketball team, and is totally sexy," Alice explains. "We were only sophomores during his senior year, so it's not like we had a lot of access to him or anything..."

"Although Alice stalked him in the hallways like a lunatic," Summer interrupts.

"Was it my fault our class locations spring semester caused our paths to cross so many times?" Alice snakes her head and wags her finger in Summer's face. "Take it up with my guidance counselor because I had nothing to do with it."

Summer rolls her eyes good-naturedly and continues. "Y'all, Alice was obsessed with this man with a capital O. She dragged me to every basketball game and woulda sold her soul to have gotten invited to one of his famous after-parties. But we were warned they didn't let underclassmen in, so we never worked up the courage to go."

"He goes to Fayetteville State now on a full-ride basketball scholarship, but he still came back to Hopkins for a couple of games this season to cheer on his old teammates. In fact, he said hi to me at a game back in December," Alice says.

"You woulda thought Jesus Christ himself had acknowledged her with the way she carried on."

"I wasn't that bad."

Summer narrows her eyes and nods at Leonetta and me, whispering, "She was that bad."

"Anyway," Alice says, ignoring Summer, "I finally got a legit invitation to Calvin's championship party this Friday night, and I gotta find somethin' fine to wear. Because God as my witness, that man is gonna notice me this weekend if it's the last thing I do." She stands and slides her chair curtly beneath the table. "So, come on. Y'all gotta help a girl out."

We head out of the food court into the interior of the mall, past the candle store and the pretzel place. I trail along with Leonetta behind Alice and Summer, who are giggling incessantly about heaven-knows-what. If Zander saw me now—at the mall on a Tuesday night amongst a small herd of teenage girls instead of in a barn with a large herd of cattle— he'd be checking to make sure hell wasn't freezing over or I wasn't coming down with the flu.

Nothing interests Alice in the first several stores, although she and Summer do buy matching unicorn socks at one of the kiosks along the way. She eventually stops to admire a few dresses in the window of Y&M, so we venture inside. While she tosses one dress after another into Summer's arms near the front of the store, Leonetta and I mill around the clearance racks in the back.

"You gonna go with them to Calvin's party?" she asks, and I can tell she's intentionally trying to sound nonchalant.

I've never been to the type of party where you need to be on some designated list like the kids in the movies. Back at East Chester, where there were only two hundred kids in the entire student body, invitations were typically open-ended. It's just the way it was. But I'm not sure Summer's off-handed invitation earlier in the parking lot was even official. And if the guys hosting the party are anything like the kids from the pickup truck this afternoon, Fayetteville-State-Calvin and his college buddies might not be too thrilled about some new girl showing up. Especially if the new girl is me.

"I dunno," I tell her. "Do you think I'll be welcome?"

She shrugs. "I don't see why not."

Given the ease of her continued browsing, I'm pretty sure she didn't pick up on my insinuation. I try again, this time more overtly. "Do you think I'll be welcome even though I'm white?"

She lifts her eyes to meet mine, her mouth pressed into a thin line before saying for a second time, "I don't see why not."

She turns away from me to peruse a rack of shirts, and I worry I've upset her. I'm not intentionally fixating on race. I just keep imagining what might happen if I was to accidentally say something offensive to someone who isn't as forgiving as Leonetta or Alice or the kids from lit circle. The parking lot incident proves people are already incensed about the two of us being friends. I can't risk making things worse for the others by showing up where I'm not welcome, especially when I'm still learning what's appropriate and what isn't.

Before I have a chance to explain myself, I notice a sales clerk approaching Leonetta from behind. Easily in her mid-fifties and constructed of pure sinew, the saleswoman's eyes and lips exhibit the tell-tale creases of a chain smoker. Leonetta is still aimlessly sliding blouses along a rack when the clerk accosts her.

"What exactly are you doing?" she asks Leonetta brusquely, the way a mother might address a three-year-old with her hand caught in a cookie jar.

Leonetta jerks back, as if she's forgotten herself, and holds her hands above her head in an apologetic posture. "Nothing, Ma'am. I'm just looking."

The clerk eyes Leonetta's oversized purse which is zipped shut and crossed tightly against her chest.

"Are you sure you didn't slip something into your bag?"

Without considering the consequences or whether it's even my place to speak up, I jump to Leonetta's defense. "She's been right here with me the entire time. She didn't take anything off the rack."

Leonetta throws me a sideways glance, and I can't tell if she's relieved or offended by my intrusion.

"It's fine," she says, glowering at the clerk as she opens the zipper of her purse. "You're welcome to look inside. I didn't take anything."

She holds her purse open for the woman to scrutinize and after a brief inspection of the contents—a small wallet, a makeup case, two tampons, a bulky keychain, and three paperback novels—the woman takes a step back, suspiciously, as if she's still not convinced of Leonetta's innocence.

"I should have known," the clerk murmurs just loud enough for us to hear as she turns away. "Nothin' in this store 'ill fit you anyway."

I watch helplessly as Leonetta's shoulders slump and her eyes close in what appears to be defeat.

She's mortified.

And I am enraged.

The woman didn't even apologize for her rudeness or her wrongful accusation.

"What just happened?" I growl at Leonetta, still glaring after the clerk as she slinks away.

Leonetta steps back, chin tucked, eyes downcast. "It was nothin'. And I appreciate you sticking up for me, but I don't need saving. I can take care of myself."

I'm appalled by what I've witnessed. Horrified. Nothing about her interaction with the store employee was routine. There was no inquiry about the quality of her day. No cheerful appeal to be of assistance. Only an empty allegation and an unwarranted search. I reach out to Leonetta's arm, but she flinches at my touch.

"I know you don't need saving, Netta, but I can't understand why you let her do that. It's not right."

She raises her head, finally meeting my gaze, and I'm unnerved by the mixture of fear and anger brewing in the shadowy depths of her eyes. I'm still trying to make sense of it all when she softens, taking me by the arm and leading me toward the front of the store.

"There are rules, Tess. Rules about being black."

I have no idea what she's talking about.

"What sort of rules?"

We stop at the store's entrance and she leans against the window, letting her bag drop to the floor. "My dad is a college professor. He holds a Ph.D. in sociology. He's a smart man. But he's black." She pauses as if to let the weight of this set in. "He always taught me to remember the blackness is what other people see first. Not the education. Not the degree. Not his kindness toward other people. Just the color. He taught me the rules once I was old enough to understand about the color. Rules about what I can and can't do if I want to stay out of trouble."

I remember the rules my dad taught me as a child. Don't climb the silos. Don't play on the tractors. Don't jump from the hayloft. Don't walk behind the cows. Simple rules. Common sense rules. Rules designed to keep me safe because the farm was a dangerous place for a little girl.

I can't imagine Leonetta needing rules because of her skin color. Unless, for her, everywhere is a dangerous place.

"Tell me," I say.

She folds her hands, bringing them to her face in a gesture of reverence, and it feels as though she's considering whether to reveal a truth that's not really hers to share or mine to understand.

"If I tell you, it's not because I expect you to be my savior. I can handle things on my own. If I tell you, it's because I trust you genuinely want to understand what it's like to be me."

I know better than to speak so I only nod.

"Keep your bag zipped, always within arm's reach. Get a receipt no matter how small the purchase. Never run if there are police around. Dress nicely, regardless of the occasion. Don't go for a walk after dark. Don't speak to an adult unless you're spoken to first. Swallow your pride. Don't go out with more than three friends at a time. And always, always keep your hands where they can be seen."

She can't look at me, and I recognize the indignity of her disclosure. She's embarrassed by the rules.

"That's the worst list I've ever heard," I tell her, and as I say the words I'm overcome by an unexpected emotion.

Sadness, of course.

But also, anger.

It's clear why my dad never taught me those rules. Why I'm oblivious to receipt management, don't have friend limits, and have never restricted my walks to daylight hours. Racial discrimination is the reason she must worry about these things while I remain blissfully unaware. That she's somehow able to suppress her anger over this injustice is unfathomable to me. As she stares at her shoes, I struggle for something appropriate to say.

"That's really unfair, Netta, and everything about it sucks. Thanks for helping me understand, though."

Before she can respond, Alice beckons to us from deep inside the store. "Come see if you like any of these," she calls over her shoulder before disappearing into the dressing room.

Without hesitation, Leonetta picks up her bag and begins walking between the racks. "It is what it is," she says. "And you're welcome. Now come on. Alice needs us."

Somehow, she lets go of what's transpired, and I try my best to follow her lead, focusing instead on Alice and the bevy of dresses she's selected. She shows us a red one. And a black one. And a black one with white stripes. And a pink one with tiny yellow flowers and a halter top.

"I like the striped one best," Summer tells her decisively. "It makes your arms look amazing and narrows your waist."

"Netta?"

"You look smokin' hot in all of them," she says, ever the

diplomat. "But if it helps, I'll agree with Summer and go with the striped one."

Finally, Alice looks at me.

"I like the striped one, too," I tell her. "But you can't buy any of them."

She raises an eyebrow. "Why not?"

It's not my place to share Leonetta's truth, that much I know. But there's no reason she shouldn't explicate herself.

With a nod of understanding, Leonetta explains what happened with the sales clerk as succinctly as she can. Alice immediately holds the dress at arm's length, studying it as if it's a hazardous waste. "You're right. All these dresses are garbage," she says, shaking her head as she slips the striped one onto the rack with the others. "I won't buy from a store where the employees are racists," she says loudly, taking Leonetta by the arm. "I'm happy to take my business elsewhere."

Minutes later I'm standing inside Sizzle, a store I never knew existed much less imagined patronizing. Although the calendar claims it's February, the store's inventory begs to differ. Tank tops and sheer tees hang on the walls. Shelves are lined with booty shorts adorned with chains and emblazoned with skulls and cartoon characters. I pick up a pair of tie-dyed hot pink shorts and hold them across my hips, trying to imagine how I would ever climb into the barn loft or shovel bales of hay without ripping the seams wide open. They clearly aren't designed for manual labor so much as attracting the attention of the opposite sex.

"Oh, my God, I found my dress," Alice cries, encouraging the rest of us to the back of the store.

An employee uses an extension pole to lower it from the display rack above the counter. It's fitted and bejeweled with sequins the color of a rich, ripe plum. Alice's eyes widen as the employee drops it into her arms, and she carries it with reverence into the dressing room, while Summer, Leonetta, and I loiter close by. Moments later she appears.

There's an audible gasp from Summer who takes a tentative step toward her friend. "It's beautiful," she says in a hushed whisper.

I search my brain for the right adjective to describe how she looks. Before putting it on I thought perhaps it would be too over-the-top, but Alice's taut curves reveal the majestic nature of the dress.

"You look like royalty," I tell her.

She spins around, giving us a 360-degree view of the ensemble. "It's not too risqué?"

"If you want Calvin to notice you," Leonetta says, "this is the dress."

Alice fingers the price tag dangling below her left armpit. "It'll use half my savings from Krispy Kreme, but it'll be worth it, right?"

Alice had filled me in about her job as a clerk at the donut shop during one of our early study sessions, confessing her desire to eventually work in a place where she doesn't have to spend time behind a register. As I look at her now, glowing radiantly in a dress capable of turning every head at the party, I feel certain Alice will be the CEO of some major corporation someday. She's the type of person who knows what she wants and isn't afraid to go after it.

This Calvin guy better be worthy.

Alice pays for the dress with a stack of fives and tens and carries it proudly through the mall, slung on a hanger covered in a protective plastic sleeve. As we pass back through the food court, Summer stops abruptly.

"Y'all, I've worked up an appetite with all this shopping. Who wants something from Dairy Queen?"

"Girl, now you know I gotta fit into this dress," Alice

protests.

Summer glares at her. "You're a bean pole. One vanilla soft serve won't kill you. And besides, it's my treat."

The rest of us agree there's no better way to end an evening of shopping than with ice cream. Leonetta chooses an Oreo Blizzard, Summer a strawberry sundae, and Alice and I opt for plain vanilla cones.

We sit at a four-top with Alice's dress carefully draped across a chair at an adjoining table. Leonetta takes a bite of her Blizzard before asking, "What's so great about this Calvin guy anyway? I barely remember him."

Before Alice can answer, Summer interjects. "He checks every box on her list."

"What list?"

"The 'Eleven Reasons Why Calvin Watkins is the Perfect Man' list."

"Is this one of *the* lists?" I ask, remembering the steno notebook.

"Of course," Alice replies, licking a trickle of ice cream dribbling down her cone. "We have lists for everything."

"So, what's on it?" asks Leonetta.

Summer disappears into her bag and reemerges with the steno pad. In seconds, she's flipped to the appropriate page.

"Eleven reasons why Calvin Watkins is the perfect man," she begins. "Number one: athletic."

Alice makes a check mark in the air with her free hand. "Check," she says. "Basketball phenom."

"Number two," Summer continues. "Taller than me."

Another check.

"Number three: doesn't sag."

"Doesn't what?" I ask.

"Sagging," Alice explains, "is when a guy wears his pants so low his whole butt hangs out. But I don't want the world seeing my man's boxers. He needs to hike up his pants where they belong and wear a belt. The way Calvin does."

I'm familiar with the way some of the guys wear their pants really low so their underwear shows above the waistband, but I had no idea it had a name. There's no end to my ignorance.

"Number four: book smart and street smart."

"Isn't that two things?" Leonetta asks.

"It's about smartness in general," Alice explains. "And he's in college, so that's good enough for me."

"Number five: has his own car."

"Silver Escalade."

Already down to my cone, I begin munching away, listening to the remainder of the list while considering what my own inventory of necessary guy qualities would include. Of course, my only frame of reference is the boys I grew up with. The ones back in Iowa with their farmer's tans and baseball caps, who were capable of rewiring a tractor carburetor without ever looking at a manual and could carry a baby calf across their shoulders as if it weighed no more than a backpack. Guys who always respected their mommas and would usually hold the door for you, especially if your hands were full. The ones who were sensitive and funny and serious, all at the same time.

As I'm creating this mental registry, I admit to myself I'm not making a list of traits I'd find desirable in *any* guy.

I'm listing the traits I find desirable in *one* guy.

"Number eleven," Summer is finishing. "Doesn't wear glasses."

"What if he wears contacts?" Leonetta asks.

Alice shakes her head. "We have perfect vision in our family. Have for generations. Even my great-grandmomma at ninety-one-years-old doesn't wear glasses, so you can better believe I'm not gonna risk tarnishing my children's gene pool by being with a guy who wears glasses."

"But what if he's nice?" I ask, remembering poor Jasper Green, my seat partner on the bus in kindergarten, with his thick, horn-rimmed glasses and eyes as big as saucers. Despite having a smile capable of melting a polar ice cap, I'm certain he's never kissed a girl, which nearly breaks my heart. Why hadn't anyone ever seen past those glasses?

"Nice only goes so far," Alice says with a wink.

chapter 14
Steppin' Out

Friday, February 15

Geometry's the only class the four of us have in common which is how Alice, Summer, Leonetta and I end up walking together to the basketball pep rally during last period Friday afternoon. The gymnasium is already swarming with students by the time we arrive, and we're forced high into the bleachers, caught in the undertow of spectators rising with the tide.

It's the first time I've witnessed the massive assemblage of the entire student body all in one place—almost a thousand teenagers preparing to send our Golden Eagles into victory against the Westover Wolverines.

We are loud.

We are enthusiastic.

We are smelly.

There's a huge, blue tarp covering the gymnasium floor, but before I have a chance to ask Leonetta about it, our principal, Dr. Emmett, crosses the space in her signature pumps. As she approaches the microphone in the center of the room, a murmured hush spreads across the crowd.

"Ladies and gentleman, welcome to this afternoon's pep

rally. It's an honor leading such a fine group of players, and in a minute, Coach Dunn and I will be presenting them to you. But first, as a special treat, it's my pleasure to introduce M.A. Hopkins's very own Legacy Step Team."

The crowd erupts around me, pounding their feet and pumping their fists. Although I have no idea what's going on, I'm too transfixed by the small group of students filing onto the tarp to bother asking. Dressed in matching black suits and patent leather loafers, they fan out in a V formation, place their hands behind their backs, and lower their heads. Immediately, the crowd falls silent for a second time.

"I told you they'd be here," Alice whispers to Summer.

To my right, Leonetta's leaning forward, hands on her thighs, grinning broadly in curbed anticipation of whatever awaits us. Realizing the significance of the moment, I turn back to the group as the first note of music blares over the loudspeaker. There's the sound of a violin, followed by a backbeat and a man's voice. I can't understand what's being said until I catch the words 'North Carolina' just before the crowd explodes. As the first stanza begins, two members of the team begin to dance, stomping their feet in time to the music. Then two more join in, followed by the rest of the group until, pair by pair, all twelve of them are stomping and clapping between their legs and above their heads and between each other's legs. They're perfectly synchronized with one another, slapping their thighs and shoulders so quickly I can barely keep track of their moving hands and feet. The crowd cries out with each mention of the word 'Carolina' and almost everyone is singing along to this song I've never heard before.

On my left, Alice rises to her feet and begins to dance, repeatedly, albeit accidentally, knocking into my knee. I'm scooting over, trying to give her extra space to move, when I notice one of the members of the team is a white guy. Upon closer inspection, I recognize him as Brad Wilson, a friendly, outgoing kid from my American History class. This gangly brainiac, who sits in the front row of Ms. Krenshaw's class and contributes daily to discussions about the New Deal and Roosevelt and the Conservative Coalition, is out there on the gym floor dancing like he was born to step. His wide-open expression mirrors the joy on the faces of his fellow teammates, and I'm transfixed by them, moving as a collective whole, absolutely killing it.

Leonetta edges into me, cheering with an unbridled enthusiasm I can't help but admire, and I wonder if anyone has ever tried running over the members of the step team for hanging out with Brad the way they did to Leonetta for befriending me.

I suspect not.

The routine continues until the music fades and only the steady percussion of feet and hands remains. There are back flips and acrobatics from the team and cheers and screams from the crowd. The air around me is pulsating and, embarrassingly enough, I'm tapping my foot.

As if, Tess. As if.

At the end, the team freezes, back in their original positions, arms lowered, chins tucked. There's a beat of silence before the gymnasium erupts into applause. In one fluid motion, I'm out of my seat, cheering with my friends until my palms are sore from clapping and my throat is raw from yelling.

Zander would have loved this.

Dr. Emmett returns, tapping on her microphone to silence the crowd. She thanks the step team as they march back into the locker rooms and without further comment, invites Coach Dunn to begin the presentation of the varsity men's basketball team. I don't think the crowd can get any rowdier than they already are, but I'm wrong. As each name is announced, their intensity grows, until in a fevered crescendo, the two captains' names are read aloud. Seniors Darius Jordan and Kendrick Watts sprint onto the court, arms outstretched, playing to their adoring fans. They showboat to the center of the room, high-fiving the other members of the team until, after what seems like an eternity, everyone settles down so Dr. Emmett can speak again.

"It's been an honor watching you gentlemen play this season, and I know I speak for the entire faculty, staff, and student body here at Hopkins in wishing you the best of luck tonight in the county championship game against the Wolverines."

There's more applause. More stomping. People calling out the names of the players as they retreat back into the locker room.

Moments later I'm being corralled like a herd of my own cattle through the gymnasium doors into the hallway for dismissal. I'm trying to keep track of Leonetta, as we haven't solidified our plans to get ready for the party, but I quickly lose her in the crowd. Luckily, moments later, she appears beside me, notebook in hand.

"Just use Google maps to get to my house," she says, handing me a scrap sheet of paper with her address. "My dad's got Bible study tonight, so we'll have the house to ourselves if you come after six."

*

Later that evening, Dad pokes his head through my bedroom door, taking note of the duffle bag full of potential outfits and makeup I've packed to take to Leonetta's.

"Heading into the field for a training mission?" he teases. "Don't forget your helmet."

"Just going to Netta's," I tell him.

"That's a lot of stuff to take to a friend's house," he says, stepping into my room. He's dressed in his fatigues, having just gotten home from work, and I double take, still unaccustomed to seeing him as a soldier. "You spending the night?"

I shake my head.

"Then what's with all the gear? Where else are you going?"

I'd never asked to go anywhere back in Iowa. I came and went as I pleased. Granted, there were only a handful of places *to* go and I was usually with Zander, but just the same, I'd never been subjected to any sort of interrogation like the one I was facing now.

"To a party with the basketball team after the game."

"You going to the actual game?"

I hadn't even considered attending the game.

"No."

"But you're going to the party afterward?"

"Yeah."

"And you were invited to this party?"

I swallow. Hard. I try not to make a practice of lying to my dad. "Alice was invited and she invited me. I'm going with her and Netta and Summer."

"But you weren't technically invited by the person throwing the party. A person you have yet to mention, by the way."

I try to act casual, tossing a sweatshirt into my bag in the hopes of hiding the paltry stash of makeup Leonetta asked me to bring. "Not technically. But I think it's enough to know somebody who's invited," I tell him. "It's at Calvin Watkins' house. He's a basketball player." I leave out the part about him being a former Hopkins player and a current FSU player because what Dad doesn't know won't hurt him.

He's leaning against my doorframe now, and his sideways

smirk tells me he's enjoying this cross-examination. It's something he's used to doing with Ashley but has never had to do with me.

"Will there be drinking at this party?"

I sigh heavily, throwing myself across my bed. "I dunno, Dad. Maybe. Probably. But I'm not going there to drink. I'm going there to support Alice. There's gonna be a guy there tonight she's crazy about, and she's counting on me to be her wingman."

Dad likes Alice. They've taken to playing chess together after tutoring on Thursday nights.

"Our girl's finally getting the hang of the game, isn't she?" he laughs, clearly feeling good about how she's taken to chess under his tutelage.

"I wish I was catching on to geometry as easily," I say, glad for the change of conversation. I make a show of glancing at the clock while rising to my feet. "So anyway, I probably should get going. I won't be too late getting home so you don't have to wait up."

"I probably will anyway," he says, easing into the hallway to let me pass. "And, Tess?"

"Yeah?" I turn to him and there's a look on his face like I haven't seen since our days in the barn together. It resembles peace, but not quite.

"I'm glad things are okay for you here. I was worried."

I shrug. "Grow where you're planted."

chapter 15
Hair Apparent

Friday, February 15

Leonetta ushers me through the front door wearing a hat, which, at first glance, I'm convinced is made of an old pair of black tights. There's no way all her hair is squashed underneath the snug fitting cap, and I'm barely into the foyer before I blurt out, "Where's your hair?"

She reaches to touch her head as if she's just now realizing her state of affairs. "Under the bonnet."

"The what?"

She shakes her head and laughs her hearty, soulful laugh. "Girl, you might be the whitest white girl I know. Have you been livin' under a rock for sixteen years?"

"Yes?"

"I believe it," she says, waving me further into the house. "It's a satin bonnet. I wear it when I'm not wearing my hair."

She leads me through a modestly furnished family room into a dim hallway, lined with childhood photos of her with a man I presume to be her father. What I don't see is a single image of her mother.

"I thought you said your hair's underneath."

"My *real* hair is underneath. My other hair isn't."

My head is spinning. I'm completely lost in the conversation. Real hair and other hair and bonnets. I follow her into her bedroom which looks pretty much exactly like mine. Twin bed. Tall dresser. Desk. Chair. A smattering of clothes on the floor. The only noticeable differences are our comforters (hers: green and purple stripes; mine: orange and yellow flowers) and our wall art (hers: a canvas print of some Caribbean island; mine: a Sam Hunt poster). She plops down onto her bed and invites me to do the same.

"My hair is not like your hair." She says this matter-of-factly. She isn't complaining or bragging. She's simply giving me an education.

"Okay," I say.

"My hair is dry and breaks off easily, so I've never been able to grow it very long."

"But it's long all the time. You wear it in a pretty bob."

"The bob isn't my real hair. It's a wig."

I gawk at her, bamboozled. Aren't wigs for old people? And cancer patients? And Dolly Parton?

"I have a couple different ones, and I also have extensions, but they're expensive and take way too long to put in. And I ain't got time for that. So, I mainly stick to my wigs."

I'm still looking at her, completely lost for words.

"You don't know what extensions are, do you?" she asks.

I shake my head.

She gets up and opens her closet door. Its contents are predictable: two pairs of sneakers and a pair of sandals on the floor, a few blouses on hangers beside half a dozen dresses which are clearly reserved for church, three hats I assume are also for church, and a terrycloth robe. What I'm not expecting is the rod lined with sections of hair, each one neatly secured to a hanger with an elastic band. There are straight ones and curly ones and wavy ones. A few have colors woven through them, pinks and purples and blues. She selects one of the longest, lifting it carefully off its hanger, and hands it to me for inspection.

"This is my hair. Well, not mine as in 'I grew it out of my head,' but mine as in 'I bought it so I own it.'"

I finger the hair gently, with the same care as it was presented—clearly a cherished possession. It's soft and silky, feeling very much like my own hair.

"What's it made of?" I ask.

"It's human hair. Just like yours. Most of my extensions are from China or India. Men and women sell their hair, and in some places, they shave their heads for religious reasons and the hair is donated for extensions. Like anything else, there's good stuff and bad stuff and you get what you pay for. You don't want fallen hair, like the hair collected after a haircut or whatever, because then the cuticles line up in different directions. Some up, some down. I had extensions made from fallen hair one time, and it was a hot mess. Nothin' but tangles." She wears an indignant expression. "The one you're holding is Remy hair which means the hair is collected into a braid before it's cut, assuring the cuticles are all facing the same direction when the extension's created."

"That's fascinating," I tell her. "I had no idea. So how do you..."

She laughs at my hesitation. "Wear them?" she finishes.

"Yeah."

She eyes me, somewhat skeptically, but then the uncertainty falls away and she removes her bonnet. Beneath, I get my first glimpse of her actual hair, the hair I believed I'd been seeing all along. It's short, though not as short as Alice's, nor so chicly styled. I'm curious about how many people have seen her this way, without a wig or the extensions. I'm certain, outside of her beauticians and immediate family, the number is probably small, which is why it feels almost sacred to gaze upon her now. How lucky I am to share this confidence with her.

"So basically," she begins, lifting a section of hair on the back of her head, "they sew it in underneath my own hair and then blend it together so it's seamless. If it's done well you can't tell where my hair starts and the extension begins. Like I said before, though, it's expensive to have done because it takes hours. Like six or eight hours. So mostly I only get them put in for special occasions. Weddings. Birthdays. The first time I had a solo in my church's choir."

My own hair gets virtually none of my attention. I wash it. Condition it if I have time. And most days I throw it into a ponytail because it's what I've always done. The barn was never a place for a loose, flowing head of hair. Unlike me, however, Leonetta clearly spends an incredible amount of time and consideration on her hair.

"What about the wigs?" I ask, my eyes wide with fascination.

She returns the extension to the closet and drops to the floor, onto her hands and knees. She digs around under her bed and comes up with three boxes. After returning to my side, she opens the first box. There are two mesh organza bags with wigs inside.

"That's your hair!" I exclaim, immediately recognizing the one on top as the bob she's been wearing since I've known her.

"Not anymore," she says. "I was gonna change it up for the party tonight. My aunt Bev gave me one for Christmas that I haven't worn yet. Thought tonight would be as good as any for its debut."

I'm thrilled by the prospect of seeing her transformed and encourage her to put on the new wig right away.

"It's not that simple," she says, sliding it out of the bag. "This will have to be combed through, straight-ironed, and set. I'll work on it while you get yourself ready."

It seems my 'getting ready' and her 'getting ready' are two completely different tasks. While I try to decide between which skinny jeans and lip gloss to wear, she frets over a barely noticeable bend in a section of the wig and whether the shirt she wants to wear is missing a button.

"I can sew it for you," I offer, discovering the shirt is indeed one button short at the bust line. "If you have a needle and thread."

We work together, side-by-side, she on her hair and I on the button. She's humming an unfamiliar tune, deep and soulful and full of longing, and as I listen to her, I'm struck by the novelty of our togetherness. Of me, in a room with another girl, getting ready for a party as if it's the most typical thing in the world. It probably is for most everyone else. But not for me. Not for Tess Goodwin—best friend to Zander, chess player, and farm hand. For me, this is the most peculiar thing I could have ever imagined for myself.

And I'm surprisingly okay with it.

"Whatcha think of the step team's performance today?" she asks as she begins the laborious process of putting on the wig.

"I thought they were amazing," I tell her honestly. "I've never seen anything like it."

"You obviously haven't spent much time livin' in the South."

"It's really popular here?"

She's lining the part on her head with the part in the wig, and I'm impressed by how perfectly they match. I can't tell where she ends and the wig begins.

"It's more popular in historically black colleges than

anywhere else. Places like Fayetteville State, Shaw, and Elizabeth City. In the early 1900s, sororities and fraternities would sing and dance as a way of initiating new members into Greek life. Stepping grew outta that."

"Do they perform very often for the school?"

She nods. "During football season, the winter concert, spring talent show, and sometimes graduation. They compete, too, all over the country."

"No wonder I'm having trouble finding people to join my chess club when they have step team as an option." I look up from my sewing. "I mean, look at Brad Wilson. He's on the step team, and I could totally see him playing chess if I would've gotten to him first."

"Really. And would that be because he's white?" she asks.

I flinch involuntarily, wondering if she's keeping a tally of all my thoughtless comments. "Because he's a total geek," I explain.

"Oh, I see," she says, still adjusting her wig in the mirror. "You might be interested to learn two other members of the step team, James Washington and Cliff Lewis, are both in the running for senior class valedictorian. And they're both black. So why aren't you able to imagine them as part of your chess team? They aren't geeky enough for you I suppose? Or is it just because they're black?"

Immediately, I panic. Backpedaling through my thought process, wondering how my innocuous, off-handed comment could have possibly come out so poorly. I've never been so embarrassed or ashamed. I stammer, trying to come up with something to explicate myself when I notice Leonetta's expression reflecting back at me in the mirror. There's no mistaking the disappointment in the downturned corners of her lips.

"You gotta watch that kinda talk, Tess," she says.

"Microaggressions are hurtful, not just to me personally but to our whole society. And, I feel what you're saying. Brad's a total brainiac. From here on out, though, it's probably a good idea not to assume only white folks can be nerds."

I secure one final knot behind the button on her shirt and toss it onto her bed. I keep my chin tucked, too embarrassed to hold her gaze. "You're right, Netta. You gotta know I wasn't intentionally being disrespectful, and I certainly didn't mean to hurt your feelings. Anyone can play chess, not just geeky white kids. I have no idea why I even said that."

I'm mindlessly poking the pad of my finger with the sewing needle, drawing blood before she responds after a long moment. "You said it because you have your own biases you carry around with you. We all do. We can't help it. We're human. But that doesn't give us a free pass. You gotta check your privilege, keep an open mind, and consider other people's feelings before you open your mouth. If you do that, you'll be okay."

I don't know that I deserve it, but I'm humbled and thankful for her clemency. That we're having this conversation at all is a testament to Mrs. Fields who certainly knew what she was doing putting us together. I couldn't ask for a better friend than Leonetta and make a mental note to stop into the office Monday morning and thank our intermediary.

"He's a total anomaly out there with the rest of the step team, though, isn't he?" Leonetta continues.

"No more of an anomaly than you and I are," I say, finally glancing up.

She's still facing away from me, looking into the mirror, making final adjustments to her hair. Our eyes lock as she shifts her gaze to where I'm sitting behind her. "We're the best sort of anomaly," she says, turning around so I can take in the fullness of her transformation.

It's nothing short of miraculous.

"Netta, you look beautiful," I gush. "I love it."

She turns back to the mirror, studying herself. "I do look fine, don't I?"

"Like the reigning queen of gorgeous."

"Then what are we waiting for?" she asks, snatching her shirt off the bed. "You and I have a party to attend."

chapter 16
Hindsight

Friday, February 15

Leonetta and I circle the block three times before resigning ourselves to a parking spot almost a quarter mile away from Calvin Watkins' house. We pass Summer's car along the way, confirming she and Alice are already inside.

As we walk together down the sidewalk—the music of the party increasing in volume with every step—I'm reminded of all the parties I attended back in Iowa. All the backyard birthday parties with bobbing for apples and pin the tail on the donkey. All the middle school bowling parties when going to Sidetracks was all the rage. All the bonfires where couples paired off beneath the stars with stolen Budweisers from their parents' refrigerators. Zander accompanied me to all of them. He was my anti-wingman, the reason I never partnered off with anyone else. Even when he had a girlfriend, he never ventured far from my side, a buffer for Lacey's rude remarks, a shield from would-be suitors.

Am I expecting Leonetta to fill his role tonight as my new security blanket?

"Wonder if Alice has accosted Calvin yet?" she asks,

breaking me from my thoughts as we climb the steps to the front door.

"I guess we're about to find out," I say. For a moment, I hesitate at the door, wondering whether it's appropriate to knock or just walk in. But Leonetta doesn't falter, nudging past me to swing it wide open, revealing the chaos within. Two guys stumble past us out into the night, and we hurry inside.

Music is blaring and people are everywhere, packed into every corner of the house and spilling into the backyard. I catch a glimpse of three members of the basketball team, Lashanda from lit circle, and a couple kids from history class. But instead of venturing off to say hello, I stay close to Leonetta, my constant navigator, as she maneuvers us past the couples making out, past the girls dancing on the dining room table, and past the keg and beer pong into the kitchen where we stumble across Alice and Summer. They're leaning against the wall beside the refrigerator, talking with two guys, neither of whom I recognize from school. But then again, school is a very big place.

"It's about frickin' time!" Summer cries, noticing us across the room. There's a Solo cup in her hand and from the ridiculously high octave of her voice, I can safely assume it's not filled with pop. She's nuzzled against someone who looks nothing like her boyfriend, Private First-Class Travis. This guy is tall and lean but clearly not military given the generous beard he's sporting. Seeing her with someone else doesn't surprise me, though, especially after hearing about Travis's most recent indiscretions. What surprises me instead is finding Alice deep in conversation with a bespectacled coed.

I nudge Leonetta with my elbow, and she leans down.

"That's not Calvin, is it?"

She shakes her head. "It's Marcus Robinson. He graduated last year."

I point to my face. "He's wearing glasses," I say.

To this, Leonetta only shrugs.

"Come say hello," Summer calls across the kitchen, waving us over.

Introductions are made. Alice is with Marcus and Summer is with Kevin Ferrell, another recent Hopkins graduate. I didn't think it was possible for Alice to look better in her dress than she did in the Sizzle dressing room, but she looks even more like a runway model now that she's made-up and properly coiffed. Both Summer and Alice compliment Leonetta on her hair, and although she shrugs them off, I can tell she's secretly pleased by their approval.

"Kevin and Marcus are old friends of Calvin's," Alice explains, adjusting the hem of her dress which keeps riding up.

This vital bit of information brings the confusion of the situation into focus. The girls aren't actually interested in Marcus and Kevin, they're simply using them as a means of getting closer to Calvin, their only option since Leonetta and I arrived so late.

I immediately morph into wingman mode.

"Is Calvin around?" I say nonchalantly to Kevin. "I'd like to say hi since it's his party and all."

Alice widens her eyes, but I can't tell if she's impressed by my ingenuity or horrified by my boldness. Or if maybe it's something else altogether.

Kevin cranes his neck, straining to see out the kitchen window into the backyard. "He's outside," he says. "I guess I can introduce you if you want." His voice is incredulous as if what I've proposed, being introduced to the host, is the most ridiculous thing he's ever heard. Here in Fayetteville, it probably is.

I try to play it cool as if it's no big deal either way, but the damage is done. A look passes between Kevin and Marcus—

can you believe this girl?—but a second later we're all traipsing through the back door into the brisk, night air.

They lead us to where a few guys are leaning against the deck rail. Some are smoking, all of them have beers, and the tallest is well over six and a half feet tall. His features are defined: strong brow, prominent cheekbones, full lips. He's definitely Calvin.

"S'up, bro," Kevin says to him, bumping fists and shoulders before pointing to me. "This is Tess. She's from Iowa. She wanted to come say hi."

I'm concentrating on making my face look casual, like being at a college basketball player's party is something I do all the time. I can tell, though, by the smile on Calvin's face I'm failing miserably. He extends his hand.

"Well, hello there, Tess from Iowa," he says. His voice is deep and smooth and incredibly sexy. I don't wonder why Alice is obsessed with him.

"Hey," I squeak as his hand engulfs mine.

"Been here long?"

"About fifteen minutes."

He chuckles, giving me a wry smile. "I meant have you been here in Fayetteville long?"

I shake my head, feeling like an idiot. "Oh. Only since the first week in January."

"Must be some change, Iowa to Fayetteville."

I nod, unable to summon the power of speech much less a cohesive thought. Suddenly, I remember Alice. I remember I'm supposed to be breaking the ice for her, talking her up so he'll want to get to know her better. I'm supposed to be playing the matchmaker.

I turn to make the introductions. "These are my friends, Summer and Leonetta and Alice. They're not from Iowa."

He nods at them, laughing affably at the stupidity of what

I've said. Then he says to Alice, "I remember seeing you around Hopkins my senior year. You still there?"

Alice is visibly shivering in her form-fitting dress but manages to respond in the affirmative. Noticing how cold she is, Marcus slips off his own jacket, draping it around her shoulders.

"Thanks," she says.

There's an awkward moment of silence between us and everything seems to stop. It reminds me of when I was little, of the quiet numbness associated with slipping my head under the water during a bath. The constant thrum of the bass and the singing and laughter from inside fade away. Now all I can hear is the beating of my own heart.

I can't believe I've just blown it for Alice. Or then again, maybe I can.

"It's cold so I'm gonna go back inside," I announce, pulling my sleeves down over my hands. "It's nice to meet you, Calvin. Thanks for, uh, throwing such a great party." I pivot on my heel and head straight for the door, convinced Alice, and possibly Summer as well, will never speak to me again.

Back inside, I scan the room of strangers searching for a familiar face but don't recognize a single soul. What I recognize instead is how lost I feel. I don't belong at this party or even in Fayetteville for that matter, and all I want to do is run to the car and drive myself home, where it's safe and no one will be embarrassed by my social incompetence.

A quick glance out the window confirms Leonetta's still on the deck with the others. They're all laughing together, probably about what a simpleton I am, and my heart breaks just a little.

By the time I reach the front door, I've convinced myself Leonetta won't mind catching a ride home with Summer. I'm reaching for the doorknob when someone calls my name from behind. I waver, the metal knob cool against the palm of my hand.

"Tess!" the voice cries again, and before I can stop myself from turning around, Lashanda Jones appears by my side. "Where you goin', girl? You just got here. You ain't even had a drink or nothin'."

I avert my gaze. Being in different grades, Lashanda and I don't get many opportunities to socialize outside lit circle, and I hadn't considered the possibility that our comradery would extend beyond the classroom walls. Still, I've already made up my mind to leave.

"I gotta go," I say, motioning toward the street.

"Oh," she says with obvious rejection in her voice. "I just thought, I dunno, maybe we could hang out or somethin'. But if you gotta go..."

There's a sincerity in her eyes which suggests she might genuinely be interested in spending time together. On my way in I'd noticed her standing by herself in the corner behind the beer pong. Is it possible she's as miserable at this party as I am?

I check my phone because it seems like the most reasonable thing to do and reply, "Nah. I guess I've got a few minutes."

Half-an-hour later, in the blissful quiet of the master bathroom, we've discussed our next lit circle selection, *Wuthering Heights*, how obnoxious Monika Moore was for shaking all the cans of soda which exploded at the AV club's bake sale last week, and what effect the conflict in Syria might have on our fathers. It turns out her dad is in the 82nd Airborne Division with mine, and she's nervous about him deploying to the Middle East. We're still discussing how she handled her dad's most recent deployment to Iraq when Leonetta opens the door.

"There you are. I've been looking all over for you," she says to me, looking truly relieved. "Checked all the bedrooms and saw more of Jamal Brady and Brenda Dillard than I bargained for." She sticks her finger down her throat as if to gag herself. "Anyway, I'm glad I found you because I thought you might wanna see what's happening downstairs."

As happy as I am that Leonetta's still willing to be seen with me, I'm not sure I want to know what's going on.

"It's a good thing, don't worry," she says with a laugh, heaving me off the floor. "Come see."

As Lashanda and I follow her down the staircase, the party overwhelms us: the rhythm of the R&B, the pungent smell of warm beer, and the crowd of people who have overtaken the space. Leonetta grabs my hand and leads me to the living room where all the furniture's been pushed against the walls to make room for the horde of dancers in the center of the room.

"What am I looking for?" I yell into Leonetta's ear.

She throws out her arm, pointing to the far left. "Over there. Look who's dancing."

I stand on my tiptoes to look for Calvin, figuring I'll be able to pick him out above everyone else, but I've forgotten I'm at a basketball party. Everyone's gigantic. Just the same, I'm hopeful I didn't ruin everything after all, and that he and Alice are on the dance floor falling in love. A moment later, I catch a glimpse of Alice through a break in the crowd. Only she's not dancing with Calvin.

She's dancing with Marcus.

And she's radiant.

I turn to Leonetta who's grinning like a madwoman.

"Marcus?" I say.

She nods vigorously.

"What about the glasses thing?"

She shrugs.

"What about Calvin?"

"What about Calvin?" someone says.

Leonetta's eyes bulge out of her head, and I know immediately I've shoved my foot back in my mouth. Slowly, I turn around to face whoever's behind me.

And of course, it's Calvin.

"How's it goin' Tess from Iowa?" he says.

"Okay," I tell him.

"You're not dancing."

I shrug. "I'm not a big dancer."

"At my parties," he says, taking my hand as he drags me into the living room mob, "everyone dances."

Before I can formulate a more plausible objection, I'm dancing, or at least moving, with this guy who's not Zander— arms in the air, hips swaying in time to the beat of the music. He's singing along with the song. He knows every word. And he's looking sweetly down at my face as if the lyrics are meant for me.

"The way you move, sexy lady..."

A blush spreads across my cheeks, and I redirect my attention on the ornamental rug beneath my feet. Calvin's no more interested in me than he is in having a heart attack right here in his mother's living room, but still, here he is, trying to show me a good time. He must feel some sort of obligation to be nice to me, thanks in no small part to my earlier bout of Midwestern awkwardness.

The steady gaze of the other girls watching us together fuels my growing embarrassment. They're probably curious as to why he's dancing with me instead of them and might be a little pissed off as well. I want to tell them, "Please! Take him! I have no idea what I'm doing out here!" But I don't. I just keep dancing, and Calvin keeps singing.

The songs fade, one into the next, and we're on our third

dance before I remember Alice and how being with Calvin might be misconstrued as a betrayal. Spotting her across the room, I stop dead, my feet frozen. Calvin leans down, sensing I have something to say.

"I'm thirsty," I tell him. "I'm gonna go get a drink of water."

"I'll come with you," he says.

"No," I say, probably a little too forcefully. "I'm fine. Just, uh, stay here and keep dancing. There're lots of other people around."

He shrugs and ruffles the top of my head with his enormous hand. "You got it, kid. But don't be a stranger."

I give him a half-hearted smile and head for the kitchen where there's plenty of beer and liquor but not a single bottled water. The request for water had been merely a ruse, but out of the living room sauna, there's no ignoring how sweaty and thirsty I truly am. I help myself to a glass from the cabinet and fill it with water from the tap. It's lukewarm with a metallic aftertaste, but after chugging it down I begin to feel better. I'm getting a refill when Leonetta appears by my side.

"This might go down as one of the weirdest nights of my life," she says.

I finish the second glass of water. "You and me both."

"I'm ready to go whenever you are," she says.

"What about Alice and Summer?"

"Summer got a text a few minutes ago from Travis and ran outta here like a woman possessed. I have no idea what happened. Guess we'll find out Monday. Anyway, I asked Alice if she wanted you to give her a ride home, but she assured me Marcus is gonna get her home instead."

I raise an eyebrow. "So much for not tarnishing the gene pool."

"So much for it," she says.

chapter 17
Infamous

Monday, February 18

The hallways are crowded as they always are before first bell Monday morning, but instead of engaging in the usual pleasantries, people seem to be avoiding eye contact with me, some even stepping out of my way as I pass. I head upstairs, chin to my chest, eyes down, trying to convince myself I'm imagining the weight of their stares trailing behind me. But I'm forced to admit it's more than just my imagination when I notice Leonetta waiting for me outside homeroom, a concerned look on her face.

"Are you okay?" she asks, placing a sympathetic hand on my shoulder. If I was only disturbed before, now I'm really freaking out.

"Yeah. Why? What's going on?"

Her face drops even further as she glances nervously over her shoulder. "You didn't see any of them?"

"Any of who?" I ask, stepping away from the door.

She sighs heavily before leaning down to whisper into my ear. "Not who. What. The flyer? Did you see the flyer?"

Brad Wilson throws me an apprehensive look as he slides

past us into homeroom. I have absolutely no idea what's going on, but the combination of his furrowed brow and the tone of Leonetta's voice is definitely cause for alarm. "No, I didn't see any flyer. But it seems like people are staring at me. What's going on?"

She takes a deep breath, slides a piece of paper out of her binder, and hands it to me. Printed on the sheet is a photograph of Calvin Watkins dancing with me at the party Friday night. Under the photo, it reads: TESS GOODWIN IS A SLUT.

The paper flutters in my unsteady hand, and Leonetta takes it back before I accidentally drop it. My mouth goes completely dry, and I bite my lip, fighting to hold back tears. "Why would someone do this? Why would anyone say I'm a slut?"

Leonetta grabs my arm and drags me into the closest bathroom where we huddle together in a stall. "I have no idea who took the photo, but there's no question in my mind about who printed the flyers..."

"Flyers? Plural?" I gasp, considering the many ramifications of widespread distribution. The entire student body will see them. The teachers. The administration. What if they believe the posters? What if they think I'm a slut?

I crumple against the stall door as the bathroom spins around me, and it feels as though I'm right back in Iowa, reliving the whole Lacey Pemberton fiasco all over again.

"How many of those are out there?" I ask once I'm finally able to speak.

The profound pity on her face is enough to make me want to remain holed up in the bathroom for the rest of junior year. "They're hung all over the school, Tess. Hundreds of them. But Summer and Alice are already out there ripping them down."

Although it's almost laughable someone feels threatened enough by the idea of Calvin and me together to warrant this level of aggression, heat rises to my cheeks involuntarily as outrage threatens to overtake me. How dare someone spread such a vicious lie? Dread and fury build in equal parts until my gaze catches Leonetta's, and I'm reminded of my friends who are out in the hallways trying to protect and defend my honor.

A deep breath works to suppress the anger as their kindness fills me instead.

"You think it was Monika?" I ask.

"It wouldn't be anyone else."

"But why? You think she assumes something happened between me and Calvin?"

Leonetta shrugs. "It doesn't matter what she assumes happened, only what actually happened, which was nothing. And the truth is, even if something did happen between you two, it's none of her damn business. She's just jealous and angry you got further with Calvin than she ever has. He wouldn't give her the time of day." She takes the flyer and rips it into tiny shreds before flushing it down the toilet.

First bell rings, and I jump involuntarily.

"We're late," I say.

Leonetta rolls her eyes. "We're not goin' to class. We're ditching with Summer and Alice. I told you they're already out there. We thought it would be better to let the halls clear before you and I join them."

"There are really that many?"

She can't look me in the eye. "That girl musta printed an entire ream."

*

There's a distinct sound of paper being torn as we round the corner of the science hallway. Summer and Alice turn their heads as we approach but continue ripping posters off the wall. Even from a distance, their sympathetic expressions make me want to cry.

"Oh, Tess," Summer says, embracing me in a hug once we make it to the end of the hall. "Monika is the absolute worst, and everybody knows it."

"That's right," Alice adds. "And not a soul in this building believes her lies about you or anyone else for that matter."

What I can't believe is how many pages are already collected in the trash bag at their feet or how cruel Monika truly is. I join the procession, carefully removing papers and tape from the walls, leaving no evidence of Monika's hatred behind.

"Thank you guys so much for ditching class to take these down. I'll never be able to repay you."

"Oh, girl, you don't have to repay us," Summer says, throwing another handful into the bag. "This is what friends do. And besides, it's not like you're the only one who's had a run-in with the queen of the heifers."

This is news to me. "One of you?" I ask, wide-eyed.

"Yours truly," she says.

We turn the corner down what appears to be the last of the poster-plastered hallways. As we continue tearing the pages from the walls, Summer explains how, when she was a scrawny, awkward freshman, Monika repeatedly stole the clothes from her locker during P.E. class, leaving nothing for her to wear but her sweaty uniform for the rest of the day. To make matters worse, Monika frequently stuck notes on her back declaring 'Stinky Summer' had arrived.

"It took almost two months before the gym teachers realized what was happening, but because they didn't know who was doing it, their only solution was to let me store my street clothes in their office until the culprit could be found. Of course, they never caught Monika in the act." She pushes the hair out of her face as she takes down the last of the posters.

"To this day, she'll still sneak up behind me and whisper 'Stinky Summer' to get under my skin. Too bad I could give two craps about her at this point."

I can't imagine fierce, confident Summer being bullied by Monika. "That's awful," I say. "How does she get away with treating people this way? Why doesn't anyone stand up to her?"

"Her dad's the head of the city council. She thinks she can do whatever she wants whenever she wants and get away with it."

"And does she?"

The others exchange glances and shrug. "Pretty much," Alice says.

chapter 18
Check Canopy

Saturday, February 23

One look out my bedroom window makes me glad I didn't take everyone's advice back in Iowa about donating my winter coat to the Goodwill on my way out of the state. Raindrops are cascading down the panes of glass like tears of a grumpy toddler, and from the way our American flag is whipping in the wind, it appears the personality of the day is no less temperamental.

I pad into the gloomy kitchen in my robe and slippers and am surprised to find Dad already dressed in his BDUs at the dinette with a cup of coffee and the sports section of the *Fayetteville Observer*.

"I thought your jump wasn't 'til two," I say quietly as I slip into the chair beside him, mindful of my sleeping mom and sister in the rooms down the hall.

"It's not," he replies, setting down the paper. "But I have to be to green ramp in a little over an hour to get ready. Not to mention I couldn't sleep."

There's a tremor in his hand as he takes a sip of coffee. I've never known him to be an anxious person. He never worried much about the herd or the fields or the constant fluctuation of milk prices. At least I never thought he did. Now, I begin to wonder how far his apprehension might extend, because here, in the dim light of morning, fear is unmistakable in the lines of his face.

"Are you worried about the jump?" I ask. "You said it was perfectly safe."

He takes a sip of coffee to avoid looking at me. "It'll be fine," he says. "It's been a long time, though, you know? My bones and joints are a little older than they were the last time I threw myself out of a perfectly good airplane. I just hope I don't break a hip. Cuz you know what they say about breaking a hip..."

I stare at him, dumbfounded. I don't know what they say.

"I'm joking, Tess. It's a joke. I'm not gonna break a hip. I'll be fine, I promise."

The howling wind and rain pelt the kitchen window. "Is it safe? With the bad weather, I mean. Will they still make you do it if it's raining?"

He chuckles. "We'll see. The wind is more of a problem than the rain. They couldn't care less about us getting wet, but the wind is dangerous because you don't want to get tangled in your risers. Last thing I heard, the weather's supposed to break by lunchtime, but who knows. I have to get ready either way, but you don't have to come watch if the weather's bad."

"I want to, though." I'd been looking forward to seeing him jump since he'd announced the scheduled drop the week before. "I'll take an umbrella."

"It might be miserable."

"I don't mind."

Dad closes his eyes, pinching the bridge of his nose between his fingers. He takes a deep breath before surprising me by saying, "Why don't you go get a game board. Maybe

Grandpa's. We can play 'til I have to go."

We haven't played chess together since leaving Iowa, and I jump at the opportunity to test out a new opening move I've been exploring with one of the guys in my chess club. The match is barely underway before he mentions something about it.

"Knight's pawn to G4? What're you playing at, Tess?"

I shrug but can't keep the smirk off my face. My fledgling chess club, which meets after school on Wednesdays in Mr. Wilson's room, consists of five students. Five. A school of almost a thousand students and only five have consistently shown up during the month since its inception. Mr. Wilson was quick to point out that as a mid-year addition to the extracurriculars list, many people may not have heard about it or might already have full schedules on Wednesday afternoons. He's also mentioned that the members we do have are some of the brightest in the school.

One of those members is Cameron Lewis, a squat, shy eleventh grader who's reminded me no less than a dozen times of his 161 IQ. He's not great in social situations or any time he's forced to make small talk, maintain eye contact, or deal with unexpected changes. He has no difficulty, however, communicating through his chess pieces, and after our first afternoon together, he struck me as some sort of a savant.

For three solid weeks, Cameron and I have been working on a technique for winning a game where pawn to G4 is the opener. It's called the Grob's Attack and is considered in most chess circles to be an inferior if not masochistic move. Cameron's convinced, however, the surprise value alone makes it worth using.

Dad plays exactly what I expect him to—pawn to D5. He's nothing if not predictable.

I slide my bishop to G2.

"Have you lost your mind?" Dad says. "Maybe you should eat a banana. Your blood sugar must be low."

"I'm good," I say as I balance on the back two legs of the chair, my arms tucked against my chest.

Dad immediately slides his bishop across the board to G4, taking my pawn. Without hesitating, I move my pawn from C2 to C4, noting how Dad is playing the exact moves Cameron predicted an experienced opponent would make using our planned assault. Not surprisingly, Dad moves his pawn from C7 to C6, eyeing me with the contempt reserved for a prisoner of war. He has no idea what I'm doing, and it's freaking him out.

"Maybe bringing you to Fayetteville wasn't such a good idea after all," he says, shaking his head as I move my queen across the board to B3. "Someone here is a terrible influence on you."

"His name's Cameron."

Dad glances up from the board, eyebrows raised. "A boy?"

"He's in my chess club." I'm being purposely evasive, knowing Dad is both relieved and worried by my perpetual status as a single woman. Because he and mom were high school sweethearts, he values young love. But since I'm not like Ashley, who has boys calling every night, he's concerned I might be on the fast track to spinsterhood.

He makes a quick decision to move his queen from D8 to C8, recognizing his other options would end catastrophically for him. With the board in my possession, he presses me for information.

"Do you like him, this Cameron?"

"He's nice," I say, fingering my pawn at C4.

"But do you *like* him?"

"Well," I say, "he has a genius IQ, is obsessed with quantum physics, most specifically as it relates to *Star Trek: The Next*

Generation, and won't eat anything he knows for certain has touched the ground."

He ponders this for a moment while I move my piece to D5, capturing his pawn.

"So, no squash?"

"Or strawberries."

"Or dropped slices of pizza."

"Yeah. No. He's not a fan of the Five-Second Rule."

Dad studies the board. "He's a proponent of that opening move, though?"

I shrug.

"I'm guessing this guy isn't a love connection."

"He's a really amazing guy, so he might be a good match for someone more into Jean Luke and the USS Enterprise," I say. "For me personally, though, not so much."

After considering his moves in complete silence for several minutes, Dad moves a pawn from E7 to E6.

"That's your move?" I tease, confident enough in my imminent win to mock him.

He throws up his hands. "That's all I've got," he replies.

The game and the conversation go on like this for the next several minutes, with Dad trying desperately to figure out both my angle and my love life.

"I danced with this basketball player from FSU the other weekend at that after-party. His name's Calvin Watkins."

Thanks to Cameron's technique, I've got him in check, and he's struggling to work his way out. Still, I can't stop myself from dangling this distracting bit of information in front of him, like a horse with a carrot.

His head pops up. "You mentioned his name before. He threw the party. Is he the same Calvin Watkins who's the starting center from Fayetteville State?"

"That's what I said."

"You met him?" His voice sounds impressed.

"I danced with him," I say.

"Hmm." His eyes are back on the board. "I was just reading about him in the paper. They did a spotlight piece on him since his team's going to the CIAA tournament this coming week. Seems like a great kid."

"He was nice to me," I say, the memory of how he went out of his way to include me now tarnished by the events of Monday morning.

Dad must sense the change in my demeanor. "But?"

I hadn't planned on telling him about Calvin and the slut posters, but now I can't lie my way out. I've never been great at keeping stuff from him.

"But nothing. It wasn't a thing, Dad. He felt sorry for me because I was the awkward chick from Iowa who didn't know her way around a party." I hesitate then, not wanting to give him any reason to doubt his decision to bring us here, but my mouth keeps talking before my brain has a chance to shut it down. "And this girl from my chemistry class, Monika Moore, found out I danced with him and put up a bunch of signs around school making fun of me. Summer, Leonetta, Alice, and I skipped first period and took them all down. Thanks to them, the rumor was squashed pretty quickly." I shrug and turn my attention back to the board, not wanting to see the pain I'm certain will be in his eyes.

He makes his final move, his only move, and resigns the game. Then he locks eyes with me across the table as if his life's depending on it.

"You're not the awkward chick, Tess. And did it ever occur to you maybe Calvin danced with you for the same reasons your new friends had your back at school? Because you're the smart chick? The funny chick? The loyal chick?"

I hadn't considered any of those options, but I had to give

it to my dad for trying to make me feel better. He was nothing if not sincere.

"So, from now on, I don't ever want to hear you putting yourself down again. You got it?"

What I want to say is I love you. What I say instead is, "Got it."

*

The skies have broken by the time I pull into the parking lot at Sicily Drop Zone. It isn't anything like I imagined. Although, with no frame of reference, I don't know quite what I was expecting. The field is expansive, open and empty in every direction. Flanking the narrowest stretch are the same log pole pine forests which dominate all the natural space here in the sandhills of North Carolina. There are two sets of bleachers beyond the border of the parking lot where a handful of spectators has already staked their claims, and to the left, a food truck selling hot dogs and funnel cakes.

I slip my copy of *Wuthering Heights* under my arm and tuck my hair under a knitted ski cap, making sure to cover my ears, before crossing the gravel toward the bleachers. The seats are wet, speckled with raindrops from the morning's deluge, and I'm contemplating wiping a section off with my sleeve when a harried-looking mother surrounded by four preschoolers tosses me a towel.

"This ain't my first rodeo," she says, smiling. "I must be a glutton for punishment."

I dry off a small section of bleacher with the towel and return it, thanking her for her kindness.

She turns to me as she's wrangling one of her boys out of a mud puddle. "This your first jump? I only ask cuz you look kinda nervous, but you got nothin' to worry about. It's a cool thing to watch."

"Yeah. First time," I admit.

She motions toward the sky, where a shaft of sunlight is now peeking through the clouds. "Your boyfriend up there?"

I'm taken aback for a second, wondering why she would assume such a thing, then it dawns on me that this is Fayetteville, where lots of young women from town date Bragg soldiers.

Before her brood, was she one of those girls?

"Actually, I'm here to watch my dad," I say. "I've never seen him jump before."

"Well you're in for a treat," she says. "This is my husband's first time as a jumpmaster. He graduated from school last week and was adamant about us being here to see it." She rolls her eyes as she runs off to prevent her youngest child from chasing after someone's Pomeranian. "If you ask me, he's got it way easier than I do. It's gotta be less painful jumping outta the plane than wrangling these maniacs."

I smile after her and open my book with the intention of passing the time until the planes arrive, but I can't concentrate on Heathcliff and Catherine. Their fictional lives seem far too removed from the real-life anxiety I'm experiencing.

Although I typically don't mind being alone and wasn't terribly upset by Mom's decision to stay home with Ashley to help with her science fair project, I long for them now as I find myself the lone dilettante amongst a sea of confident, seasoned spectators. What I wouldn't give for a single affirmation from them about Dad's chances of survival.

"You're being silly, Tess. Your dad's perfectly safe," Mom would say, were she beside me on the bench now.

Without them, however, I'm left stewing over the safety bulletin on Gruber Road which read '14 DAYS NO DIVISION FATALITY' as I passed by on the way to the drop zone. I can't help but wonder what took the life of the soldier two weeks before and pray whoever it was became the victim of a shark bite or a chocolate chip cookie overdose and didn't lose their life as the result of a faulty parachute.

Oh, God, I pray. Let it have been anything but a faulty parachute.

My experiences with parachutes, although limited, have always been pleasant. For most of my life, I only associated them with the enormous rainbow-striped swatches of loud, crinkly fabric my elementary school teacher, Mr. Whalen, brought out on days he lacked the strength to referee another round of dodgeball. We would all hold onto a spot around the perimeter and squeal with delight as he tossed balls atop the parachute for us to shake off like popcorn, pumping our arms up and down until all the 'kernels' exploded onto the ground.

Scanning the western sky for signs of approaching C-130s, I recall my first field day as a kindergartener. It was special because our parents were invited to join us at the final station of the day: the parachute. Without the delay or embarrassment many of the other parents exhibited, Dad dashed to my side, as enthusiastic as the surrounding six-year-olds. I remember the way he grinned, towering above me like a giddy giraffe while we listened to Mr. Whalen's instructions. As the whistle blew, we lifted our arms, raising the parachute into the air as high as we could until the whistle blew again and we all slipped under the fabric, trapped with the air beneath, creating a rainbow-colored dome above our heads. Crouching side-by-side underneath this dome, my dad whispered to me, "Of all the princesses in the Kingdom of Colors, you, fair maiden, are the loveliest," and I had said, "I love you, too, Daddy."

The memory of the parachute harnessing the air to bring simple joy to a group of kindergarteners is strangely reassuring. Because if it had the power to do that, certainly it would keep my dad aloft, carrying him safely to the ground.

"I hear them," the oldest of the woman's four boys calls out, pointing to the left with one hand while shielding his eyes with the other. "And I see them too. Here they come."

I jump to my feet at the same time the boy begins chanting "Check canopy, check canopy, check canopy, check canopy," igniting my already frazzled nerves.

"Timmy, stop," his mother snaps, throwing me an apologetic gaze. "He does this every time. He remembers the announcements from Airborne School. He must've heard the jumpmasters say it a million times that day. I'm so sorry."

But Timmy continues his incantation.

"Check canopy, check canopy, check canopy, check canopy, check canopy."

I try to ignore him, concentrating instead on the planes, which are now close enough for me to make out their propellers. I don't know which plane Dad's in and wonder briefly if I'll be able to recognize him. As the initial stream of soldiers begins spilling out of the first plane, however, it becomes obvious there'll be no way to tell one jumper from the next. Every one of them looks exactly the same.

"Check canopy, check canopy, check canopy, check canopy, check canopy."

The only way to know for certain he's safe is to watch them all. To try and follow every jumper from the gaping hole in the side of the plane to the ground. But there are dozens of them. Hundreds even. And they're falling so quickly I have trouble figuring out where to look.

"Check canopy, check canopy, check canopy, check canopy, check canopy."

The second plane is emptying out, each soldier an unwieldy figure hurtling toward earth, laden down with a parachute pack on the back and enormous rucksack on the front. Parachutes stream out behind each of them before catching the air to inflate, giant olive umbrellas as numerous as the stars in the sky.

"Check canopy, check canopy, check canopy, check canopy, check canopy."

By the time the final plane approaches the drop zone, every parachute has opened. Every soldier has reached the ground safely. Statistically, though, this means the chances of something bad happening now are increasing with each passing moment. The first jumper appears out of the plane and my breath catches.

Please be okay, I say to myself.

As each soldier materializes in the sky, I say it again.

Please be okay.

Please be okay.

Please be okay.

Please be okay.

"Check canopy, check canopy, check canopy, check canopy, check canopy."

We are together, son and daughter, both of us praying in our own way for our fathers' safe passage.

As the last jumper lands, the boy falls silent, and I let out a very deep breath.

chapter 19
Kings and Queens

Wednesday, March 6

Cameron and I are three sessions into a new game using the Barnes Opening, pawn to F3, which most chess aficionados consider to be the absolute worst starting maneuver. Not only does it prevent the development of the pawn itself or open any lines for other pieces, the move hinders the development of the White king's knight by denying it its most natural square. Worse yet, it weakens White's kingside pawn structure, opens the E1–H4 diagonal against White's uncastled king, and opens the G1–A7 diagonal against White's potential kingside castling position.

In short, the move is suicide, and there's a reason no one ever uses it.

No one, that is, except Cameron.

He's especially quiet sitting across the picnic table from me today, and as I'm waiting for him to take his turn, his silence reminds me a bit of Zander who was known to shush me if I tried to carry on a conversation while he was thinking through a complex sequence of moves. He would often complain he couldn't concentrate with my 'blathering,' so chatting about useless drivel became one of my techniques to use against him in the event I became desperate enough to win.

As much as I like Cameron and have become accustomed to and even fond of his quirks, it's Zander I'd rather be playing with on this seasonably warm afternoon. With the blossoms budding on the redbud trees, it wasn't hard to convince the entire chess team that our psyches and vitamin D levels could stand a move outside to the picnic tables for some sunshine.

A mother cardinal works diligently on her nest, gathering pine needles off the ground and delivering them to a narrow grouping of branches in the tree above. It makes me curious about my tree, my bur oak, and whether it, too, has begun to bud. I make a mental note to ask Zander about it the next time we talk, but inexplicably, the thought of our upcoming conversation hurts my heart. Our Sunday afternoon chats, undoubtedly the highlight of every week, are also the times I dread the most. They are the painful reminder of how far away we are, in both physical and emotional proximity.

*

The first time the two of us faced separation was during the summer before seventh grade. Along with a few other members of his 4-H program, Zander entered one of his father's spring calves into the state fair two hours away in Des Moines. Unlike pies or crafts, those entering livestock are responsible for their animal's care for the duration of the fair. With no one else to feed the calf or muck the stall, Zander was forced to stay.

And I couldn't stand the thought of him leaving me behind.

"Why don't you come with me?" he offered from the lowest branch of our tree as I bemoaned the utter tedium that would become my life once he headed to the fairgrounds the following week.

I turned my face from the waning sun, looking down at him from my perch above to check if he was serious. He was grinning, his eyes hopeful. Was he nervous about being at the fair alone?

"I can't leave Dad," I told him. "He needs my help."

He scoffed. "Ashley can help for once. That girl hardly does anything."

He was right. Ashley was rather lazy, not to mention so easily distracted from her chores it was less trouble to pick up her slack than nag her into submission. Her ineptitude was the whole reason Dad needed me around.

"I guess I could ask Mom and Dad," I relented. "But don't get your hopes up. There's a good chance they'll say no."

But they hadn't said no. They actually supported the idea, encouraging me, as long as I was going anyway, to enter one of our chickens as well.

That week at the fair, Zander and I tucked ourselves into sleeping bags each night on the straw-covered earth of the cattle barn, exhausted from the events of the day. As we lay together, side-by-side, amongst the pungent odors of the livestock and oppressive heat that was part and parcel to summer in Iowa, we'd promised one another we would return to the fair every year, no matter what. Even once we were old and gray with bad hips and wrinkles.

"We'll pick something different to enter each summer," Zander said, "and come together so neither one of us has to be alone."

*

This August he'll be entering the dairy goat his mom bought at the farmer's market last summer for him to raise. And I know, for the first time ever, he'll be going without me. I wonder if he'll bring someone else along or if he'll go it alone.

I decide immediately he'll fly solo. He is, after all, practically a grown man, and he certainly doesn't need anyone's help taking care of a stupid goat for a few days.

I'm imagining him sleeping alone on the floor of the livestock barn when Cameron, in an unprecedented show of boldness, begins to speak while contemplating his next move.

"Are you going with anyone to prom?"

He asks without emotion making it difficult to discern his motivations. And while it may be true he says everything without emotion, this particular question comes with a heap of potential consequences depending on how I chose to respond.

"I'm planning to go with Leonetta and Alice and Summer," I tell him truthfully, gaze locked on the board, not wanting to give anything more away. Part of me is worried he's about to ask me himself, and I'll be forced to let him down. It's not that I'd have any problem going with Cameron as a date, I just have no interest in going to prom with any guy.

At least no guys from Fayetteville.

"Oh," he says simply, sliding his pawn out of my knight's range.

I try to concentrate on my next move. On my next series of moves. Should I protect my bishop? Sacrifice my third pawn? But I've lost focus, unable to track more than a few moves in my head, and there's no denying his interest in my prom plans has me flustered. He has a tender heart, and the last thing I want is to upset him, but now I can't help wondering why he asked.

"What about you?" I blurt out before I can stop myself.

"Me what?" he says without looking up from the board.

"Prom? Have you asked anyone to prom?"

His face is inscrutable. "People like me don't go to prom."

There's something about the way he says it, so matter-of-factly, as if it's written somewhere in the Old Testament on a tablet sent by God.

"Why not?" I challenge him, straightening from my hunched chess position to assert a more commanding posture.

He shrugs.

"That's not an answer, Cameron," I say.

"It's your turn," he replies, ignoring my line of questioning altogether.

I cross my arms and cock my head. "I'll take my turn as soon as you tell me why 'people like you,' whatever that's supposed to mean, don't go to prom."

He lifts his eyes slowly from the chess board and in one giant, sweeping motion, throws out his arms, sending the board and all our pieces tumbling onto the ground.

Several beats pass as we both sit in stunned silence, waiting for the other to react. I'm getting used to his outbursts and overreactions, and although I no longer take them personally, it still takes a second to compose myself. The last thing I want is to enrage him further, and since it's clear he has no intention of cleaning his mess, I dutifully slide off the end of the picnic table bench and begin collecting our scattered pieces. Cameron, for his part, doesn't move.

"The way I see it, you don't need to be on the shortlist for prom king or queen to deserve to go to the dance. Everyone deserves to go to prom. If you don't want to, that's on you. But if you want to and choose not to because you're nervous or scared or feel like you don't have anybody to go with, that's another story." I hesitate for an instant, wondering if what I'm about to say will be helpful or make everything worse. "If you want to go, you should come with me and my friends. We'd love to have you along."

I finish gathering the last of the pieces—a black king and white queen—I have to crawl under the table to reach. After tossing them all into a box, I stand to face Cameron who remains stoically seated in exactly the same position.

"Well?" I say to him.

Before he can answer, Mr. Wilson calls to us from his room's second-floor window directly above our heads.

"I just got a call from the NC Chess Association and you better do whatever it is you all do to prepare for battle because the delegation from M.A. Hopkins was accepted into the NC State Regional Tournament next month."

Cameron's face brightens almost imperceptibly.

"For real?" I call to Mr. Wilson.

"No joke," he says.

I turn to Cameron. "I guess we're gonna compete together."

He shrugs. "Then we might as well go to prom, too."

chapter 20
Corn Rows

Monday, March 18

Ashley misses the school bus again this morning.

After dropping her off, I'm late to first period. Sadly, this isn't the first time, and after I hand in my late pass and slink to my seat, Ms. Krenshaw's still growling at me for interrupting her class.

"Getting to be something of a habit for you, Miss Goodwin," she says, waving my tardy slip above her head. "One more of these and you'll have earned yourself an ASD."

"Yes, Ma'am," I say, defeated. Alice slides a stick of gum across my desk. Juicy Fruit. Just what the doctor ordered.

The rest of history passes without incident but in chemistry, Leonetta is noticeably missing.

"Did you see her this morning?" I ask Alice as we loiter by the door, waiting for her to arrive.

"No. But I don't usually. Did you?"

I scrunch up my nose, recalling my frazzled morning. "I was late, remember?" Leonetta spent the weekend in the Caribbean at her mother's wedding. "Think she made it back from Jamaica?" I ask. "Maybe her flight got delayed."

Alice shrugs. "I didn't hear from her one way or the other. Maybe she decided to stay a little longer."

I take out my phone to text her, but the late bell rings before I'm able to press send. Mr. Hogan strolls through the door, and I slip my cell into my pocket as we scramble to our seats. He throws me a dirty look for having my phone out but doesn't dare say anything to Monika and her herd of heifers in the back of the room, still carrying on like it's Saturday night instead of Monday morning. I'm pretty sure he's as scared of her as the rest of us.

She eventually tears herself away from her posse and comes skulking to her seat beside me, asking casually, "Where's your friend?"

Although I still have no definitive proof about who hung the slut posters, we both know she's responsible, which is why I haven't said a word about it, refusing to give her the satisfaction of knowing she upset me. Now, her unprovoked recognition of my existence catches me off guard, and for an instant, I don't realize she's talking to me. The malicious undertone of her inquiry tips me off, though, so I keep my eyes turned down, hoping I'll be able to ignore her.

"I'm talking to you, Old MacDonald," she says, her voice clipped. "I asked if you know where your friend's at?"

I don't look up. "Alice?"

"No. Not Alice. The other one."

She doesn't have to say it. Leonetta.

"Haven't seen her," I mumble as class begins.

Monika chuffs. It's a horrible sound. A laugh capable of making my skin crawl. She leans close to me, closer than the two of us have ever been before, and whispers in my ear.

"She's probably out there in the middle of the road throwing herself in fronta oncoming traffic. Or at least that's where I'd be if I was her."

She leans back in her chair, fumbling in her purse for a pen, effectively ending our conversation.

I replay Monika's words in my head a dozen times before it hits me.

She's seen Leonetta. Here at school. Today.

But Leonetta's not in class, and Monika's convinced she should be out trying to kill herself.

Oh, God, I think. *Something's terribly wrong.*

My hand shoots into the air, and I'm on my feet before Mr. Hogan gives me permission to leave class.

"This is highly unusual," he says to me, scribbling off a hall pass for the bathroom. "We just came from class change."

"Bad beans for breakfast," I say, clutching my midsection. "I might be a while."

I'm out the door before he has a chance to respond but take a moment in the hallway to assess the situation as I would a game of chess. Although I'm already several moves behind, some matches aren't won through extensive analysis but on intuition alone. I'm certain my fearless guide Leonetta is around somewhere, but because she seems to know the sizable square footage of the building better than its architect, finding her might prove difficult.

I decide to begin at the beginning and set off in the direction of the choir room, the place she starts her days. On my way, I shoot her a quick text, asking if everything's okay, and am discouraged but not surprised when I don't get an immediate reply. She's not lurking anywhere near the choir room, so I continue along her presumed route to her first-period Spanish class. I keep checking over my shoulder for Monika or one of her minions, unnerved by the eerily abandoned hallways and tightly shut classroom doors. Only a sea of lockers spreads out before me as I make my way to the foreign language wing, and I pop my head into each of the women's rooms, checking for feet beneath stall doors as I go.

The bathrooms are deserted as well.

There's no sign of her near the Spanish room, so I continue on, repeatedly checking my phone for a reply as I make the return trip toward chemistry. I'm almost back, chastising myself for my inferior sleuthing skills, when a rustling sound from behind the closest stairwell draws my attention. I turn the corner to investigate.

Leonetta is almost unrecognizable with her hair braided in tight rows against her head, tiny shells beaded onto the ends. She looks like someone else entirely. Someone from a foreign country. But there's no one else it could be sitting propped against the wall, legs splayed before her, reading *Wuthering Heights*.

"Netta? What are you doing here?"

Her head jerks up from the book and her tear-stained cheeks tell me everything I need to know. She pats the floor beside her, an invitation to sit.

"What happened?" I ask, sliding down the wall beside her.

She closes her novel and tosses it into her bag. Mascara is smudged beneath her lower lashes and her signature red lipstick is smeared across her cheek as if she's wiped her face in anger, probably with the back of her hand.

"Triflin' heifers," she says.

"Monika?" I ask, already knowing the answer.

She nods. "Said I look like a tired, fake Cicely Tyson."

I stare blankly at her, having absolutely no idea who Cicely Tyson is.

"She's a famous actress and the first black woman to wear cornrows on TV," she says, accustomed to my ignorance.

I reach out to touch one of the smooth shells woven onto the side of her head. "Is that what these are called? Cornrows?"

She gives the smallest indication of a smile. "Yes, girl.

Cornrows. My whole family wore them for Mom's wedding."

Oh, God. The wedding. Monika's drama almost made me forget all about it. "How was it?" I ask now, hoping I don't seem rude for not remembering to inquire on my own.

She stares off across the stairwell as if I've asked her to explain Einstein's theory of relativity. "It was fine," she says finally. "It was nice visiting my sister and brother. They were in elementary school last time I saw them."

The nostalgic quality to her voice conveys an unspoken longing, and it's clear she has no intention of returning with me to class.

"You never mentioned having other family," I say, settling in beside her.

"They're half-siblings, from my mother's second marriage. I have another half-sister too, on my dad's side. But I'm the only kid the two of them had together. They were only a couple for a little over a year."

I let this sink in, the idea of having other family members spread all over, not living under the same roof. The idea of being separated from my mother by half an ocean, while she raises siblings I barely know. The loneliness associated with being apart is unfathomable to me because as much as Ashley drives me crazy, I can't imagine not seeing her every day.

"They're all younger than you?"

"Katrina is older. She lives in Memphis with her husband and little girl, Trish. My dad had her before meeting my mom. Aayla and Hasan are younger. Twelve and fourteen. They're from mom's marriage to Omar."

I'm staring straight ahead at the pale-colored wall tiles of the stairwell. My head's swimming with questions I'm not sure are appropriate to ask. None of the families I knew back in Iowa were as complicated as Leonetta's. Or as interesting.

"Can I ask you a question about your mom?" I say, hedging

my bet she'll be as open to me as she's always been.

"Yeah. Of course."

I hesitate. She's already been upset once this morning. The last thing I want to do is upset her again. But I decide to go for it, wording my question in what I hope is the most innocuous way possible in an attempt to keep her mind off Monika. "I'm glad you're here, of course, because my life would suck without you, but why did you decide to live in the U.S. with your dad instead of in Jamaica with your mom?"

She sighs heavily, her chest rising and falling with what seems like the weight of a hundred lifetimes. "My parents' marriage was short. My mom was a young Jamaican woman, only nineteen-years-old when they met. And, like I told you before, my dad was already established as a well-regarded, American college professor. He was also almost twice her age. He was on a year-long sabbatical, researching the sociological effects of poverty on the people in my mother's town, and they fell in love. She got pregnant with me, they married, hastily, but by the time I was born they'd come to appreciate their differences were too great for them to ever maintain a relationship, much less raise a child together."

She pauses, coming to the part of the story where she tells me how she came to grow up in the United States instead of Jamaica. It's obvious the separation is a wound that's never fully healed, and I take her hand.

"When my parents decided to split, my mother couldn't stand the thought of leaving Jamaica on her own, if the U.S. would have even allowed it. My father, of course, had to return to the States. To his career. To his obligations. He didn't have the option to stay. They decided, together, I would be better off living in the U.S. with my dad than in Jamaica with my mom. I'll never know if they made the right decision, but when I think of how different my life would have been if I'd stayed on with her..." Her voice trails off. After being harassed by Monika and her crew, maybe she's thinking Jamaica might have been the better option.

"It must have been hard, growing up without her," I say, squeezing her palm against mine.

She shrugs. "Lots of kids grow up without moms. And I have my dad. So that's something."

"It is." I rack my brain for something to help get her out of the stairwell and back to class. Something to take her mind off of her own troubles. "You know, there was this girl Lacey back in Iowa who was like the Monika of East Chester High. Total queen of the heifers."

Leonetta laughs, so I go on.

"In September of eighth grade, one of the kids in our grade, Connor Jenkins, had a birthday party—a big bonfire and cookout in his backyard. Everyone was invited because his mother considers herself a pillar of the community and would never dream of letting him leave anyone out. My friend Zander and I tried to bail because we knew the jerky kids were gonna be there, but our moms forced us to go."

"So there's at least a few benefits to not havin' a mom around, huh?" she says with a quiet lilt. She's trying to make me smile, but the melancholy of her tone is unmistakable. I give her shoulder a gentle nudge and confirm, with a roll of my eyes, my mom can definitely be a pain. She responds with a sideways grin, so I continue with my story.

"Anyway, the party was going along fine until after dusk when one of the kids took out a bottle of his dad's homebrewed moonshine."

"Gross," Leonetta says.

I nod in agreement. "Somehow we all ended up playing Truth or Dare. People challenging one another to taste the disgusting drink, throw stuff into the fire, tell who they wanted to kiss." I pause now because I'm no longer in the stairwell with Leonetta. I'm beside Zander, back around the fire, the searing heat on my face and my hands, smoke and teenage angst wafting through the air. For a moment, I forget what compelled me to dredge up this painful memory.

Then I remember Leonetta and all the ways she's been a friend to me since we met. The way I need her to know, in this moment, she's not alone.

"Zander, being Zander, opted for a dare. They told him he had to go five hundred paces into the fields behind the fire and count to a thousand before he could come back. And because night had already fallen and the field was a scary place, even for middle-schoolers, he was allowed to take one other person with him."

I don't know what went through Zander's head at that moment—if he was scared of going into the field alone or if he considered taking someone other than me. And I'll never know if things might be different for us now if he'd chosen another kid to go with him into the darkness that night.

"He picked me, of course," I say to Leonetta, who's now hanging on my every word, "because I was his best friend." I explain to her how, with considerable provocation, we made our way into the field, one step at a time, mindful of the rats and snakes that lived there and the treacherous footing of the uneven soil. "I don't remember what we were talking about. Probably nothing important. We were deep in conversation, the way we always were, before we realized we were so far into the field we could barely make out the glow of the bonfire behind us."

I place my hand on my abdomen, remembering the searing pain I'd experienced standing there with Zander in the middle of the Jenkins' field. We were surrounded by the decomposing husks of drying cornstalks, only days away from harvest, and the pungent stench had been overwhelming, causing me to gag. Seeing my distress without knowing quite what to make of the situation, Zander eyed me warily in the moonlight and asked if I was okay. I assured him I was fine, that it was only a stomach cramp, but I wanted to return to the party. I fell three times on the way back, and by the time we reached the clearing beside the fire, the pain in my abdomen had grown so acute, it was all I could do to stay upright.

"If I had known I was getting my period for the first time, maybe everything would have been different. But I had no idea what was happening out there in the cornfield with Zander. The pain. The nausea. By the time we got back to the party, I'd made quite a mess of myself. I'd fallen on the way back and knew my hands and knees were covered in mud, but I didn't realize blood was seeping through the crotch of my jeans. Of course, even in the dim glow of the fire, Lacey Pemberton noticed. That girl noticed everything. I've often wondered if there was something I could have said or something I could have done, but there was nothing. No way of knowing what was about to happen. So, I stumbled into Connor's house and called my mom to come get me. I was completely unaware of the spark I'd ignited."

Leonetta's eyes are wide as if she knows what's coming. As if she can already imagine how cruel one person can be to another. Because she knows firsthand how jealousy can make people say and do horrible things. That people like Lacey and Monika are cut from the same cloth.

"By the time I got to school Monday morning, the rumor had already spread, as if I'd taken a match to that cornfield and set it ablaze myself. There was talk Zander had forced himself on me. That he took advantage. Caused me to bleed."

"But he didn't," Leonetta gasped.

"No, of course, he didn't. He would never. It was a vicious

lie spread by a vengeful, jealous girl who hated being left behind when Zander took me into the field instead of her."

"Did Zander get in trouble?"

"At first, but in the end, everyone was satisfied it was a misunderstanding. They believed Zander hadn't harmed me in any way. I'd simply gotten my period at the wrong time in the wrong place." The words sound both ridiculous and slightly ironic coming out of my mouth. Because for most girls, it would have been mortifying enough to have the whole school privy to the details of your first menstrual cycle. But to have faced only that would have been a walk in the park for me. "So anyway," I say at last, "if I could go back to school and face Lacey, you can go back to class and face Monika. Because you and I both know you're way tougher than I am. And in my opinion, your hair is on fleek."

Leonetta raises an eyebrow skeptically. "On fleek?"

"Lit?" I offer. "Snatched?"

She tosses her book into her bag and hoists herself off the floor, extending her hand to help me up. "Just stick to being little ole Midwestern you and don't worry 'bout learning the lingo, m'kay?"

"Ten-four," I say, giving her a salute.

"Better," she acknowledges as we begin making our way back to chemistry. "And thanks. Thanks for coming to find me and thanks for sharing your stuff. You're a good friend."

I give her arm a squeeze. "Back atcha."

chapter 21
Purple Coneflower Boutonniere

Sunday, March 24

Even after almost three months away from the farm and all its endless responsibilities, I still wake up every morning at 4:45 like clockwork, even on the weekends. Which is why I'm not surprised to be startled out of an exceptionally realistic dream only to find it's not even five o'clock.

My head is fuzzy in the disorienting sort of way that comes along with not quite remembering where you are or how you got there. Only moments ago, tucked safely inside the familiarity of my dream, I'd been in the barn with the herd. With Sunshine. I'd been milking her by hand, something we rarely did since it was never particularly effective. The cows' teats become less receptive to manual expression after being mechanically milked for so long, so hand expression is often a lesson in futility. Just the same, it's what I'd been doing in my dream: milking Sunshine. My forehead rested against her flank as I milked her, and I was conscious of how solid and stable she felt beside me. Her body was warm, and I matched the pace of my squeezing to the rhythmic grinding of her teeth as she chewed her cud. The milk shooting into the pail below was creamy and fresh-smelling, and I felt somehow that Sunshine was happy to share it with me.

I don't remember much else of the dream, but what tendrils remain are enough to drive me to tears. Since arriving in Fayetteville, I haven't cried for the herd, for my farm, or for Zander. Not once. But for some reason, the images of Sunshine leave me welling up, spilling over for their loss. I cry for Minnie and the infected hoof I nursed her through, singing to her as I cut away the painful, damaged section of bone. Bella, who would moo if she saw me approaching in the field, the bovine equivalent of a salutation. And sweet Annie, who was born blind in one eye, causing her to bump into things due to a lack of depth perception. There's a sudden urgency fueled by longing. Where they are now and what's happened to them in my absence?

Is anyone being mindful of Minnie's hooves?

Does Bella moo at her new owner in the fields?

Are the door jambs padded to protect Annie's head at her new home?

Dad knows, of course, but I haven't plucked the courage to ask him about our girls. There's a part of me who still doesn't want to know, who wants to keep imagining the farm as it was while I lived there, not as it exists today. There's someone else who knows too, of course, but I haven't asked him either. And he hasn't offered.

Suddenly, I can't wait until the afternoon to talk to Zander. I want to talk to him now, but it's not even four o'clock in Iowa. The only reason he'd be up this early on a Sunday morning would be if the barn was burning down.

I make several unsuccessful attempts at falling back to sleep, but after tossing and turning for the better part of an hour, I finally give up. At my desk, I turn on my lamp to try and study for an upcoming math test on the Pythagorean

Theorem, but despite my best intentions, my mind keeps slinking back to Iowa.

And the herd.

And Zander.

Finally, at 8:27, I pick up my phone. Surely, he'll be awake by 7:30, and if he isn't, I reason he ought to be. Surprisingly, his mom answers on the third ring.

"Good morning," she says in a voice as familiar to me as my own mother's. "Tess?"

"Hi, Miss Nancy," I say. "It's me. I hope I'm not calling too early, but I was hoping to speak with Zander if he's up."

She chuckles. "Oh, yeah. He's up. Been out in the barn with his daddy since sunrise. One of the cows is about to give birth, and we think it might be twins. Musta left his cell here on the table by mistake in all the excitement."

Hearing this, it's like she's taken a vise to my heart. How I would love to be there.

"Oh," I say, conscious of my invasion. "Well, no reason to call him in. I'll try again later."

"Nonsense," she tells me, and before I have a chance to protest again, I hear the banging of their kitchen's screen door as she heads into the yard. I can imagine her crossing the thin stretch of grass between the house and the largest barn where the cows are kept. Then she calls out, "Zander! Tess is on the phone!"

I can't make out what he says in return but a moment later, he's breathing heavily into the receiver.

"Hey!" he says brightly. "Did I order a wake-up call?"

I'm embarrassed for not having the patience to wait for our scheduled time later in the day. He's going to assume I have something pressing to discuss. Something more urgent than the well-being of my herd.

"No," I stammer. "I just woke up early. You know. Old

habits. And I had a lot on my mind and no one else to talk to."

He steps into the house, slamming the screen door behind him as his mom had done only seconds before. After crossing the kitchen into the foyer, I hear his footfalls on the steps.

"We think one of the cows is having twins," he says, ignoring my awkwardness and starting right in on the conversation. "Dad's worried something's gonna go wrong or they're gonna be runts, but we'll see. He's got me out there keeping watch, but that cow's barely dilated. I've got plenty of time for a chat." His mattress groans beneath him, and I can picture him sprawled across his unmade bed in his t-shirt and work pants. "So, what's up?"

I take a labored breath, psyching myself up for what I've been wanting to ask for weeks. But now that the opportunity has finally presented itself, I stumble.

"I, um... I wanted to tell you I'm going to be competing in the regional chess invitational in Durham next month. A real tournament." It comes out all in one breath, and I feel like a fraud. The chess competition is the last thing I want to talk to him about.

"That's amazing!" he gushes, and I'm placated by the warmth of his enthusiasm. "You're big time now, girl. What do you get if you win?"

"I have no idea," I tell him. "I haven't even thought about winning. I guess I would move on to the North Carolina state competition, but who knows. And it's a long shot anyway. I'm not good enough to win."

He scoffs. "You are."

I tell him about Cameron and his obsession with figuring out how to win using unorthodox opening moves. "I beat my dad using Grob's Attack. Cameron worked out this entire match and Dad played right into it."

"You'll have to teach it to me, next time we play."

An uncomfortable silence follows since neither of us is positive if there's ever going to be a 'next time.' There are no guarantees.

"So, what's going on with everyone at school? Anything exciting?" It's a stupid question, but it's all I've got.

"All anyone's talking about is prom. Prom this and prom that. It's enough to make me wanna be homeschooled."

"It's the same here," I tell him, remembering Alice and Summer's newest list, Eleven Reasons Never to Wear Chiffon. "Everyone's lost their minds."

Zander clears his throat. "You going? I mean, did anyone ask you to go yet?" There's an edge to his voice bordering on jealousy.

Alice is planning to go with Marcus. They've been inseparable since the party at Calvin Watkins', who coincidentally has been relegated to Alice's B-list. Summer, of course, is going with her boyfriend, Travis, despite Alice's objections. Leonetta and I are planning to go together. And then, there's Cameron.

"Nah. Probably a group of us going together. Leonetta, Summer, Alice..."

"Oh," he says mildly. "Just the girls."

"Something like that," I say, without explaining specifics. "What about you guys? Are Claire and Will still together?"

"Yeah. They're disgusting. You should see them."

I laugh. "I'm sorta glad I don't have to. It's almost worth moving half-way across the country to miss it. What about Lacey? Is she still with Connor or has she moved on?"

"Still with him, believe it or not. Those two deserve each other, though. Keep all the negativity in one place so the rest of us can steer clear."

Before leaving Iowa, I'd always imagined Zander and I might go to prom together as friends. Mostly because it would be fun but also because he'd look amazing in a tux, a native wildflower pinned to his lapel. A purple coneflower perhaps. The cows always devoured the wild varieties out in the field.

"What about you," I say before I'm sure I want to hear the answer.

"Oh, me?" he stammers. "Yeah. I'm going. Judy Lewis asked, so whatever. I'll go."

Immediately, I regret having inquired. I swallow hard, trying to dislodge the lump that's taken up residence in my throat. Judy Lewis. Beautiful, smart, full-busted Judy Lewis. Imagining them on prom night together, his arm around her waist, her heaving bosom out in plain sight, turns my stomach.

To keep myself from obsessing, I change the topic to the only other subject on my mind.

"What happened to my cows?" I blurt out.

There's a pause full of strained silence. It hangs heavily between us, telling me everything I need to know without the aid of a single word. Zander will have nothing good to report.

"Tess, does it really matter anymore?"

I hold my breath. I don't respond.

"If I tell you, it's not gonna make you feel better. It's only gonna make you feel worse."

He's right, of course, but I've made my peace with the herd being gone. I've overheard my dad's phone calls. Seen letters in the mail from the auctioneer. I know the truth. I just need to hear it from him.

"Tell me," I say. My voice is clipped. Hushed.

He sighs, unconvinced. "There, uh, was an auction last month, but you already knew that. Buncha guys came in from neighboring counties. There were even a few from outta state. The farm itself was sold to some young couple from Colorado. They didn't want the cows though since their plan is to convert all the fields to corn for ethanol. They want to save the planet or something. Who the hell knows? Anyway, most of the herd was sold piecemeal to other dairy farms. A handful went to slaughter—they were too old to sell."

My gut seizes for a second time. I don't know if I can bear any more sadness, but I have to know.

"And Sunshine?"

He makes a noise reminiscent of a cough. He's trying to keep his composure.

Because he can't bring himself to tell me Sunshine's dead.

"She's here. Here with me at our farm. She didn't go for much. Only a few hundred bucks. Dad let me take a little outta my college fund to buy her."

I'm gobsmacked. I wipe tears I didn't realize were falling with my sleeve. I have absolutely no response and keep sniffling into the phone. I can't imagine why he would do it. Why he would take money away from his education for a stupid, worthless cow. A worthless cow no one else even wanted.

No one else but me.

"Thank you," I whisper once I've steadied my breathing. "Why didn't you tell me about all this before?"

"Your dad made me promise not to say anything 'til you asked. He said to give you time to come around on your own. And if you never asked, I was never supposed to tell you."

I'm not sure whether to be grateful or affronted by Dad's foresight.

"Does he know what you did? Does he know about Sunshine?"

He hesitates. "No," he says finally. "We didn't tell him."

His voice, heavy with emotion, confirms his motivation for spending his hard-earned dollars on Sunshine. It was the same reason my dad kept her in the first place, long past her prime. Long past the age other farmers would have put her out to pasture.

He kept her because he loves me.

*

That night back at my desk, I'm still trying to study for the stupid geometry test, but my mind keeps wandering to Zander. I turn the page of my spiral notebook, tucking the Pythagorean Theorem notes underneath to reveal a clean sheet of paper. At the top of the page I write:

Eleven Reasons Why I Loved Being a Farm Girl
1. The smell of freshly harvested wheat.
2. Watching the barn cats chase crickets in the hay loft.
3. Muddy boots.
4. Watching the first rays of morning spill across the field from the top fence rail.
5. Fresh milk.
6. Dusty overalls.
7. New life.
8. The rumble of the combine.
9. Frost on the corn stalks.
10. Wet cow noses.
11. Capturing the heart of a farm boy.

chapter 22
Smothered and Covered

Saturday, April 6

"One for *Resident Evil 6*," I tell the nondescript teenage girl behind the movie counter. She hands me my ticket, and I file into the theater behind Leonetta and the others. I can't believe I'm paying good money to watch a movie based on a video game I've never played and probably never will. There's no doubt the selection was made by Travis or Marcus, what with the flesh-eating zombies and scantily clad Milla Jovovich wielding a semi-automatic weapon on the marquee. Talk about being in the guys' wheelhouse. Still, it was nice of Alice and Summer to invite Leonetta and me with them on their double date, so I won't complain out loud about the guys' horrible taste in films. At least I'm not sitting home by myself on a Saturday night.

Ashley, of course, headed out early with a crew of friends to the bowling alley. She practically lives there on the weekends. More surprising was Mom and Dad's reservation at the Japanese steakhouse for dinner, leaving me to fend for myself for the night. When Alice's text came in, I'd been grateful for the invitation. There's only so much homework a girl can do before she's no longer able to keep the melancholy at bay.

After stopping at concessions for extra-buttered popcorn, a pop, and Jujubes, I follow the others into the theater. Marcus chooses our row, way down in front, and Alice takes the seat beside him. They're holding hands and talking quietly to one another in hushed tones and wordless gestures. It's fun to witness this side of her, the part she reserves only for him, all giggly and nervous. Summer takes the seat beside Alice and, of course, Travis slides in beside her. Unlike Alice and Marcus who can't keep their hands off each other, I haven't heard Summer say two words to Travis since they pulled up in his pickup truck. The discord between them is palpable, as if they're warring factions embroiled in a no-win standoff. Something must have gone down between them before they arrived, making me curious about what compels them to stay together, especially given his proclivity for cheating on her. It doesn't make any sense.

Leonetta wriggles into the aisle seat leaving the chair on Travis's right side for me. I keep waiting for the awkwardness between us to pass but even after hanging out together half-a-dozen times, being around Travis still feels strange. There's something charming about him, and if we'd met under different circumstances, we might've had a shot at being friends. But given his track record of unfaithfulness, I'm hesitant to grant him the benefit of the doubt, especially given his current status—discreetly reading his texts while Summer and Alice chat beside him. Because although it's possible he's gotten an important message from his commanding officer, I'm more likely to believe he's checking on intel from other girls.

I shift my body away from Travis, leaning closer to Leonetta until our shoulders touch. She smiles warily, having also witnessed his nonchalant display, and like me, chooses to keep her mouth shut. I get the feeling, however, she won't remain silent forever. Her candid sensibilities won't allow it.

Before we can share any more than a curious glance at one another, the lights go down and the movie begins. An hour and forty minutes later the final credits begin to roll, and as I'm working the crick out of my neck, I notice Alice and Summer are gone. In their place are two empty seats between the guys.

I lean past Travis to call down the row to Marcus. "Where'd they go?"

He straightens in his seat, adjusting his shirt across his shoulders and shrugs. "They skipped outta here about fifteen minutes ago. I guess they went to the bathroom and decided to wait for us out there."

I can't blame them for bailing early. The movie's plot was so generically predictable, there was absolutely no reason to stay. What I can't understand is why Alice wouldn't have at least come back in to be with Marcus.

"Something's up," Leonetta whispers in my ear, and I nod in agreement.

The two of us hurry into the lobby, leaving the guys to watch the credits on their own. We discover Summer and Alice sitting on the floor beyond concessions, leaning against the wall. It's obvious, even from across the lobby, Summer's been crying. She wipes the mascara from under her eyes with the edge of a tissue as we approach.

"What happened?" I ask.

She turns her head, dejected. "Nothing, except for me being a stupid idiot. Again."

Leonetta holds out her hands, pulling them both off the floor as I glance over my shoulder for Travis or Marcus. There's no sign of them yet.

"Don't say that," Alice scolds. "You're not a stupid idiot. You're brave and strong and beautiful. He's the idiot."

"So, what did happen?" Leonetta asks again as we make our

way outside to the parking lot, the unseasonably crisp night air cutting at our faces.

"The same crap," Summer moans, closing her jacket protectively across her chest. "He got all pissed because apparently he tried to call me last night while I was at Cora's house—you know, the shy girl who lives at the end of my street who's always begging me to come hang out? Anyway, I accidentally left my phone at home and my sister answered and told him I was 'out' which set him off." Her intonation changes now into a weak impersonation of Travis's much deeper voice. "Why didn't you tell me where you were going? Why didn't you tell me who you were with? What are you hiding? If you have so much free time, why didn't you want to spend it with me?" She sighs. "Now he's doing this passive aggressive thing where he pretends he's the perfect boyfriend and nothing's wrong while he waits for me to say something else to set him off. You should've heard him baiting me during the movie. He's jonesing for a fight."

Alice rolls her eyes. "He's only worried you're gonna start talking to somebody else the way he does. And it would serve him right if you did."

"It would serve who right?" a voice says from behind us. I don't have to turn around to recognize who it is.

Alice glowers at Travis who's appeared beside Summer, draping his arm possessively around her shoulders. There's a coldness to his expression, daring Alice to say something more, to accuse him of something, justified or not.

"It's nothing," Summer mumbles under her breath, and I'm taken aback by the way her demeanor's completely changed since he arrived. The confident, self-assured woman I know has been replaced by a sullen, insecure version of herself and my heart breaks for her. There's a moment of awkward tension while Travis takes us all in, but we don't have to wait long to find out whether he heard Summer complaining about him.

"You still got your panties all in a wad about earlier, and now you're crying about it to your friends? I already told you I wouldn't need to get upset if you would be considerate and tell me where you are and who you're with so I don't have to go tracking you down." He glances at the rest of us. "And we're not coming out with you for waffles. I don't make a habit of hanging out with people who talk trash about me behind my back."

Leonetta tenses beside me, her hands gathering into fists. She takes a step forward toward the soldier. "She's not a child. She can make her own decisions about whether or not she wants to go for waffles."

Travis ignores her and without another word turns with Summer, who's still caught under his arm, toward where his truck is parked on the far side of the lot. As they begin to walk away, she glances back over her shoulder, giving us a desperate look, but she doesn't attempt to break free of his grasp.

"Should we go after her?" I ask the others, but Alice shakes her head as she watches Travis and Summer round the corner of the theater.

"No. Let her go. Just pray that douche ships off to Syria sooner rather than later."

"Yeah," Leonetta agrees, "and then pray he isn't able to find her again when he comes back home."

*

At the Waffle House, we fit comfortably at a four-top, with Alice and Marcus on one side and Leonetta and I on the other. We have everything covered and smothered, scattered and topped, and once we've finished rehashing every dreadful minute of *Resident Evil,* all that's left to discuss is our friend's equally dreadful situation.

"What's the deal with Travis?" Marcus asks before shoveling a gigantic forkful of hash browns into his mouth.

"I want to say he wasn't like this in the beginning," Alice tells him thoughtfully. "But thinking back on how he treated her when they first started dating, I guess there were probably indications of the crap you saw today if I'd been looking for them."

"Like what?" Leonetta asks.

Alice pushes the runny yolk of her egg around her plate with her fork. "I dunno. Like, he was too good to be true when it came to checking in with her. He was always calling, wondering where she was or what she was doing. It was sweet at first, him thinking about her all the time. But it got annoying once she started having to check in with him whenever she wanted to do anything or go anywhere. Like she needed his approval."

"You think he's worried she's gonna hook-up with someone else?" Marcus asks. "Since she's still in school and he's out there in the world." I get the sense he might be harboring these same fears about Alice, although perhaps he doesn't want to say anything since their relationship is still so new.

"Yeah. Absolutely. But he's not just worried," Alice says. "He's petrified. Because he knows if he can do it to her, she can do it right back." She looks reassuringly at Marcus now and says, "But he broke their trust early on with all sorts of lies. We don't have that problem, do we?"

He smiles at her, taking her hand. "No. We sure don't."

There's something bittersweet about watching Alice and Marcus together. The way they look at one another with such reverence and respect—the way most girls can only dream of being cherished by someone they love. And although they've only known one another a couple of months, it seems as though they've been together forever, two old souls trapped inside the bodies of these young lovers.

So easy for them. So effortless.

So different from Zander and me who are the exact opposite. Two people who have known each other forever but can't seem to put the pieces of their collective puzzle together. Or are afraid to for fear of ruining everything else.

I consider, as I'm watching them pick food from each other's plates, it might be time to open myself up to the idea of finding my own significant other. Someone who might not be a perfect match for my list but might be good enough to share a plate of waffles.

My stomach lurches at the thought. The idea of replacing Zander as the peanut butter to my jelly is unthinkable. I'd almost rather starve.

As I've been mulling over my own tragic love life, Alice has begun telling us about the beginning of her friendship with Summer. About how they met in Spanish class freshman year, the result of a random assignment pairing. At first, she explains, she'd wanted nothing to do with her. Figured they wouldn't have anything in common. But as she got to know her over the course of the project, she realized just how amazing Summer actually was.

"I mean, seriously, her name's Summer. Which technically isn't even a name. Could I expect to become friends with someone named after a season?"

The rest of us laugh, but not at Summer's expense. Because it was true. At first glance, Summer looked and sounded like the type of girl most people loved to hate. Petite. Busty. Adorable. She was the sort of person you assumed made it to the top of the food chain by clawing her way to the summit; securing her post atop the bodies of every person she stabbed in the back along the way. But she wasn't like that. Because when it came to being a mean girl, Summer Phillips was far too nice.

"I'll never forget the day I saw her on her hands and knees, sorting through trash from the cafeteria's compactor, helping Aaron Barker look for his missing retainer. There was absolutely nothing in it for her. Aaron wasn't cute or funny or frankly appealing in any way, so it's not like she was trying to get him to like her. No teacher made her stop to help him as a punishment. She set her things to the side and got right down into the garbage with him because, as she told me later, he looked like he could use some help. That was it. *He looked like he could use some help.*" Alice's eyes widen, punctuating the ridiculousness of her statement. "Anyway, that's when I knew I could trust her to be my friend. Any person who's nice enough to dig through disgusting, stinky garbage to look for someone else's orthodontia is someone I want on my team, you know what I'm sayin'?"

We all nod in agreement as I try to imagine Summer elbows-deep in refuse. It sounds exactly like something she would do.

"She and I created our first list that afternoon in Spanish class: Ten Reasons Trash is Gross.

"I thought your lists always have eleven reasons," Leonetta chimes in.

Alice wags a finger. "Took us half a dozen before we decided to switch to eleven. We only did ten reasons in the beginning."

Marcus is wearing a curious expression, his eyebrow raised suspiciously. "What lists?"

Leonetta and I snicker, knowing of at least one particular list he would be especially interested in reading. Alice goes on to explain about the lists and how their friendship grew around them, and as I'm listening and laughing along with the others, I'm struck by how content I am, happy even, to be sitting among this group of people. A year ago, I would have never pictured myself eating waffles at eleven o'clock in a greasy spoon with a new group of friends. But here I am. And I could totally get used to this unexpected way of life.

chapter 23
Heathcliff and Catherine

Tuesday, April 16

I'm early to lit circle for literally the first time ever and, while I wait for everyone else to arrive, find myself skimming my now well-worn copy of *Wuthering Heights*. For me, *Wuthering Heights* has always been one of those novels prone to transformation with repeated readings, but as I glance at a particularly compelling passage from the early pages of the book, I realize it's not the story that's changed.

I'm the one who's grown.

I was thirteen the first time I read Bronte's seminal masterpiece. Having only read a handful of other classic works of literature by which to compare it, I'd been discouraged by Heathcliff and Catherine's unrealized love affair. I fixated upon the story's main character, certain Heathcliff would eventually metamorphosize into the classic, romantic hero I'd been envisioning: dark and brooding at the start, fiercely loyal and adoring by the end. Of course, he never did and I was devastated, tossing the book aside, certain its pages held nothing more for me.

The following summer, out of boredom and lack of

inspiration, I'd reread the book, more cautiously this time knowing Heathcliff would remain malevolent and abusive until his death. Through this filter I was able to concentrate on other facets of the work, most importantly Edgar, Catherine's dutiful husband, whose cowardice and naivety made him as unlikable as Heathcliff. This rereading provided little insight about the true nature of love I'd been expecting to find, and only served to reaffirm my disappointment.

When Leonetta mentioned *Wuthering Heights* was on our spring reading schedule for lit circle, I'd initially balked, as this particular Bronte sister had always left me wanting. But the selection was the selection, and I convinced myself fresh insight might be gained through discussion with this new group of friends.

"*Wuthering Heights* is two love stories in one. True or false?" Mrs. Alexander begins once everyone has arrived.

Rashida speaks up immediately. "True. Heathcliff and Catherine. The younger Catherine and Hareton."

"Anyone disagree? Anyone argue it's only Heathcliff and Catherine's story?"

Everyone shakes their heads. "Two love stories," Will says, giving a thumbs-up to Rashida.

Mrs. Alexander looks pleased with our assessment. "If that's the case, what's the point? There has to be a reason Bronte chose to present us with two love stories in this one novel."

"We're obviously supposed to compare them," Lashanda says. "One's good. One's bad. One works out and one doesn't."

A murmur of agreement floats around the room.

"But why?"

I consider Mrs. Alexander's question—why Heathcliff and Catherine were never able to find happiness together while the younger Catherine and Hareton were. And suddenly it hits me.

"Heathcliff and Catherine never embrace change," I say. "Young Catherine and Hareton do."

Mrs. Alexander beams at me. "Go on," she says.

I'm still mulling it over, flipping through the novel for an example to share when Leonetta pipes up.

"Heathcliff and Catherine act like children their entire lives," she says. "They never grow up. Their feelings for each other never mature. They keep fixating on what they had as kids, the relationship of their youth, but instead of growing up and becoming mature adults who deal with change effectively, they stay frozen and that's why they can never pull it together."

"Yeah, yeah," Roy pipes up. "Like how Catherine keeps going on about wanting to go back to the moors where she was a kid and doesn't remember much of her life since she was twelve."

"A grown woman would make her decision and go with it," Rashida adds. "Either go all in with the highfalutin guy and give up on Heathcliff altogether or choose love and say screw society and its class system. But she waffles between both without committing to either. She needs to change and she doesn't."

"Heathcliff is no better," Leonetta adds. "He carries the same grudges with him from childhood all the way to his deathbed. He never accepts change; he lets it tear him apart which is why he never turns into the proper romantic hero we expect him to become."

Listening silently to the group's spot-on analysis, I'm struck by the lesson Bronte is attempting to teach us about love. What she's been attempting to teach us all along.

Love which doesn't grow and accept change is destined for destruction.

Oh, God.

Zander.

There was a point, before Connor's bonfire party, when our relationship shifted. Hormones were probably to blame, but the sad truth is we did begin to see one another as more than the friends we'd always been. Looking back now, it's obvious. The way he would linger outside the barn on evenings he knew I was out there, making up reasons to come around. The times I caught him staring at me in math class instead of solving for Y. The way he'd casually find ways to brush against me, letting his hand rest against mine a little too long.

Then that night happened. The cornfield. The blood. And everything after.

Someway, somehow, we'd both decided without a word between us we could never be together in that way.

Our love could never grow from childhood friendship into something more.

We would always be just friends.

Love which doesn't grow and accept change is destined for destruction.

But now our separation has stripped away the complexities of friendship to reveal a simple truth. I'm capable of loving him in a different way. In an adult way, with romance and passion and longing.

How easy it would be to act upon this revelation if he still lived next door.

If only I wouldn't have squandered our final years together platonically instead of exploring the possibility of becoming a romantic couple. Why did we even care what the people in town thought, with their righteous stares and presumptuous natures? We should have let them talk. Let them say what they would about the two of us. Because we knew the truth—what we had together was pure and wholesome and true.

It was okay for love to change from something simple and childlike to something deeper and far more complicated.

Not changing would be the destructive thing.

These truths crash down upon me, consuming me whole in the way my dad always warned the feed would should I ever find myself trapped inside the silo. It spills over my head, building around me, threatening to suffocate me if I don't keep pushing myself to the surface. It might be easier to surrender myself to it. To let it all overtake me.

To allow myself to love him.

"You okay?" Leonetta whispers, breaking me from my trance. A line of sweat has beaded along my brow.

I look at her, her soulful, ebony eyes full of compassion and concern.

"I don't know," I stammer. And I seriously don't know. What I *am* certain of is I don't want to be here anymore. Here at lit circle. Here at M.A. Hopkins Senior High School. Here in Fayetteville. I want to be in my barn or up my tree. Anywhere but here.

I stand without making eye contact with anyone else in the room, especially Mrs. Alexander who'll block me from leaving if given the opportunity. I gather my books hastily into my arms and run for the door. After skidding into the hallway, I make a beeline out to the student parking lot.

By the time I get there, Leonetta is already waiting for me, leaning against the hood of my car.

"Shortcut," she says as I approach. "There's a delivery corridor behind the closest stairwell to Mrs. Alexander's room. Comes out right over there." She nods toward a door on the side of the building, not twenty feet from where we're standing.

Despite the storm raging inside me, I grin at her. She's a good friend. A great friend. I should've known she'd come after me.

"What's going on?" she asks as I sidle up beside her.

I consider saying 'nothing' and leaving it at that. I don't want to talk about my epiphany, but I can't lie to her. She'll see right through me.

"You remember the guy, Zander, my friend from back in Iowa?"

"The one you talk about all the time?"

I glare at her. "Not *all* the time," I say.

It's her turn to raise an eyebrow at me.

"Okay, I talk about him sometimes," I concede. But then I stop. I can't find the words to go on.

"What about him?" Leonetta urges, nudging me with an elbow.

"I..." I've never said the words aloud and it's harder than I thought it was going to be. "I love him," I say finally.

She makes a small sound. A bit like a laugh but more like a contented coo, as if she's a baby and I've been tickling her toes. "I know," she says.

It feels almost like she's punched me in the gut.

"You know?" I say. "How is that even possible? You've never even met him."

She lays a hand on my shoulder, and if it had been anyone else doing it I would have thought it condescending, but since it's Leonetta I'm certain she's being sincere.

"Honey, that wistful look you get whenever you talk about him... There's never been any doubt in my mind about your feelings for him." She narrows her eyes at me, searching for something in the lines of my face. "Don't tell me you're just now figuring it out."

Am I just now figuring it out?

"I'm afraid we might end up like Catherine and Heathcliff because we're exactly like them, and I don't want that for us. We were kids together. We grew up together. We have this thing between us that's so much bigger than simple friendship.

When Catherine says 'I am Heathcliff,' I totally relate. Because I *am* Zander, whether I want to be or not. I can't separate myself from him because so much of who I am is tied to who he is. Our history is long and deep. But since we've been apart, things have changed." I take a deep breath, surprised at how easily all of this is flowing out, but I focus, forcing myself to come to the point. "What destroyed Catherine and Heathcliff was their refusal to embrace change. They didn't let their love mature. If my friendship with Zander is going to survive, it's what we need to do."

Leonetta shrugs. "So, you gonna tell him?"

My heart stops. "Tell him I love him?"

She slides off the hood of my car. "Yeah."

"I don't know if I can. At least not right now. Not while we're so far apart." She scowls at me. "I will, though, eventually. Maybe this summer if he comes to visit."

"What if he never comes to visit?" she asks.

Tears pool in the corners of my eyes. "He'll come," I tell her. "He has to."

chapter 24
Zugzwang

Saturday, April 27

Dad's battalion is on DRF 1, which stands for Division Ready Force—battle-ready status. What this means is he's not supposed to go too far outside Fayetteville because if something catastrophic were to happen in the world, his unit could be expected to deploy in less than three hours. As my most enthusiastic groupie, however, even threats of the apocalypse couldn't dissuade him from accompanying me to the regional chess competition in Durham. After the hour-and-a-half drive, he still can't keep the excitement out of his voice as we enter the venue.

"It's killing your mom not to be here," he tells me as we approach the registration line in the lobby of the Courtyard Hotel where the tournament is taking place. "But Ashley still needs to be driven everywhere, so..."

"I know," I say, taking a step forward as another participant receives her nametag and packet ahead of me. "It's okay. I'm glad you were able to come," I add. "I just hope you won't get in trouble for being here."

He drapes a confident arm around my shoulder as we

continue to shuffle forward. "You worry about winning today, and I'll worry about my Commanding Officer. Besides, if I get a call, I can make it back in time. You just might need to catch a ride home with one of your teammates." He squeezes me into his chest. "Nothing's gonna happen, though. I promise."

The line continues to grow behind us, and we fall into comfortable silence for several minutes. Then, with an air of wonder, he asks, "How does this whole event even work?" I can tell by the way he's watching the torrent of people streaming through the door, he's impressed by the sheer number of participants and spectators the tournament has attracted. "I've never seen anything like it."

I take another step forward and begin explaining it to him, hoping a simple recitation will ease my mounting anxiety as well. "Each school sends at least one team. Each team consists of four members. For our school, it's me, Cameron, Devon, and Kallie. We each get to play three games, win or lose, and we get points for winning. The team with the most points at the end of the competition wins. The school gets money, and I think there's some kind of trophy involved."

"Wouldn't it be exciting to win?" he says as we take another step forward.

"I don't have high hopes," I say. "We're sorta the Bad News Bears of chess."

We reach the table. "Well," he says, "even though none of you have ever played in a tournament before, you shouldn't be intimidated. You've beaten me, and I'm a helluva player."

I roll my eyes at him as I accept my name tag and schedule from a frazzled-looking volunteer. My three timed matches are at ten o'clock, one o'clock, and three o'clock. Awards are presented at four o'clock. It's gonna be a long day.

"Hey, Tess!" a voice calls from across the room.

Cameron, his mother Corrine, and our teammates Devon

and Kallie have set up camp at a table in the corner of the hotel lobby. After introductions are made, they offer us glazed donuts from the Krispy Kreme box they brought. While we eat, the four of us pass around our registration sheets, comparing schedules, and I'm excited to discover, depending on how quickly my games end, I should have an opportunity to watch each of my teammates play at least once. And everyone should be able to watch me since I'm the only one who has a game in the first timeslot at ten o'clock.

Moments later the welcoming announcements crackle over the loudspeaker. "Everyone scheduled to play in the first round should report to their assigned locations immediately. Spectators should move into the allotted viewing areas indicated by the yellow sections on your map. Thank you all for your participation in today's tournament and remember, in the words of the great chess champion Emanuel Lasker, 'When you see a good move, look for a better one.'"

"Go get 'em, kid," Dad says, backing away toward the spectators' area. "You got this."

I manage a weak smile, overwhelmed by the fear of disappointing him. I want to make him proud. I need to make him proud.

It isn't long before I'm three-quarters of the way through my first match. Having randomly selected the black pieces at the start, I began the game at a decided disadvantage, having to react to my opponent's opening move instead of choosing my own. I'm used to this though; for most of my life, my dad never let me play white. Only black.

His tutelage carries me through to the end of the match as I place my opponent, a buff, sweater-vest-wearing senior, in checkmate.

Spectators aren't allowed to cheer or applaud to avoid disturbing other ongoing matches, but as the judge confirms my win, I can almost hear my dad breathe a sigh of relief from across the room.

He's not the only one.

Cameron beats his first opponent with little to no effort, and after Kallie loses to an innocent looking girl in pigtails who turns out to be a veritable wolf in sheep's clothes, we break for lunch. Cameron's mom heads out to get drive-thru from McDonald's, and after returning with the food, the team regroups to discuss strategies over Big Macs and excessively-salted fries.

"Interesting opening move," my dad says to Cameron in an attempt to make small talk with him after noticing he hasn't spoken to anyone since lunch began.

Cameron looks up from his burger, genuinely confused. "Interesting how?"

Dad takes a sip of his pop and shrugs. "Pawn to A3 isn't something you see every day, that's all."

"Taking your opponent by surprise is a proven winning strategy," Cameron tells him with pokerfaced conviction.

"You don't have to convince me," Dad laughs. "Tess beat me with one of your crazy openers not too long ago. I hope for your sake you're able to catch all your opponents off guard today the way she did with me."

"Of course, I will."

I can't help but smile at Cameron's confidence and hope he won't be too disappointed if his strategy eventually fails him.

"Don't you think the end game is as important as the opening?" my dad asks, and I throw him a look I hope conveys it would be best to retract his line of questioning. Debating the importance of opening strategies with Cameron is akin to opening Pandora's box.

"There can be no end game without a strong foundation. Sometimes the foundation is rooted in your own strength and sometimes in your opponent's weakness. I happen to like the challenge of making the most of my opponent's vulnerabilities."

Since he's already finished his, Dad grabs a few fries from my bag. "What happens if you go up against someone who doesn't get flustered by your quirky opening move?"

"It's called the long game," Cameron deadpans.

This sets my dad into a fit of hysterics and the rest of us, including Cameron's own mother, can't help but laugh along.

"My long game is legendary," Cameron continues, glancing around at us, the humor of his intense persona completely lost on him.

Once we've settled ourselves and placated Cameron, it isn't long before the afternoon sessions are announced. We wish each other luck, and as I head across the lobby in the direction of my second match, a curious sensation crawls up my spine—someone is watching me. I turn back to see Dad gazing wistfully in my direction, but the instant our eyes meet he rearranges his face into an enthusiastic grin. He gives me a thumbs up, and I return the gesture but can't help but wonder why he initially looked so pensive. Is he worried about my match? Afraid I can't handle a loss? Because I honestly don't care at all about the winning or the losing.

At the end of the day, all I need is the warmth of his pride. It's really all I've ever wanted.

As it turns out, I lose my second game, completely outmatched from the start. My opponent is a shrewd ninth grader from a local high school here in Durham. Her eyes are warm and wide and doe-like, causing me to immediately underestimate her. Perhaps the inability to read people is my fatal flaw.

She determines her moves with little hesitation after my turns are complete, making it appear as if the only deliberations are coming from my side of the table. This flusters me, and I begin making rash decisions, one after another, in an attempt to give her less time to contemplate her strategy while I'm laboring over my own. The technique backfires, leaving me, and by default my king, with nowhere left to hide.

Dad and I are watching Kallie from the spectator's section, waiting to be called for my third and final match when he says, "Too bad about being put into zugzwang at the end of your game." I have no idea what he means, and he must sense my confusion because he immediately explains. "You were down to your last five pieces, trying to protect your king with the rook, but since your other three pieces had nowhere to go, you were forced to move the rook simply because you had to take your turn." He runs his hands against the velvety crew cut on the back of his head. "It's called a zugzwang—having to move even though you don't want to because you don't have the option of staying where you are."

The notion of moving across the country when I didn't want to back in January and the irony of the terminology isn't lost on me. Apparently, it isn't lost on Dad either because now he's grinning at me like he's afraid of getting punched.

"Too soon?" he asks.

I do punch him good-naturedly in the bicep and say, "No. It's fine. I'm fine."

The smile fades from his lips and eyes and is replaced by genuine concern. "Are you really, Tess? Are you certain? Because I need to be sure you're okay. And if there's anything I can do to help..."

I interrupt before he becomes overwrought with sentimentality, something he's known for. I can tell the guilt of dragging me here to North Carolina is tearing at him. Perhaps it's because he still misses the farm and the life and the people we left behind, too.

"I already told you, Dad, I'm fine. It hasn't been an easy adjustment, but how can I complain when I get to come here and do this?" I stretch out my arms, indicating the tournament. "I never got to participate in anything like this back in Iowa."

He chuckles. "No. That's true enough." He keeps looking at me, searching, as though he's still not convinced. As if I'm merely appeasing him. "What about friends?" he says at last.

I shrug. "What about them?"

"I dunno. It seems like your teammates are a lot different from the ones back at East Chester." He thumbs over his shoulder to indicate the rest of the chess club. "Do you all have much in common, outside of chess?"

"No. Not really. But it's okay," I tell him. "We get along fine."

Before he's able to continue grilling me, we hear the announcement encouraging those of us participating in the final round to make our way to our assigned locations.

"That's me," I say, popping out of my seat. "See you on the flip side."

My final match encompasses all the best chess has to offer. Skill. Patience. Integrity. Thoughtfulness. And even a little bit of luck. The best part, however, is placing my opponent in checkmate and turning to the spectator's section for the first time since the start of the game. Beside my dad, grinning and waving like a bunch of maniacs, are Summer, Alice, and Leonetta. They're all hyped up as if they've come to cheer at a step competition instead of a chess tournament. As soon as my win is confirmed by the judges, I shake hands with my opponent and race across the conference room to where my small but mighty cheering section awaits.

"I have no idea what just happened," Leonetta says as I approach, gathering me into her arms, "but whatever it was, you looked like you owned it."

"She totally owned it," Alice agrees, "and that's coming from someone who knows slightly more than nothing about chess."

I laugh, still trying to get over the shock of their arrival. "Why are you here?" I ask.

Alice nods towards my dad. "Somebody gave me all the details after one of our study sessions a few weeks back. Plus, we all had prom shopping to do, and your tournament gave us the perfect excuse to venture outside of Fayetteville. Now we're certain nobody else will show up to the dance with our dresses."

Summer glares at Alice. "It was mostly to see you, though, Tess," she adds.

"It means a lot that you guys would drive all this way," I say. And it's true. I'm overwhelmed. Zander is the only other person I can think of who would drive hours to watch me play.

"We wouldn't miss it," Leonetta says.

"Seriously, girl, you've been working all semester for this," Alice adds. "We're so glad we got to see you win."

Off to the side, Dad's grinning, hands in his pockets staring at his shoes. He knows he's the reason Leonetta, Alice, and Summer are here, and it placates his guilt over moving me in the first place. He sees for himself I'm okay. And I have friends. Real friends.

Friends who will drive hours to watch a thirty-minute game of chess they couldn't possibly care less about.

Because what they care about is me.

It's not long before the final matches end, and Kallie, Devon, Cameron, and his mother join us in the center of the conference room waiting for the awards to be announced. We've all done pretty well but are still surprised to discover we've placed eighth out of over thirty teams. We congratulate one another with hugs and high fives and fist bumps.

"Not bad for our first year," Cameron concedes. "We'll win the trophy next year."

It's funny, but it feels to me like I already have.

chapter 25
Soul Food

Saturday, April 27

Cameron and the other members of the chess club take off right after the awards presentations, leaving the rest of us loitering in the hotel's parking lot.

"What're you doing about dinner?" Alice asks, searching her purse for the keys to her car.

"I dunno," I say, glancing at Dad. The two of us hadn't made any plans outside of the competition itself.

"We were talking about going to this place called Mo's Soul Food, around the corner off I-40. My dad always took me there as a kid for mac and cheese. His way of apologizing for dragging me along to university functions," Leonetta says. "You wanna come with?"

I open my mouth to decline, concerned for my dad's feelings, but Summer pipes up before I can respond. "We should totally go celebrate your big win. And you're welcome to join us too, Sergeant Goodwin," she adds quickly at the end.

He brushes off the offer with a wave of his hand, knowing the request was only extended out of polite obligation. "Nah. I appreciate the invite, but you girls should go on without me.

Truth be told, I oughta be getting back to Fayetteville sooner rather than later. I'll hit a drive-thru along the way."

"You sure, Dad?" I hate bailing on him after he gave up his entire day for me.

He grins, fishing keys out of his pocket as he turns toward his truck. "Had my heart set on listening to my entire Pink Floyd playlist on the drive home..."

"Oh God, no." He knows how I feel about his obsession with seventies British rock bands, effectively handing me a guilt-free pass. "You're positive you don't mind?" I ask again as he climbs into the driver's seat.

"Have fun. Enjoy the mac and cheese. Don't come home too late. And Tess?"

"Yeah?"

"I really enjoyed watching you play."

*

The girls don't say anything about the exchange between my dad and me as we pile into Alice's car. Two plastic dress bags hang from the garment hook above my head.

"Looks like you guys had a successful shopping trip," I say.

"Yeah, we did," Alice says enthusiastically from the driver's seat. "Go on and look at them. Mine's the blue one and Leonetta's is the orange."

Between the plastic clothing protectors and cramped conditions in the back seat, it's hard to tell what I'm looking at. From what I can tell Alice's is tiny and sequined and the color of the sky at sunrise. By contrast, Leonetta's is a swath of tangerine satin.

"Seeing them on the hanger doesn't do them justice," I tell them both diplomatically. "But I'm sure they're gonna look amazing on." Then I notice there's no plastic bag for Summer. I hesitate to ask.

"I'm not going," she says flatly, her face to the window, expression hidden. What I catch instead is Alice's mournful glance into the rearview mirror.

Something's wrong, and I reach out tentatively to touch her arm. "What happened?" I ask.

"I broke up with him," she says with a tiny shrug.

The car shudders, tires crunching over the gravel parking lot at Mo's. Before I can grill her on the details of the breakup, Alice shuts off the engine, and I follow the others into the vestibule inside the diner's double doors. We're led immediately to a booth at the far corner of the sparsely populated restaurant by a bored and haggard-looking waitress. I wait until after she takes our drink orders and lumbers off before properly attending to Summer's heart.

"You wanna talk about it?" I ask her, eyeing Alice and Leonetta skeptically in an attempt to assess how bad the situation is.

She shrugs again, dolefully perusing her menu. I can tell by the way she's angrily flipping the pages she's not actually reading any of the options.

"Another girl?" I prod.

She nods.

"I'm sorry," I manage, because what else is there to say.

"We've been trying all day to convince her she should still go to prom with us. Especially since I'm the only one with a date at this point," Alice says. "If anyone should be feeling like the odd man out, it's me."

Summer closes her menu defiantly. "I don't feel like the odd man out. I feel like a stupid idiot for putting up with his crap for so long. It would have been nice if he could have held out being such a raging douchebag a little while longer. Long enough to get through prom at least." She shakes her head. "That jerk forced my hand, though. Because seriously, a self-respecting woman can only put up with so much before she has to bail. Enough is enough."

Although curiosity is eating me apart, I don't ask for the specifics of the actual breakup or what ultimately led to her decision. As much as it isn't any of my business, prom obviously isn't something she's keen on discussing. So, I let it drop.

But Alice doesn't.

"If you don't want to go solo with Netta and Tess, you could always go with Cameron."

Summer furrows her brow, dubiously. "Cameron, the chess kid?"

The waitress arrives to deliver our drinks and takes our orders. Alice chooses the fried catfish, Summer the chicken and waffles, and Leonetta and I get the macaroni and cheese.

Alice takes a sip of her pop before turning to Summer. "Did you not notice the way he was lookin' at you today?"

Summer rolls her eyes, but there's no way she missed him stealing glances at her while he thought no one was looking.

"He's coming with us anyway and think of how much it would mean to him if you went with him as his date."

Summer softens, settling herself into the corner of the booth where the back of the torn plastic seat meets the window. "He's a sweet kid," she says finally, looking at me across the table as if this is all somehow my fault. "But I'm not asking him. He's gonna have to pluck the courage to ask me if he wants to go as a couple."

"I'll mention it to him," I say, wondering whether he has the social graces to pull off something of this magnitude, even knowing Summer's already agreed to say yes. "But I can guarantee he's not going to ask using rose petals to spell out WANNA GO TO PROM? in your front lawn."

Bo Wysong asked Lacey Pemberton to prom using rose petals the year before. Of course, the entire town knew every detail of the proposal by the following morning after her mother sent pictures of the event to the local newspaper. It was no coincidence Bo chose the day before the weekend edition came out to stage his elaborate request. Zander and I were positive Lacey masterminded the scheme, orchestrating the entire proposal from behind the scenes so she'd make the front page of the paper. Typical Lacey.

Our food arrives and, after slathering her waffles with butter and syrup, Summer waves off my warning. "He can ask me at lunch. With regular words. Anything, as long as I'm not the one inviting him."

Alice looks encouraged about Summer's willingness to join us. "Fair enough. And besides, it's not like any of this is even going to matter in the whole scheme of things. I'm only concerned poor Cameron might fall head over heels for you because of this."

"Who knows? Maybe it'll be a love connection," Leonetta says through a mouthful of mac and cheese.

Summer gazes out the window into the parking lot, but her eyes are unfocused as if she's a million miles away. Quietly, she says, "Don't worry. I won't be here long enough for him to fall in love with me."

Alice sets her fork on the edge of her plate, steadying herself with both hands against the table. No one speaks, and all I can hear is the muffled conversation and clanking of silverware from the kitchen. That and Leonetta's labored breaths.

"My dad got his assignment yesterday afternoon, so it's official," Summer continues, unwilling or unable to make eye contact with the rest of us. "We're going to Fort Huachuca in Arizona. He's going to be an instructor there for at least the next two years. We leave May 17."

Although I can tell she's trying, Alice can't stop herself from interrupting. "And you waited all day to tell us this because...?"

Of course, the reason she's guarded her secret for the past twenty-four hours is obvious to me. Why she's been hushed and aloof instead of her typical vivacious self. Knowing how she feels about Travis, we should have guessed her impassivity wasn't simply a result of their breakup. It was from holding in this heart-wrenching information capable of reducing us all to tears.

And so, before Summer can reply, it's my turn to interrupt. "She waited all day because there's not much worse than telling the people you love that you have to leave them. Because until you say it aloud, there's still a chance it might not be true." I tap her foot gently under the table and she glances up at me. Our eyes lock and an unspoken understanding passes between us. I can empathize with how hard it's going to be for her to leave Alice behind. "It sucks."

She nods her reply, too overcome with emotion to respond with words.

As the tears fall, Alice gathers Summer against her. "It's gonna be okay," she whispers into Summer's head of chestnut curls, and I can't help but wonder who Alice is trying to convince: Summer or herself?

Realistically, it's both.

We're quiet for several moments—silent forks, brooding hearts. Finally, Leonetta says, "They're making you leave before the end of the school year? That ain't even right."

Summer nods. "The Army doesn't care about disrupting families. All they care about is having soldiers where they need them when they need them. They say jump and we jump." She pushes what remains of her waffle around her syrup-laden plate with her fork. "I guess I should be glad he's not slated for the Middle East. At least not yet."

Simply hearing the warzone mentioned causes a pinch

in my chest. A growing pit I've been quietly preparing to fill with the pain of my dad's possible deployment. But instead of turning inward to dwell upon my own loss, I focus on the situation at hand, making the conscious decision not to waste time being depressed about Summer's impending departure. Looking back, Zander and I foolishly squandered our final weeks together, pushing one another away instead of enjoying the time we had. I won't allow the four of us to make the same mistake.

What my friends need now is a mission. Something to unify us and take our minds off Summer's departure. And I've got just the thing.

I clear my throat, wiping cheese from the corners of my mouth with my napkin as I say, "I overheard Monika talking to Jayelle in chemistry yesterday. Apparently, she found out someone named Latrina bought her same prom dress, and now she's trying to get her dad to pass some citywide mandate preventing girls from wearing identical dresses to the same dance."

There's a mischievous gleam in Alice's eye. The first I've seen in quite some time. "You're kidding?" she says.

I shake my head, twirling the ice nonchalantly in the bottom of my glass with my straw.

"That's ridiculous," Summer says. "Why doesn't she just get another dress? Lord knows her daddy will buy her whatever she wants."

"True," I say. "But she doesn't want another dress. She wants the dress she already has. Said she looks, and I quote, 'hot as sin' in it, and I don't think she'll stop until she's sure she's gonna be the only one wearing that dress."

Summer swallows her last bite of waffle. "Her dad may be a county commissioner, but he doesn't have the ability to pass legislation about stupid prom dresses. Monika has to know that. She's talking to hear herself talk."

Having taken the bait, Alice leans across the table at me, grabbing for my arm. She can't resist the opportunity to see justice served, even if it's her own brand of justice. "Tell me you know what this dress of hers looks like."

"I might have seen a picture of it on her phone."

Summer's brow arches in understanding. "No way, Alice, don't even think about buying the same dress. You don't want to take her on. It's social suicide. And besides, you already bought a perfectly nice dress."

Alice scoffs. "Please. I can put up with anything Monika dishes out. And I'll take the other dress back. It'll totally be worth it to bring that triflin' heifer down a notch." She shimmies her shoulders, running her hands along the length of her torso. "And you all know I'll look better than she will in that dress."

"No doubt," Leonetta agrees.

"The look on her face when she sees me in her dress..." Alice looks seriously around the table at the three of us. "Showing her up is the least I can do. A little retribution for the way she's treated you all."

"You don't have to," Leonetta says, but there's no mistaking the muted anticipation in her voice.

"Are you kidding?" Alice smiles. "That's what friends are for."

chapter 26
Coming and Going

Saturday, May 11

I'm having trouble recalling the last time I wore something
other than jeans or cutoffs as I stand in front of my bedroom
mirror, struggling to secure the zipper of my prom dress. The
fastener's lodged uncomfortably between my shoulder blades,
and as I try to shimmy it into position, a vague image of a long-
forgotten floral sundress comes to mind. Mom insisted I wear
a dress to my eighth-grade graduation and although I resisted
at the time, I'm beginning to realize how blessedly simple it
was compared to the intricate ensemble Summer's chosen for
me to wear to prom. I'm still contorted, all angles and elbows,
cursing under my breath when Dad appears at my bedroom
door.

"Well look at you," he says, whistling from against the door
jamb. "My little farm girl's all grown up."

I roll my eyes over my shoulder at him as I turn my back in
his direction. "Thank God you're here. Can you zip this thing
up?" I ask, holding my hair over my nape.

His hands warm my bare shoulders as his deftly fastens the
zipper, and I'm relieved to finally take a proper breath.

"Lotta straps on that thing," he says, propping himself on the corner of my desk as I admire myself in the mirror. "How'd you figure out where your head was supposed to go?"

I shrug, not quite certain how I did discern between the arm holes and the head hole. The dress is cherry red, with crisscross straps across the bodice and matching bands across the back. There's a hint of cleavage showing and the skirt flows gracefully from my waist to above my peep-toe heels.

"You don't think it's too much?" I ask, his approval paramount in all things.

"I think it's perfect."

Although I flush at the sincerity of his compliment, his melancholy tone draws my attention, and I brace myself for what I fear is coming: a sentimental oration about how I'm growing up too fast and how he wishes I could stay his little girl. He's prone to fits of sappiness, especially about matters which are out of his control. I cross my arms beneath my bust and raise an eyebrow.

"Go ahead, Dad. Say whatever it is you need to say. You can get it off your chest but don't make me cry because I suck at makeup and I've already had to redo my eyeliner three times this afternoon."

He sighs. There's a painful edge to it catching in his throat, and it serves as a cautionary beacon, a warning I'm ill-prepared for what he's about to say. But instead of speaking, he stands, stretching the small of his back. Finally, he says, "It's nothing. Another conversation for another time."

He makes for the door but I stop him, tumbling over myself in my heels. If my steady push toward adulthood isn't what has him wrought with sentimentality, there's only one other thing it could be.

"Tell me," I whisper, steadying myself against him. "You're leaving, aren't you?"

His nod is almost imperceptible, the slightest motion I've ever seen, but the affirmation is clear in the lines of his face, the way they deepen with worry as he stares at me.

"When?"

"The end of June," he says.

"How long?"

His eyes cut away, unable to maintain my gaze. "Until they let me come home. Nine months. Could be a year."

I'm quiet for a moment, lost within myself, trying desperately to calm the churning maelstrom building beneath the surface. Rationally, I've known this day might come. Fighting against Assad with the Syrian people was one of the reasons he re-enlisted, and his unique decoding abilities were the reason the Army was willing to take him back.

Leaving was not only possible. It was probable.

He wells up, tears pooling in the corners of his eyes, and I need to look away. Seeing him cry only reminds me of how hard it was for him to leave the farm back in January. Leaving his family behind in Fayetteville will be harder still. But he's not a farmer anymore, and he won't be able to live with himself if he doesn't do what he's been trained to do as the soldier he's become.

"We'll miss you," I say at last, my voice wavering. "I'll miss you."

He takes a deep breath, pulling me to his chest. "I wasn't going to say anything yet. Especially not on your big night. I don't know how you see through me, but you've always been able to. Anyway, I'm so sorry I upset you."

Before I can respond, my phone starts buzzing from beneath a pile of dirty laundry on the floor.

Dad takes me by the shoulders, holding me at arm's length, and smiles. A weary, splintered sort of smile that nearly breaks my heart. Inside are all the apologies he wants to make and promises he wants to keep. "Take the call. Then come find Mom and me before you leave, okay? She wants to take some pictures."

I tell him I will, and as he closes the door behind him I fumble for my phone. I assume it's Leonetta or Summer, calling to check on my progress or to confirm our meeting time, but instead, the name on the screen makes my heart race.

"Zander?" I say by way of greeting, hoping he can hear me over the distinct hum of a tractor engine in the background.

"Yeah. Hey, Tess. How's it going?"

His voice simultaneously soothes my soul and sets me on edge. Hearing it reminds me of home. Of lazy, summer afternoons in the barn. Of carefree days, full of tree climbing and snowball fights. But it also frightens me. I'm not sure why he's calling instead of sending a text. It's not Sunday. It's not even his week to call. Immediately, I assume the worst: something's happened to his family or maybe Sunshine.

"I'm good. But I'm the one who's supposed to call you tomorrow, remember?" I say.

He chuckles. "Yeah. Consider this a bonus call for the week. I just couldn't wait to tell you the good news."

My mind races, unsure of what could be so pressing he couldn't just send a text or wait one more day to share. I catch a glimpse of myself in the mirror, bedazzled like an ersatz princess off to the ball without a prince, and it strikes me he might be calling with some news about his own prom. An image of him with beautiful Judy Lewis—all doe-eyed and giggly—bubbles into my head. What I wouldn't give to have him with me tonight instead.

"What good news?" I say finally, making my voice as pleasant as my somber mood will allow.

"I bought the plane ticket. I'm flying into Fayetteville the second week of August as long as you're sure your mom and dad won't mind me staying at your house. And as long as you promise to drive us to Wilmington so we can see the ocean for the first time together."

I mentally boot Judy out of my head and replace her with an image of us at the beach. Salty, humid air. Sand beneath our toes. All our weeks of wistful planning and hopeful longing materialize into fruition.

I'm trying to recover, still reeling from his declaration but something about the second week of August digs at me. Then I remember. The Iowa State Fair is always the second week of August.

"What about the fair?" I ask.

My response is met with silence on the other end of the line. A moment later he replies in a wounded tone which slices through me, clean to the bone. "After all our planning, now you don't want me to come?"

Burdened by the weight of our unexpected conversation, I crumple into a pile on the floor, my gown crushing beneath me. But I don't care. All I want is to straighten out things with Zander. I only wish I could do it face-to-face instead of over the phone.

We never were very good at phone conversations.

"No," I gasp into the receiver. "That's not it at all. I want you to come visit. More than anything." I pick nervously at my freshly manicured thumbnail waiting for him to reply. "I just don't understand why you're giving up the fair to come here instead. You've never missed a single one."

I hear him shifting positions, perhaps switching the phone to his other ear before he says, "And neither have you, until now. We always said we'd go together. I decided if you're not going then I'm not either."

My heart aches. A splendid, bursting-full-of-joy kind of ache.

"What about your goat?" I whisper.

This makes him laugh, breaking the tension and bringing him back. "That goat is nothing but a glorified pain in my ass. The only ribbon that beast might win is *Most Likely to Roll Around in His Own Filth.*"

Now I'm laughing with him, remembering how Billy did have the unfortunate habit of sleeping in his own manure. We're still sharing stories about his stupid goat, reminiscing about what an ornery creature he's always been when my call-waiting beeps.

"We can hang up if you need to get that. I oughta be getting back to the barn anyway. It's almost time to milk."

I don't want to hang up. I want to keep talking about farm life. I want to finalize our trip to the beach. I want to keep hearing his voice.

"It's probably Summer or Leonetta about tonight."

"What's tonight?" he asks.

"Prom," I say as indifferently as I can.

"Oh, that's tonight, huh?" His voice is light. Casual. Because, of course, he knows I'm not going with another guy. "Send me some pictures, okay?"

"Sure," I tell him, although I doubt I actually will. "Gotta go."

"Call me tomorrow so we can hash out the details of my trip?"

I assure him I will and disconnect, switching over the line to discover a telemarketer inquiring about my current credit score. I hang up without pause and silently curse the invention of call waiting for ending my conversation with Zander so abruptly. I unfold myself from the floor, attempting to smooth the wrinkles out of my dress, and as I take one last peek at the mirror on the way out the door, I reconsider sending Zander a photo.

Because in the words of Monika Moore, I look 'hot as sin.'

chapter 27
Let Freedom Ring

Saturday, May 11

Summer keeps throwing out the word *fierce* to describe how we look in our gowns and, judging by the length of time Alice's mom, Renee, has been snapping pictures of us under the sprawling willow in her front yard, she wholeheartedly agrees. After filling her phone's memory, Renee takes a break to search the house for an old digital camera. During the brief posing hiatus, Cameron and Marcus strip off their tuxedo jackets and Leonetta and I take off our shoes, tossing them to the side. Sweat beads on the back of my neck, dampening my hair into ringlets as a triumphant Renee finally returns, rearranging the girls one last time in an attempt to find the perfect color composition between my red, Alice's hot pink, Leonetta's orange, and Summer's baby blue.

"How about rainbow order?" she cries out in a way only a former Miss Georgia Peach would. "First Tess, then Netta, then Summer. And Alice, you go on the end."

"Do rainbows even have pink?" Summer whispers to me through gritted teeth.

"They do now," I reply with a smirk.

We go on like this for another five minutes until happily, mercifully, Renee's camera battery dies. Summer, Leonetta, and I waste no time hightailing it barefoot across the lawn to my car, anxious for a welcome burst of air conditioning. I've already turned it to full blast by the time a much slower Cameron slides cautiously beside Summer in the back seat. Once everyone's settled we head off behind Marcus and Alice who lead the way out of the neighborhood in his truck.

Prom is being held at the Officer's Club on base, but since Bragg is a closed post, we're forced to take the long way around, doubling back to the only gate allowing students access to the dance. We're almost there, and even Cameron is singing along to the radio at the top of his lungs with the rest of us when I notice flashing lights in my rearview mirror. Immediately, I turn down the music.

"Is that a cop or an MP?" Summer asks as the scream of sirens closes in on us.

"I can't tell," I say, straining to read the logo on the front of the cruiser. "But I'm going the speed limit, so it shouldn't matter either way."

A moment later the Cumberland County police officer rushes past us only to immediately slam on his brakes, sliding in behind Marcus's Chevy Tahoe. We pass them both from the left-hand lane as the officer pulls Marcus and Alice off the side of the road.

"What the heck?" I say, slowing down to adjust my mirrors in an attempt to see what's happening behind us. "Should we turn around?"

"No," Leonetta snaps. "Keep going. They'll be fine. Marcus'll know what to do."

My heart is racing, not only from the lingering fear of getting pulled over but in anger over Marcus's detainment. "He was right in front of us so there's no way he was speeding.

Why would the cop pull him over out of nowhere like that?" I struggle, trying to remember if he had a broken tail light or an open gas cap, but I don't recall seeing anything out of the ordinary.

"I'm sure it's nothing," Leonetta says, although the tone of her voice implies she's not convinced. Then I remember her father's rules.

"You think he's being profiled?" I ask, watching her reaction from the corner of my eye as I navigate the Volkswagen onto base.

"I dunno. Maybe." She turns around, angling to see out the back windshield. "Let's hope not."

Cameron pipes up from the back seat. "Maybe it's one of those sobriety check points. It is prom night after all. Cops are gonna be out."

I consider this but am convinced there's another reason the officer pulled Marcus over instead of me. Leonetta must notice the flush of my cheeks. "It's gonna be okay," she tells me. "They'll be okay."

*

The Officer's Club is adorned with so many red, white, and blue streamers and American flags draped from the ceiling, it looks more like an Independence Day Celebration than a Junior/Senior Prom. In response to the recent increase in family member deployments, the senior class chose *Let Freedom Ring* as their theme. For the love birds like Alice and Marcus, it's not particularly romantic, but not having to hear Ed Sheeran crooning all night suits me fine. Bring on the John Phillips Sousa. Besides, between worrying about Marcus being detained by the police, Cameron's potential for social awkwardness, and the altercation that's sure to develop once Monika discovers she and Alice are wearing the same dress, there won't be much time for romance anyway.

Instead of heading straight downstairs to the ballroom, we decide to wait for Marcus and Alice in the main level vestibule. We're in line to have our pictures taken by the professional photographer when I spot them shoving through the double doors. I race over to them, leaving my place in the queue.

Alice looks flustered, her eyes wide, face flushed. Marcus, on the other hand, appears unfazed.

"Is everything okay?" I ask as they approach.

Marcus waves me off, taking Alice by the hand as they cross the atrium. "It was nothing. We're fine. Just a misunderstanding."

She scoffs at him before turning to me, clearly enraged by what transpired. "It wasn't nothing. It was awful. We had to get out and stand on the side of the road like common criminals while the officer searched the car for God-knows-what. Drugs, alcohol, food wrappers? He didn't find anything, though, thank goodness, because there was nothing to find."

It's not hard to imagine how mortifying it must have been for her to have to stand there on the shoulder, gawked at by passing onlookers while the car was inspected.

"Why'd he pull you over in the first place?" Summer asks, joining the conversation with Cameron at her heels.

Marcus shrugs. "Something about random checks because of prom and trying to keep drivers safe. It wasn't a big deal, and we're here now so let's drop it." Alice still doesn't look convinced as he lifts her chin with his hand and places a gentle kiss on her lips. "Don't let it ruin our night, huh?"

She sighs in acquiescence, but I can't help feeling torn. Neither of us was doing anything wrong, but the officer intentionally passed me by, making the conscious decision to pull Marcus over instead. Since there could only be one logical explanation for his choice, how should we react? Is it better to be like Marcus and accept the unjustness of it all? To assume following the rules will be enough to keep him safe, despite being singled out simply for being black? Names from the news like Terence Crutcher, Jordan Edwards, and Walter Scott pop into my mind. Did these black men assume their obedience would protect them? If so, perhaps it would be more prudent to be like Alice, wary of the prejudicial policies which lead some to anticipate the worst from an entire race of people.

I'm still pondering the unfathomable inequality of our world as we descend the stairs to the ballroom. Below me, I notice Alice adjusting her plunging neckline to accentuate her cleavage, preparing not only for her entrance but also for the inevitable fallout associated with wearing the same dress as the queen of the triflin' heifers. The dress, in all its pink deliciousness, fits her body like she was born to wear it, emphasizing her elegant features and killer curves.

If Monika wasn't such a jerk, I might almost feel sorry for her.

From the landing, a quick scan of the faces below confirms Monika has not yet arrived. Even with her brief detainment by the police, Alice still beat our adversary to the punch. She'll be the one to debut the hot pink masterpiece.

After successfully tracking down the dress in her size at a bridal boutique in Pinehurst, Alice spent the better part of a week plotting her own brand of retribution against Monika. It's with great pride that I watch her now, Marcus beaming on her arm, making the final descent down the massive staircase into the ballroom. Most of the students are watching the stairs in anticipation of their own friends' arrivals, and I'm not surprised to hear catcalls and whistles from many of the guys below. For her part, Alice takes it all in stride, neither showboating nor shrinking like a timid violet. Leonetta and I follow several steps behind, in awe of her grace and confidence.

She's certainly going to need as much as she can muster once Monika arrives.

We claim an unoccupied table in a corner of the room farthest from the buffet line, and the guys hurry off to gather drinks for the rest of us.

"Cameron's doing awesome at this whole prom thing," Alice says to Summer who nods in agreement.

"He's a nice guy," Summer says. "Quirky, but nice. And he did better at the proposal than you thought he would, Tess."

I don't tell her that hot gluing pawns to a chess board to spell PROM? was my idea.

"The chess thing was a sweet gesture," Alice agrees. "But I'm worried about how he's gonna handle the confrontation with Monika once she eventually shows up."

I can't take my eyes off the staircase, watching for her arrival. My stomach's in a knot, but Alice appears remarkably calm, despite being the one actually wearing the dress.

"I already gave him a heads-up that things might get ugly between you two. I told him he should stay out of it and let the rest of us handle everything," I tell her.

Alice raises an eyebrow at me. "What do you mean 'the rest of us?' We've already discussed it, and this is my deal."

"No way," Summer says, shaking her head vehemently. "We stay together tonight. Marcus and Cameron, too. There's safety in numbers."

I blanch at Summer's use of the word safety, wondering if Monika and her friends pose a legitimate physical threat. The pain in my stomach intensifies, and I wonder whether I've gotten my friends into something more dangerous than I initially anticipated.

The dress was supposed to be something to bring us together. Not something to put us at risk.

There's no time for Alice to object or for me to fixate on

my growing apprehension because, a moment later, Monika appears at the top of the stairs.

"She's here," I cry out, louder than I intended.

Alice grins. "It'll take a few minutes for people to realize we're wearing the same dress and for word to get to her." She rises to her feet, using the table as leverage. "Unless I go over there and say hello myself."

"Don't you dare," Leonetta says, taking Alice firmly by the arm. "This isn't a game. Let her come to you if she even has the guts."

We wait in anticipatory silence until the guys return, drinks in hand.

"You'd think they were serving cocktails instead of soft drinks with the size of the line over there," Marcus says, handing Alice her Diet Coke. No one laughs at his observation, forcing him to acknowledge our anxious stares. "She's here?" he asks.

Alice nods.

"Okay then. It's time for us to dance."

*

On the dance floor, Marcus is a one-man show, gyrating to Drake's newest release like a man possessed. He pulls Alice close, swaying in time to the beat, but before I have time to feel weird about my own pitiful moves or the way they're dancing together, he's got me by the hands, drawing me into the fold.

"Come on, Tess from Iowa. You got this."

The song ends, flowing seamlessly into the next, and it isn't long before I'm almost having a good time, troubles forgotten. Summer and Leonetta flank me on both sides and we're laughing with sweet Cameron, who seems to have temporarily forgotten himself, caught in the moment with the rest of us doing some ridiculous version of the cabbage patch.

We are one teeming mass of camaraderie.

But the magic comes to an abrupt end as Monika and her cadre approach.

"Nice dress," she says to Alice above the music, eyes dark, full of malice.

"Thanks," Alice replies with a shrug, still dancing. "It was on clearance." I have no idea how she's able to keep her composure in the face of Monika's venomous gaze but she does, adding innocently, "Hope you didn't pay full price."

My own muscles tighten involuntarily, and beside me Leonetta's jaw clenches, her hands balling into fists. She stops dancing, ready to defend Alice in whatever capacity she may need.

Monika ruffles, swallowing hard to hold back anger as a small group of onlookers surrounds us, forming a circle in the center of the dancefloor. She must know losing her cool here could end in expulsion or even arrest. She's weighing her options, deciding her next move in this real-life game of chess. With the opening moves and middle game played long ago, it appears we've arrived at the endgame.

It's time to play your remaining pawns, Alice. We're here for you. Use us.

Monika takes a step forward, asserting her dominance. She assumes she has Alice in check. "You're gonna regret the day you bought that dress, bitch. Your life is about to be turned upside down."

Alice stops dancing, at long last, giving Monika her full attention. As lean in stature as she is, I've never seen her looking so formidable.

"I have the right to wear any dress I please, especially looking as amazing as I do in this particular dress. And the reason I have that right is because this is a free country where I am entitled to life, liberty, and the pursuit of happiness." She places her hands on her hips, narrowing her eyes. "This dress makes me happy, so I will continue to wear it. You, however, can feel free to change if standing beside me is making you uncomfortable."

"You better watch your back," Monika threatens, losing her temper as she takes another step forward. "You have no idea what I can do to you."

"No. I'm done watching my back. We're all done watching our backs because we're done dealing with you. You're a bully, Monika. A bully." She slows her speech, punctuating every word. "A weak. Scared. Bully. The only reason you didn't want Latrina or anyone else to wear this dress is because you were afraid you'd be outshined. And now you have been. So, what?"

Two faculty chaperones are pushing their way across the dancefloor. If one of us is going to make a move, now is the time.

Leonetta's hand slips into mine as she says, "You spend all your time tryin' to break our spirits and our bodies hopin' to make yourself feel important, but it'll never be enough. Because you're really just a coward, hiding behind your family's wealth and prestige, thinkin' you have some sorta magical power over the rest of us. But it just ain't the truth and tonight we're taking our power back."

I take a deep breath, supported by Leonetta's faithful presence. "You don't scare us with your threats anymore, Monika," I say, turning heads with my boldness. "Because we don't need your validation. Not as long as we have each other."

Leonetta squeezes my hand, both of us blinking back tears. Tears of anger. Tears of fear. Tears of pride. Never in my life have I had a group of people so willing to stand up for one another. Back in Iowa, my so-called friends turned their backs on Zander, forgetting who he was and accusing him of horrible things. I was the only one who stood by his side while everyone else turned against him. How different things might have been for us if his friends had defended him instead of allowing Lacey's narrative to spread.

"Yeah. Leave 'em alone, Monika," says a voice from the crowd behind me, startling me from my thoughts. A glance into the group reveals Lashanda Jones from literature circle stepping forward. Beside her is Rashida Burns. "You got a lot of nerve," she says to Monika.

"Yeah. Get outta here," someone else calls.

"You're canceled," shouts another.

The crowd is growing on every side and people are nervously shifting around me. With Leonetta still holding tight on my right, I'm startled by the warmth of someone else's hand on my left. I turn to see Brad Wilson, the white kid from the step team smiling down at me.

"If you come for them, you gotta come through me," he says.

Beside him, a second member of the step team comes forward. "And me," he says.

"Me too," adds another.

Behind Alice, Roy and two other members of lit circle step out of the shadows. "Us too."

Others continue chiming in, adding their voices of solidarity to the growing consensus as the chaperones finally make their way through the throng of onlookers to the center of the circle where Alice is still nose to nose with Monika.

"What's going on here?" asks Mrs. Hawthorne, a reserved member of the science department sporting a waist-length jacket and beige capris pants.

"Nothing much," Alice tells her, smiling broadly at Monika, the lilt of her voice like bubbles in champagne. "We were just admiring each other's dresses, that's all."

Monika opens her mouth to speak but nothing comes out.

Alice has her in check.

"Move along then," Mrs. Hawthorne instructs. "Don't make me get administration involved in your apparel dispute."

After a flash of hesitation, the crowd disperses back into the rhythm of the music, to their tables, and to the buffet line, which has recently opened for dinner. Monika glares at Alice with a look capable of melting steel. In response, Alice gives her a little wave, turns on her heel and says, over her shoulder, "Have a great night!"

Checkmate, Alice. Checkmate.

We follow our friend back to our corner table. If I am walking, I don't notice. It feels more like I'm floating on air.

"What kind of badass group of people have I hooked up with?" Marcus says proudly as he collapses into his seat between Alice and Summer. "Y'all showed that girl what's what."

I have no idea what will come of our altercation with Monika. Perhaps she'll gather a band of supporters to come after us in the school parking lot Monday morning. Perhaps she'll steal my backpack. Pour urine on my lunch tray. Spread horrible rumors about me contracting an STD. In the end, though, she won't do any of those things. She'll keep her distance, at least for now.

But if for some reason she does come after us, we'll be okay. Because we're not alone. We have each other. These classmates. These friends.

And we'll always have each other's backs.

chapter 28
Promises, Promises

Sunday, May 12

It's just after midnight as we make our way across the parking lot to where my car is parked under a scraggly looking maple outside the Officer's Club. The cool, damp night air is a welcome relief to the stuffy confines of the ballroom and I gulp it down, happy to be done with the stress of the dance. Alice and Marcus head off in the opposite direction to his truck, but we've agreed to meet around the corner at Wilson Park to hang out a bit longer before officially ending the night.

"That was fun," Summer says as we cross the pavement, her strappy sandals in one hand and clutch in the other. "You have a good time, Cameron?"

He smiles and nods, and although he doesn't say anything I can tell by his musing expression it was one of the best nights of his life. So much for not being the type of kid who gets to go to prom.

"I did," Leonetta says. "I haven't danced that much since... Well, since ever. I didn't even dance that much at Mom's wedding."

Given the condition of my aching feet, I could have done

with a little less dancing. But then again, the dancing wasn't what made the night particularly special for me anyway. It was what happened in the quiet murmurs and stolen glances around the periphery of the event. In the classmates who whispered their thanks to us for standing up to Monika. Who gave hugs for pointing out it's not okay for her to treat other people with such disrespect. I was unaware she'd held such a large percentage of the student body in her crosshairs, but given the sheer number who waylaid us during multiple trips to the buffet, it seemed the confrontation was long overdue.

I'm still mentally congratulating our little group for a job well done when a voice calls out from beside a nearby dumpster. Whoever it is sounds anxious and not especially sober.

"Summer?"

Our heads whip around in unison to discover an inebriated Travis stumbling out of the darkness into the glow of an overhead street light. Summer's eyes narrow. Her grasp tightens around her purse. "What do you want?" she asks.

His face is puffy. Eyes bloodshot, as if he's been crying. He takes a cautious step forward, almost losing his balance, and I can't tell if his nerves or the alcohol are to blame.

"I'm leaving," he says at last, raising himself to full height as if the declaration should warrant our veneration.

Summer shrugs, nonplussed, telling him to have a nice trip before continuing her trek to the car.

"For Syria," he adds poignantly, his words halting her mid-stride.

Knowing Summer was going to be at the Officer's Club tonight for prom, he's been holed up behind the dumpster, waiting to say goodbye. Although most of me hates him for the way he's treated her in the past, a part of me can't help but feel sorry for him, disheveled and abject in the darkness.

Summer doesn't turn around, keeping her back to him as she says in a tone heavy with both regret and sadness, "Be safe over there, okay?"

I expect him to say goodbye then. To blow her a kiss. To amble away. What I don't expect is for him to pull a ring from the cargo pocket of his shorts.

"Summer," he says. "I can't go if I don't have anyone to come back home to."

She's still facing away from him, staring blankly into the night, so of course she doesn't see the ring. She doesn't speak for a moment, but once she finally does her voice is firmer than I expect it to be. "Stop. I'm not doing this. We broke up, remember?"

As the seconds pass, I'm silently willing her to turn around, to witness what's truly happening. To see the terrified look in his eyes.

"Summer. Please. I love you."

Maybe it's the tenderness of his words, the anguish of his voice, or merely her own curiosity that compels her to face him, and I hold my breath in anticipation of her reaction to finding him on bended knee.

"Oh, Travis," she sighs, her eyes glistening in the lamplight. "You're not ready for marriage and neither am I. You're scared. Scared of the war. Scared of leaving. Scared of being alone. And even if I take that ring tonight and promise to wait for you 'til you get back, you're still gonna be scared. That's not gonna change. And we're still never gonna end up together. You have to know that."

A long awkward moment passes as Travis struggles to his feet, brushing loose gravel from his palms as he rights himself. "Please," he implores her again, holding the ring out for her to see. "Give me a second chance."

Even as a reluctant bystander, my heart is breaking for

them both because, despite her callous exterior, I can tell by the way Summer bites at her bottom lip that she still has feelings for the guy. And although she may never love him again the way she once did, there's no mistaking her tenderness toward him.

She shakes her head, solemnly. "I can't, Travis. I'm sorry."

"Please?" he cries like a feral animal, staggering toward her, arms outstretched.

If I was surprised by Travis's unexpected proposal, I'm even more astounded by Cameron's reaction to the soldier's persistence. With a voice I've never heard him use and a bravado I was certain he didn't possess, he steps between them and says, "She said no. No means no. Now leave her alone."

Travis blinks as if coming out of a daze. As if he's wholly unaware there's been an audience standing courtside, privy to the drama playing out between them. He turns to Cameron, offended. "Who the hell do you think you are? This is none of your damn business."

I expect Cameron to retreat into the shadows where he's always been content to hide away from the prying, judgmental eyes of the world, but instead, he takes a courageous step forward, placing himself between the former lovers.

"It's my business because Summer is my date. And you've upset her. And I don't like seeing her upset."

"It's okay, Cam," she says, placing a gentle hand on his arm. "Thanks for standing up for me, but this isn't your problem."

As the words escape her lips I realize how terribly wrong she is. Like Cameron, I should be defending Summer against Travis the same way we all stood up to defend Alice against Monika at the dance. This is what real friends do. They support one another in the face of... complexity.

"Go home, Travis," I say in a voice more assertive than I intend. "Then go to Syria and when you come back, find a nice new girl to love. Only this time, instead of being a lying, cheating dog, treat her with the respect you forgot to show Summer. And maybe then you'll be worthy of that girl's heart and she'll be willing to wear your ring. As I see it now, though, you haven't earned that right here tonight."

He's conflicted, uncertain about whether to feel wounded or outraged. "Summer?" he pleads.

Now it's Leonetta's turn to step forward, joining the human barricade. "You heard the girl already," she says. "You blew it. Better luck next time."

Summer nods and with one last gaze into his eyes, climbs into the back seat of my car.

*

By the time we pull into the parking lot at Wilson Park, Alice and Marcus are swinging side-by-side on the swings—his legs pumping, her skirt billowing. A pang of jealousy washes over me as I call to mind an image of Zander and me on our tree's old tire swing. We spent hours together, pushing each other as high as the rope would allow in our never-ending quest to swing all the way around the branch.

How carefree those days had been.

They come to a stop as we approach, dragging their heels in the sand, then follow us to the dock along the lake shore. We carefully lower ourselves onto the weathered planks, and even though I worry momentarily about snapping turtles as I dip my toes in the water, I decide it must be safe once the others follow suit. There's a moment of contemplative silence until Alice finally inquires about our recent whereabouts, and after explaining how we were detained by a marriage proposal from Travis, the conversation turns to me.

"So, it's happening then," Alice says. "The 82nd is finally deploying to Syria."

"If Travis can be trusted," Summer says.

They are and he can. Because, of course, my dad's already shared the truth.

"They're leaving next month," I tell them. "Travis and my dad."

A beat passes as my revelation sets in. While the others consider my situation, I pick at the splintered decking, a sharp corner drawing blood as it pierces my skin. It's a tangible reminder of the emotional pain I'll endure after my dad's departure. I've never been without him a day in my life. Now I'll have to survive without him for months, if not years.

I stick my finger in my mouth, not wanting to bleed on my dress, as Summer says thoughtfully, "It's hard at first, not having your dad around. But it'll get easier as the weeks and months go by. You get into a routine, and eventually it'll become normal, being without him."

The blood tastes like an old penny, metallic and corrosive in my mouth. It reminds me of the time I fell, landing face first in our driveway when I was first learning to ride my bike. Dad had convinced me I was ready to go it alone. Assured me I could balance on my own, without his hand to steady the seat. But I had disappointed myself, careening headlong across the gravel, splitting my lip and scraping the side of my face. He'd apologized to me for letting me go before I was ready, but I knew it wasn't his fault.

Just as leaving now isn't his fault.

This time, however, I don't have to balance on my own.

"I'll be okay," I say at last. "I'll still have you guys."

"Exactly," Summer says, scooching over to drape her arm around my shoulders. "Alice and Netta aren't going anywhere, and even after I move we can still keep in touch."

I try to ignore the pang of sorrow accompanying thoughts of Summer's departure. Although I haven't known her long, I feel closer to her than most of the girls I grew up with. The same goes for Alice, and especially Leonetta. I can't believe these extraordinary girls are a part of my life and it's because, unlike in Iowa, I allowed them in. I consider how my life might have been different if I'd been open to the possibility of having more than one best friend instead of relying solely on Zander for so long.

For the duration of our conversation, Leonetta's been staring into the fog gathering atop the surface of the lake, being intentionally evasive. Something's clearly bothering her, and I put her on the spot. There's got to be a reason she's gone quiet.

She sighs heavily, picking at the polish on her nails. "I'm leaving too, right after school ends. But only for the summer. I'll be back by Labor Day."

"You're what?" Alice cries before I even have a chance to process. "I know I didn't hear you're leaving for the summer."

"I am. My mom invited me to stay with her in Jamaica for three months. Spend some time with my siblings. Get to know her new husband." She lifts her chin, catches my gaze from beneath her lashes. "I couldn't say no, even though I'd way rather spend my summer here with y'all."

Alice sits between Marcus's legs, leaning back on her elbows with her head against his chest. The anticipation of standing up to Monika long forgotten, she appears deflated like a helium balloon with a slow leak. I imagine we're a matched set, tethered to one another, unable to float away.

"Let me get this straight," she says softly. "Tess's dad is shipping off to Syria, Summer is moving to Arizona with her family, and Netta's spending the summer in Jamaica." She turns toward me, a dejected smile playing at the corners of her lips. "Guess it's gonna be you and me, girl."

"Guess so," I say.

She smiles in earnest then, rolling her eyes. "It's probably not such a bad thing considering you have to take remedial geometry this summer, and you're gonna need as much tutoring as I can give you."

Although the thought of spending my vacation solving geometric equations doesn't thrill me, spending my days with Alice is more than a fair trade-off. I only worry her company alone might not be enough anymore. That I've grown too accustomed to having all these people in my life. Me, Tess Goodwin, a girl who was perfectly satisfied to spend every waking hour with only the companionship of the boy next door can't stomach the thought of being without a full ensemble cast.

These friends.

This circle.

This community.

"Promise you'll call and text," Summer says, taking Alice's hand. "Promise."

"I promise," Alice tells her, grabbing Leonetta's hand.

"I promise," Leonetta says, reaching out to me.

"I promise," I say. And I mean it.

Chapter 29
Love Makes the World Go 'Round

Thursday, June 27

While I scrub the last of the spaghetti sauce from the bottom of the pan in the kitchen, Dad sits in the center of the family room, furniture shoved against the wall, gear splayed around him like a child on Christmas morning. I've never seen so much equipment, and as I observe him through the kitchen pass thru, I can't help but wonder how he's going to make it all fit inside his rucksack and duffle.

Two bags are all he gets to take with him tomorrow. Two bags to fit everything he needs to sustain him for the next nine months in Syria.

As I watch him now, rolling a pair of pants into a tight ball, I want to ask if he's scared, the way Travis was on prom night. I want to ask if he has the conviction to shoot another person if he must. I want to ask if he's going to miss me as much as I'm going to miss him.

What I say instead is, "How long's the flight over there?"

He jumps at the sound of my voice, disturbed from

somewhere deep in thought. "Oh, Tess. I didn't know you were still there," he replies, looking up from his bag. "What's that again?"

"I was wondering how long it will take to get there. To Syria. On the plane."

He cocks his head to the side, settling onto his heels. "They tell us it's about eighteen hours. But I'm not concerned about the time and distance. The worst part is the lack of accommodations on the plane."

"Like what?" I ask, setting down my dishrag to join him on the family room floor.

"Like we're traveling in a C-130, and it's gonna suck. The webbed seats are made of canvas straps, and they slice across the back of your legs until they cut off the circulation. We'll be crammed in like sardines, sitting shoulder-to-shoulder down the sides of the plane with cargo stacked in the middle. There's nothing but a bucket for a bathroom, and it's loud, with lots of vibration, especially on the propline. Plus, no in-flight movie or snacks."

Of course, it's easy to talk about the mechanics of it all as he explains about the plane. The preparations. The logistics. The execution. What's difficult to talk about is what it's going to be like once he's gone.

He returns to his packing list, checking off items with a Sharpie as he crams them into the duffle. Protective gloves. Sunglasses. Helmet. Utility belt. Mag light. Night vision goggles. Canteen. Heavy coat. I try to picture him using all these things, living in a war-torn nation on the other side of the world, and I can't even imagine what it will be like. Where will he sleep? What will he eat? What will he do every day?

I fold together several pairs of socks, rolling them as I've seen him do with the rest of his clothes. "What are you gonna do once you get there?" I ask.

He sets down the packing list, giving me his undivided attention. "What do you mean?"

"Like, what's your job gonna be?"

He's thoughtful for a moment, resting back on the palms of his hands. "It's a pretty complicated thing," he says. "But mostly I'll be in charge of decoding the intel we pick up on secured channels from the enemy. Hopefully, we'll prevent them from engaging in more attacks against the Syrian people. If we're lucky, we'll be able to root out cells of terrorists living in villages so they can't hurt anyone anymore."

I try to envision what a Syrian village looks like. What the villagers look like. And also, what they'll think of my dad.

"Are you scared?" I ask before I can stop myself. I don't want him to say he is, but it would be foolish to think he isn't.

He nods slowly, watching me, not wishing to give too much away. Clearly, the last thing he wants is for me to worry over him.

"Of what?" I prod.

"I worry mostly about making sure we do right by the Syrian people. Because most everyone over there is completely innocent. Lots of folks just trying to survive. Normal families living their lives. The tough part is figuring out who's who, you know? I guess I'm afraid I might not always get it right, and my mistake might cost someone their life." He pauses, reading the expression on my face. "It's all gonna be fine, though, so don't you go worrying your head about me."

His deployment to Syria is a little bit like my move to Fayetteville. Having to figure out the people in order to survive. "So how do you win?"

He raises an eyebrow. "Win?"

"Yeah. Win. Win the war. If you're gonna mess up, how do the good guys ever win?"

He must assume I'm speaking in broad generalities, not

only about the war in Syria because he pushes his equipment to the side and crawls on his hands and knees over to where I'm sitting against the wall. He edges up to me, pulling me close, and in an instant, we're back on the farm. I'm five years old again, Daddy's little girl.

"There's this saying in chess: 'Victory goes to the player who makes the next to last mistake.' It basically means during a game of chess you can make mistakes along the way and still come out ahead as long as you learn from those missteps and adjust accordingly. You don't need to do things perfectly from the beginning to eventually get it right in the end. I've found over the years the theory applies to life as well. And I'm pretty sure it will be the same for war."

I nod, considering the mistakes I've made in my own life, including the time I wasted worrying about fitting in here in Fayetteville. It makes me grateful for second chances, and I'm glad, as far as my new life is concerned, there's still time to get things right.

There's one mistake I've made, however, which might be a game ender. The years I squandered with Zander are gone, and there's no guarantee I'll ever have the chance to make things right between us. We may never get to explore being anything more than friends.

"Dad," I say, staring at my hands, disbelieving of what I'm about to divulge. "I think I'm in love with Zander."

He doesn't chuckle to himself as I expect, and when I lift my chin, wary of his reaction, his expression is serious. Wistful even. "I know," he says.

"No," I continue, shaking my head, certain he can't possibly understand. "I really love him. Like, *love* love. And I want to tell him when he comes to visit, but I'm scared of ruining our friendship."

He nods thoughtfully. "That's understandable," he says.

We're silent for several moments, and I'm flushed with embarrassment, unable to look him in the eye. I have no idea what compelled me to say something to him about Zander in the first place, and I don't know what advice I expect him to give. I'm considering an exit strategy, perhaps running from the room, but before I can get off the floor he places his hand on top of mine and says, "Don't ever be afraid to follow your heart, Tess. It's served you well this far, with your new friends here and with Zander back in Iowa. Trust your feelings and whatever happens, at least you gave love a chance. It's the best any of us can hope for."

He wraps an arm around my shoulder and places a kiss on the top of my head.

"You think I should tell him?"

"I'll be disappointed if you don't," he replies.

Chapter 30
Unexpected Visitor

Tuesday, July 16

Alice and I are halfway through the last geometry assignment in preparation for my summer school final exam. I've finally grasped the concept of quadratic equations, but the verdict's still out on whether my recent understanding is a testament to Alice's teaching abilities or my dogged perseverance. She confirms I've solved question number nine correctly, and I admit to myself it's probably a healthy combination of both.

We're alone as she watches over my shoulder at the kitchen table. Mom and Ashley are grocery shopping at the PX, and the house is silent, save for the scribbling of my pencil against the paper. We spend most of our days together—when she isn't working at the donut shop, babysitting her brother, or out with Marcus. Even still, I tag along with them on many of their dates, the third wheel of a surprisingly genial trike. If they're annoyed by my presence, they don't show it, although I do feel their pity that I should find myself so woefully unattached.

To that end, I've been working on another assignment almost as important as my final exam prep: a packing list for the beach. In a little over two weeks I'll pick up Zander from the Fayetteville airport, and along with Mom, Ashley, and her best friend Jillian, we'll head to Wrightsville Beach. As excited as I am about finally seeing the ocean, I must admit to myself I'm far more excited at the prospect of being back together with Zander after so many months apart. He is, after all, the macaroni to my cheese. Knowing this, however, doesn't keep me from lying awake at night worrying things between us might be different. Our conversations might be awkward and strained instead of easy and fluid like they've always been.

And, of course, there's the matter of my heart. I worry I won't find the words or the courage to tell him exactly how I feel.

Obsessing over Zander might be part of the reason I'm struggling with the proof for problem ten. Alice leans in to examine my error, but the doorbell rings before she finishes reading through the question.

"Hurry back," she calls to me as I make my way to the front of the house. "It's a simple fix. You accidentally took the square root instead of dividing by two."

The interruption, probably a neighbor looking for Ashley or a UPS delivery, is a welcome, viable excuse for stretching my legs. I'm hoping it's the waterproof phone case I ordered from Amazon, but nothing can prepare me for what I find instead.

For an instant, I think it's Dad, standing on the porch in his dress blues. My mind struggles to put the pieces of what I'm seeing together. The uniform. The unknown soldier. The thinly veiled dread behind his carefully composed façade.

"Miss Tess Goodwin?" the soldier asks.

"Yes," I whisper.

"Is your mother here?"

Seconds pass, both of us standing together in the doorway as I try to remember, but my mind's gone blank. There's someone else in the house, but it's Alice in the kitchen, not my mom.

I shake my head.

"Oh," he says, the corner of his eye twitching beneath the brow. "Well then, the Secretary of the Army regrets to inform you that your father, Sergeant Greg Goodwin, was killed in action yesterday in the Aleppo province of Syria, the casualty of a convoy bombing. There is an ongoing investigation. Once the investigation is complete, you will have full access to the report. On the behalf of the Secretary of Defense, I extend to you and your family my deepest sympathy in your great loss."

He goes on, but I'm no longer listening. I'm falling, both literally and figuratively. As I crumple to the floor the soldier catches me, his hands under my arms, returning me to my feet. I'm aware of the firmness of his grasp, the husky scent of his aftershave, the bile rising in my throat.

...killed in action yesterday.

"No," I whisper.

Not my father. Not my dad. He promised he would be safe. He's only been gone two weeks.

"Tess?" Somewhere far in the distance, someone is calling my name. I hope for an instant it's Dad, sneaking in through the back door, playing a horrible prank. But then I hear it again and remember Alice.

"We need to get her to the couch," the soldier says to her as I'm being shuffled across the room. I'm aware, as they ease me onto the cushion, there's another soldier present, handing me water in a glass from my own kitchen. I reach to take it, involuntarily, my hand palsied with tremors.

How long have they been here?

"Any idea where Mrs. Goodwin is or when she'll be back?" the soldier asks Alice as if I'm not even in the room.

"She's at the PX," she tells them. "I'm sure she'll be home soon."

Hours later, Alice is still by my side on the couch, idly rubbing my back with her hand as my mother speaks in hushed whispers with the chaplain in the kitchen. I've cried myself out, twice, and am barely holding it together now as Ashley lies beside me with her head in my lap, shuddering into a crumpled wad of tissue.

We sit in strained silence, and I can't stop thinking of Dad as the farmer he truly was, not the soldier the Army will remember him as. My gallant, thoughtful, magnanimous father, dressed not in sand colored camo, but in overalls quilted by the residue of a thousand memories: of grass stains and birthing fluids, tractor grease and mud. My father, who encouraged me to follow my heart by his example, reassuring me through life's greatest challenges I was on the right path. Who, more than any other person, shaped me into the person I've become. Into the person I will always be.

Tears begin anew, although I'd been certain there were no more left to shed. My body spasms, overpowered by the vast injustice of it all as I bury my head in my hands and weep. Alice pulls me close, pressing my body against her own while I try to make sense of the senseless. How will I ever survive without my dad? What type of world will it be without him in it?

Certainly not any world I want to be a part of.

Chapter 31
Goodbyes

Wednesday, July 31

After Dad died there were dozens of phone calls. Closed door meetings. Visits from strangers and friends alike. There was uncertainty. And then there was a resolution.

There was never any question about whether the three of us would return to Iowa, since, according to Mom, Fayetteville held nothing for us. She decided, however, under the Army's counsel, to wait for Dad's body to be returned stateside before leaving post. It would be easier, they told her, for everyone involved. In the space between knowing and leaving, we spoke with counselors and met with chaplains, but more than anything else we supported each other. This was especially true on the day I thoughtlessly drove past the Division Headquarters billboard and saw the fatality counter had been reset. Mom found me hours later still parked on the side of the road just beyond the wretched sign.

Dad arrived the following week, and the Army held a small ceremony for him at the main post chapel by the parade grounds. There were soldiers from non-deployed units in attendance as well as other wives and personnel. There was

Alice, who lingered nearby with a small but loyal troupe from school. And of course, there was Zander, who surprised me by showing up unexpectedly after changing the date of his flight so he could stand bravely by my side as Mom was presented with my dad's posthumous awards: his Purple Heart, his Congressional Medal of Honor, and his Bronze Star for acts of valor in combat. As it turned out, after his convoy was attacked, Dad was shot in the back trying to drag a fellow soldier out of the line of fire. Unfortunately, this confirmation of his bravery proved to be of little comfort.

Of all the people in attendance, though, Ashley was the one who ultimately got me through the day. After an emotional prayer from the chaplain, my attention fell to her, staring at the casket, her eyes bleary and bloodshot like my own. In that moment, I caught a glimpse of my father in them, right there, a part of her physical makeup as well as her heart, and I realized he would always be a part of me as well.

Now, as I sit in silence beside Zander on the floor of my empty bedroom, my twin bed, desk, and dresser already loaded onto the moving van, I find myself staring blankly at the new, purple-striped carry-on purchased for the beach which will now travel in the opposite direction back to Iowa.

My door creaks open, startling me from my thoughts as Mom pokes her head into the room. "You guys ready?"

I nod once.

"Okay. We're leaving in half an hour."

As she closes the door behind her I choke back what I want to say, which is I am *not at all* ready to leave. Surprisingly, Mom's decision to return to Iowa didn't carry the relief I'd hoped it would. Instead of alleviating some of the pain, it only intensified it. Because despite everything, I've made a life for myself here in Fayetteville. Developed friendships. Put down roots. And as I gaze out the window to watch the neighbor boys biking down the street, I admit to myself that what upsets me most about going home is leaving behind the final memories of my dad.

There's a good chance once I leave Fayetteville, I'm never coming back. I'll forget the smell of his starched uniforms. The way the short hairs bristled on the back of his head beneath the line of his beret. The black shoe polish stains at the base of his fingernails.

As fresh tears cascade down my cheeks, I find myself crying against Zander's shoulder not only for the loss of my dad but for the loss of everyone I'm leaving behind. Friends I never knew I needed before I met them. Leaving Iowa, I assumed Zander and I would eventually cross paths again. We'd visit one another and maybe attend college at the same university the way we'd always planned. But Summer, Alice, and Leonetta? There's a chance I'll never see them again.

Although my tears should be reserved solely for my dad, I can't keep my grief over him from spilling into their fonts as well in a giant tidal wave of loss. So many future memories devoid of their presence.

I'm a sniveling, blotchy mess as my door creeks open for the second time. I expect Ashley, who's taken to crying herself to sleep at the foot of my bed every night, but instead, Alice slips wordlessly into the room. And behind her, Leonetta follows.

I cannot speak. I do not rise to greet them. The sight of Leonetta is too much. Instead, she and Alice drop to the floor, wrapping me in their embrace.

"You're supposed to be in Jamaica," I sniffle after my latest round of tears subsides.

Leonetta shakes her head. "No. I'm supposed to be here. With you. I'm sorry it took me so long to get here. I can't believe I almost missed saying goodbye."

Her presence is as baffling as it is a relief. "How'd you find out I was leaving?" I ask.

She shares a conspiratorial glance with Alice which expresses an unspoken gratitude. "Alice called my dad who called my mom who insisted I change the date of my returning flight so I could get here in time to see you before you left. That turned out to be much harder than it was for Zander, though. I'm so sorry I didn't make it back in time for your dad's ceremony."

"It's okay," I tell her, taking her hand in mine. "I'm glad you're here now."

As we sit, lined up together against the wall, I'm reminded of three other women: The Fates— Clotho, Lachesis, and Atropos. But unlike the Fates who had the ability to shape destinies, I'm acutely aware I've had absolutely no control of my destiny over the past year. Every moving piece across the chessboard of my life was decided by chance, not choice. The sale of our farm. Our move to Fayetteville. The new friends I found. My father's death. It all happened *to* me, not *because* of me.

The part I love most about chess is the control. The power you have to plan ahead, influencing the outcome of the game by successfully predicting what moves come next. Life, I am finding, isn't that way at all. There's no planning. No predicting. Only adjusting to whatever's thrown your way in the hopes of making the next to last mistake.

Zander excuses himself to give the three of us a moment alone, leaving me between Alice and Leonetta searching for the right thing to say.

"I'm sorry about your dad," Leonetta says, squeezing my fingers. "He was a really nice guy."

I look at our hands woven together. The richness of her skin set against the paleness of mine. It's the most beautiful thing I've ever seen. We are completely different and absolutely the same.

"He was," I say. "He really was."

Leonetta continues, clearing her throat uncertainly. "Alice told me y'all were moving back to Iowa, but I guess I didn't figure it would be so soon. I thought maybe we'd have more time together."

I remember thinking the same thing about my dad, always assuming we'd have more time. It was the same with Zander back in the fall and with Alice and Leonetta now. But I guess that's the thing about time—it's tied to Fate, so you never know how much you're gonna get.

We better make the most of what we have while we have it.

I turn to Alice, then to Leonetta, holding their gaze long enough for them to appreciate the importance of what I'm about to tell them. "I love you guys. You know that. I love you like I've never loved any other girlfriends because the truth is, before you, there weren't any other girls I felt comfortable letting into my life. But the three of you... you taught me what it means to be a friend. A real friend. What it means to have someone else's back even when life gets hard or messy."

"Like when triflin' heifers try to sabotage you at every turn?" Leonetta adds.

"Yes," I say smiling, "especially then. But more than anything else you taught me people are just people. It doesn't matter where we're from or how we grew up because we all want the same things out of life—to be loved and respected and a part of something bigger than ourselves. I didn't appreciate that before I got here. I didn't appreciate that before I met you. I thought I was going to be so different from everyone that no one here would understand me or want to get to know me. But that wasn't the case at all, because despite our differences, we turned out to have lots more in common than I ever imagined we could. A few connective threads bound us together. And that was all it took."

Alice leans into my shoulder, trembling against it. "We're gonna miss you, Tess," she breathes.

"I'm gonna miss you, too," I say past the lump in my throat. "I'm sorry I'm not gonna get a chance to harvest with you this fall."

"It's okay," she says. "I'll send a cotton bouquet to your house. Something to remember me by."

"And maybe you can come back to visit. Or we can come visit you," Leonetta adds, her voice wavering.

"I'd like that," I tell her, but even as the words escape my lips, I fear I may never see her again.

A moment later my mom's at the door announcing it's time for us to leave. As we're saying our final goodbyes, Leonetta takes a folded piece of paper from her back pocket and presses it into my hand. "Love ya, girl," she says.

We make it to a rest stop in Indiana before I find the courage to open the note.

Eleven Reasons Why We'll Always Be Best Friends

1. Tell each other the truth, even when it's hard to hear.

2. Stick up for one another.

3. Force each other to try new things, including Tabasco and chess.

4. Loyal. Faithful. Reliable.

5. Excuse each other's weaknesses.

6. Champion each other's strengths.

7. Try to imagine the world from the other's point-of-view.

8. Never judge one another.

9. Challenge each other to be brave.

10. Fight together against triflin' heifers.

11. Love each other just as we are.

Chapter 32
New Beginnings

Friday, August 16

Dad's service is held at the funeral home across the street from the Nazarene church, and he's buried at the cemetery off Second Street. The entire town shows up to pay respects to their fellow farmer turned fallen hero, and in the days that follow it seems as though I will never have a moment to myself again thanks to the seemingly endless procession of people delivering casseroles, fresh vegetables, and sympathy cards to our doorstep.

Then, as quickly as they appeared, everyone slips quietly away, back into the blissful normalcy of their lives. Everyone, that is, except Zander.

I'm waiting for him on the stoop—two rickety, wooden steps leading to the front door of our new house in town. It's a rental on 4th Street, within walking distance of the elementary school and the old folk's home. Growing up, I passed this nondescript, mid-century rancher a thousand times going into town, never imagining I would eventually come to call it home. Never knowing the circumstances that would take me out of Iowa and back again.

Zander's truck turns the corner at the end of the street and a sense of peace washes over me. We've barely spoken in the weeks since my return, but words have been unnecessary. Everything important between us is understood, as it always has been.

He pulls up to the curb, and I don't wait for him to get out to greet me. I'm already halfway across the front lawn before he can even shift the truck into park.

"You wanna invite Ashley to come along?" he asks as I slide into the passenger's seat.

I shake my head. "Kassi's here, spending the night. They found a bunch of old Reese Witherspoon movies on Netflix and are having a binge marathon."

"Sounds like fun," he says sarcastically.

"What, you don't wanna watch *Legally Blond* with her for the thousandth time?"

He lifts an eyebrow at me as we drive away from the house. "Did they find *Election*? Because she's brilliant as Tracy Flick."

"Probably," I tell him with a playful shove. "We can always come back here later on if you really want."

We head to the shaved ice stand in the center of town, which is nothing more than a dilapidated shed managed by a twelve-year-old kid with an ice crusher and a selection of artificial flavorings in various dayglow colors. Zander pays for two blue raspberries and, with spoons in hand, we set off to our final destination.

I haven't driven by our farm since we returned, and as we approach I can't swallow down the lump forming in my throat. With the exception of a late model Toyota in the driveway and a pair of freshly painted white rockers on the porch, the house, the barn, and all the outbuildings look as though we never left. I catch myself scanning the horizon for Dad atop his tractor on his way in from the fields. Zander places a reassuring hand on my knee, jarring me from my introspection. I've been holding my breath, but this is the moment I've been waiting for. It's time to finally exhale.

"You okay?" he asks as we turn toward the Robert's Farmstead Dairy sign, crunching up the gravel drive toward his house.

I manage a weak smile in appreciation of his sensitivity and awareness of how difficult it is for me to be here. "Not now. But someday I will be." It's as close to the truth as I'm able to articulate given everything that's transpired.

We park beside his house, and he takes my hand as we cross to the fenced pasture on the east side of the property. The rough edges of his calluses press against my palm, and I recognize each of them as if they're my own. Across the field, our oak stoically endures the heavy burden of its branches. I resist the urge to run to it.

Until I notice her.

"Sunshine," I call into the breeze. "Sunshine, I'm home."

Cows, for all their endearing qualities, are not dogs. I don't expect her to break into a full gallop and race across the field to greet me the way a Golden Retriever would. Still, my heart melts when her ears twitch at the sound of my voice.

"Sunshine!" I call again, unable to hold back tears or the sudden rush of memories.

She stops grazing, lifting her face from the grass, turning toward the fence I'm now scrambling over. Zander's footsteps thud behind me as I race across the field. I slow as I approach, not wanting to frighten her, realizing she may have forgotten me in the many months we've been apart. I hold out my hand above her snout, feeling the warmth of her breath.

"Sunshine?"

She takes a step forward, pressing her nose into my palm the way she did the night I spent with her after the birth of her first calf. Tears flow freely as I press my face to hers, taking in her familiar, earthy smell while I scratch behind her ears.

"He's gone, girl," I tell her, wrapping my arms around her neck. "And he's not ever coming back."

*

As the sun dips below the horizon, Sunshine follows us back to the barn. Zander slips quietly away to tend to the rest of the herd, leaving Sunshine and me together on the floor of the stable. She chews at her cud, blissfully unaware of how my world has repeatedly imploded over the course of the past year. Spared a certain death by Zander's compassion, for her all that's changed is the side of the fence she calls home. For me, however, nothing will ever be the same. Dusk has fallen and shadows overtake the barn as we lie together on the clean bed of straw. I'm propped against her back, laughing as I tell her about how Leonetta once admitted she'd never been close enough to a cow to hear it moo.

"Can you imagine, Sunshine? Never hearing the sound of your voice?"

I tell her what I learned from Alice about cotton, how the burrs cause your fingers to bleed. "Think about what those would do to your lips," I say, knowing her proclivity for taste testing foliage she shouldn't. "And Summer says she tried milking a cow once on a school trip in Georgia, but it sounds like she didn't get any milk out since she was doing it all wrong. Maybe someday she can come here for a visit, and I can teach her how."

I have no idea how long we lie there together, me talking and her listening, but I'm certain it's close to midnight when Zander's flashlight sweeps into the barn.

"Tess? You still in here?"

"Yes," I reply, stretching a kink from my back. "I'm over

here with Sunshine."

A moment later he appears at the stall door wearing a white t-shirt and blue athletic shorts. I'd recognize his pajamas anywhere.

"I guess it's time to take me home," I say, getting to my feet. I'm ashamed of my selfishness, keeping him up so late. "I didn't realize how long I've been out here."

He shakes his head, stepping barefoot into the stall. There are two old pillows and a thin blanket under his arm. "You don't have to go," he says. "In fact, if you want, you could stay the night." A look of yearning crosses his face as he continues to ramble. "I already called your mom to let her know you might stick around, so she didn't worry, in case you wanted to stay. If not, I can take you home."

There's so much I want to say to him, standing in front of me, silhouetted by strips of moonlight creeping through the rafters. I want to explain how much I've changed in the short time I've been gone. How much I learned about true friendship from a group of girls I would have never had the courage to say hello to, much less befriend, if I'd never moved away. I want to warn him I'm no longer afraid to let other people into my life, so I won't be relying on him so much to fill that space anymore. I don't need him quite the way I once did.

Because now I imagine him occupying a different square on my chess board.

I sit back down, sliding over to make room for him beside me on the straw, and he acknowledges my invitation to stay by flicking open the blanket. As he lowers himself beside me I say, "We never made it to the beach."

"I know," he says.

"I'll repay you for the plane ticket."

He chuckles, wrapping the blanket around our shoulders so we're encased in a cocoon of woven cotton. "I don't care about the money," he says. "And I don't care if we never get to see the ocean."

I let my head fall to his shoulder and yawn, mindlessly rubbing Sunshine's back with my foot. "We'll get there someday."

He takes my hand, squeezing it with an urgent sort of desperation, and I can tell by the way his muscles tighten against mine he wants to say the words we've never spoken aloud to one another before.

"Maybe we will and maybe we won't, but I'm sorry you had to lose your father for me to get my wish."

My chest tightens at the mention of my dad. "What was your wish?" I ask.

"This. This right here. To have you back on the farm with me." He hesitates before continuing, rubbing his stubble against the back of his hand. "I missed you, Tess."

"I missed you, too," I say, my heart rocketing around in my chest. "But..."

I stop then because we've reached a pivotal moment in our friendship. He wants to tell me he loves me, and I wish I could do the easy thing and accept this path he's paving before me. Accept his love and be the Tess he wants me to be. It would be easy. So very easy.

But we've always been honest with each other. Always.

And since one of the last things Dad told me was to follow my heart, I can't lie to Zander now. I intend to keep my promise.

"But what?" Zander says, turning my face so he can see me fully. Even in the darkness, there's no mistaking the trepidation in his eyes.

"But I'm afraid this place might not be enough for me anymore. Now that I've seen what else is out there, who else is out there, I want to go explore the world."

He flinches.

"But I don't want to go alone. The next time I leave, I want you to come with me," I finish.

The tension between us slips away, and he allows me to settle back into the hollow of his chest. "After graduation, we always planned on moving to Des Moines," he says. "You wanna go somewhere else?"

"I think so," I say. "I mean, instead of staying here in Iowa, maybe we can go to college in Seattle or Baton Rouge or Poughkeepsie. All I know is there's a lot more to life than farms and cows and tractors, and I don't want to squander a single opportunity to learn everything there is to know about the world outside of Iowa. Experience new adventures. New traditions. New people."

"Poughkeepsie, huh?" he laughs. "Is there even a college there?"

I elbow him in the ribs causing him to grunt. "I dunno. Maybe not in Poughkeepsie, but there's a college out there somewhere for us in a place where we can learn more from the people than we can from the books." I turn to him, our faces so close I can smell the toothpaste on his breath, and I love him and want him to be a part of the grand undertaking that's going to be my life. "Eventually, once I've experienced the whole of the world, I might be ready to come back here and be a farm girl again. Because I love being a farm girl. I'm good at it."

"You're great at it," he agrees.

"But until then, will you think about coming with me?"

"Follow you around the country? Like, as your boyfriend?"

My breath catches at the word. "Yes. Exactly like that."

His lips are on mine before I realize what's happening, and as I quickly respond with my own, all I can think about is what took us so long to get here. "Yes," he says finally, coming up for air. "I'll go with you, wherever it is you wanna go."

We sit together in comfortable silence, and Sunshine's switching tail grows still as she drifts off to sleep. For the first time in my life, I'm surprisingly okay with the great unknown of my future. I'm no longer afraid of not fitting in. Of changing circumstances. Of new people. Because as long as I keep an open mind and an open heart, I can handle whatever life throws my way.

Zander stirs behind me, finding a comfortable position to settle in for the night. In the darkness, his voice drifts through the thick night air. "Can I ask you a question?"

"Hmm?" I murmur, adjusting my head on one of the pillows.

"At your dad's funeral, when you read everyone your list about why you love him, why were there eleven reasons?"

The nostalgia incited by his question makes me want to laugh and cry, remember and forget, leave and stay.

"You mean instead of a round number like ten or twenty?"

"I guess."

I tell him about Summer and Alice's lists. About how the lists brought us together, taught us about one another, and gave us purpose.

"Girls can be weird," he says.

"No doubt."

Crickets chirp noisily out in the fields, and in the barnyard, I hear the contented moo of a lone cow. Zander kicks me playfully with his foot.

"Maybe someday I'll make it onto one of those lists."

I smile, grinning to myself in the darkness. "Maybe you already have."

Eleven Reasons I Love My Dad

1. Always believed in me, even when I didn't believe in myself.

2. Taught me by example to follow my heart.

3. Introduced me to chess.

4. Kept me safe.

5. Encouraged me to embrace change even if I was scared.

6. Showed me what kindness and acceptance look like.

7. Never let me take the easy way out.

8. Trusted me to do hard things.

9. Allowed me to be myself.

10. Let me know he was proud of me.

11. Will always be my hero.

A Note to Readers from Amalie Jahn

"Every story is a love story –
the only question is what kind of love."

When I began writing *The Next to Last Mistake* my intention was to pay tribute to one of the most powerful forms of love I've ever experienced—the serendipitous bond of friendship between a group of young women coming of age under a unique set of circumstances. Although Leonetta, Tess, Alice, and Summer are fictional characters, the friendships they portray are not.

After relocating from Maryland to North Carolina in my early twenties, my husband's unexpected deployment during our first months together at Ft. Bragg came as a devastating blow. At the same time, three coworkers at the elementary school where I taught found themselves similarly upended, and the four of us quickly became family. As one of the few white teachers in a predominantly black school, the type of interracial friendship we shared was the norm, but it's not hyperbolic to say that the grace and wisdom afforded to me by the incredible black women at LBES forever changed my life.

Our time together proved that unique bonds of friendship

can be created when trust crosses racial lines. Those bonds continue to be amazing sources of strength for us, and it's an honor to pass along the lessons we shared from the years we spent together. During my TED Talk in 2015, I spoke about the many ways people are more alike than we are different and encouraged listeners to seek out those commonalities as a means of connecting with others. While the friendships portrayed in *The Next to Last Mistake* embody these ideals, as the connections between Leonetta, Tess, Alice, and Summer strengthen throughout the book, the girls also begin to recognize the importance of their differences. It's the appreciation and understanding of these differences which ultimately solidify the bonds of trust between them.

At its core, *The Next to Last Mistake* is a celebration of the love between four friends and the complex beauty of interracial friendship. Here are the three amazing women who taught me all those years ago not to shy away from the unknown, to seek the truth, and to be comfortable being uncomfortable. Thank you, Johnisha, Susie, and Holly from the bottom of my heart for trusting me to tell our story.

Acknowledgments

Much like raising a child, bringing a book into the world is not a solitary endeavor. From those who sparked the idea which ignited the first pages into fruition to the publishing house that delivered this book to the shelves, so many hands and hearts have gone into bringing Tess, Leonetta, Alice, and Summer's story to life.

First and foremost, a huge thank you to my husband, Drew, for providing a life where dreaming big is encouraged. Thanks for picking me up when I fall apart, for knowing dessert is the very best way to celebrate milestones, big and small, and for giving me the time and space to explore the path in front of me. I love you, and I'm grateful for you every single day.

So much love to my in-house YA fiction aficionado, Molly, for being the first set of eyes on my terrible early drafts. Thank you for eagerly awaiting new chapters, crying at all the right parts, and keeping me updated on all the current lingo. I still maintain 'lit' doesn't always mean what you think it does.

Hugs and kisses to my sweet Brody for being my most enthusiastic cheerleader. Thanks for telling all your teachers and school librarian I'm a Newberry Award winner—even though I'm not. The fact you think I could be means the world.

For inspiring me with your love and kindness, a huge shout-out to the faculty, staff, and students at LBES. You will always hold a special place in my heart. Johnisha Bagby,

Susie Brown, and Holly Ank—I am humbled and thankful you trusted me to tell our story. Wishing you nothing but happiness and a world free from triflin' heifers.

A big HOOAH to my fellow Army wives, April Pedersen, Holly Ank, and Monique Everson, for being on call when I needed help remembering specific military jargon and Ft. Bragg intel. Thank you all for your service.

Special thanks to Anne Zirkle, for tackling the initial round of edits, and to my family, friends, and critique partners who helped polish the first chapters before querying began. I truly appreciate your honesty and willingness to be a part of the journey.

Love to Heather Skinner, for brainstorming with me in the eleventh hour and pushing me to go on when I was ready to throw in the towel. Your friendship means the world to me.

Because authentic representation was paramount in this project, extra special thanks go out to Leslie & Summer Boyd, Lisa Yarrow, Kennedy Lightfoot, Christina Chisholm, Crystal & Kenzie Cofie, Kim Lindstrom, Noa Aviles, and Julie Rauschenplat for giving your time and experience to ensure every character was accurately portrayed.

Thank you to Julius Tillery for allowing me to include your amazing company, Black Cotton, as part of Alice's narrative.

To my editor, Elizabeth Turnbull, and the team at Light Messages, I'm so grateful to you for not only taking a chance on me but for seeing the potential in this quiet friendship story.

And, finally, to each of my readers who cheered me on in anticipation of the next big thing, thank you. I hope *The Next to Last Mistake* is all you hoped it would be.

About the Author

Amalie Jahn is a *USA TODAY* bestselling author of more than 8 young adult novels, including *The Next To Last Mistake*, her latest release (Light Messages Publishing).

Amalie is the recipient of the Literary Classics Seal of Approval and the Readers' Favorite Gold Medal for her debut novel, The Clay Lion. She is a contributing blogger with the *Huffington Post* and *Southern Writers Magazine*, as well as a TED speaker, human rights advocate, and active promoter of kindness. She lives in the United States with her husband, two children, and three overfed cats.

When she's not at the computer coaxing characters into submission, you can find Amalie swimming laps, cycling, or running on the treadmill, probably training for her next triathlon. She hates pairing socks and loves avocados. She is also very happy time travel does not yet exist. Connect with her right here in the present day at these social media sites:

- Websites: amaliejahn.com and lightmessages.com/amalie-jahn
- Facebook: facebook.com/AmalieJahn
- Twitter: @amalieJahn
- Instagram: @amalie.jahn.official

Visit amaliejahn.com to join Amalie's FREE Readers Group and, in addition to receiving promotional discounts, sneak peeks, and monthly newsletters, your membership will now grant you exclusive access to bonus material (shorts and novelettes) delivered right to your inbox!

IF YOU LIKED

The Next to Last Mistake

YOU MIGHT ALSO ENJOY THESE TITLES

Behind These Hands
Linda Vigen Phillips

In the Midst of Innocence
Deborah Hining

A Theory of Expanded Love
Caitlin Hicks